For her sixth novel, Sarah-Kate Lynch travelled to London, Paris, Hong Kong and Muriwai in search of the world's best afternoon tea emporiums. As a result of her tireless devotion to such research, she can now only eat things that are bite-sized and come in stacks. There must be chocolate on one level, cucumber on another, and raspberry jam in between.

You can find out more about Sarah-Kate by reading her column in the *New Zealand Woman's Weekly* (although most of it is made up) or by visiting her website at *www.sarah-katelynch.com* (although most of that is made up, too).

Above: The author engrossed in her research at The Peninsula, Hong Kong.

on top of
everything

SARAH-KATE LYNCH

BLACK
SWAN

A BLACK SWAN BOOK published by Random House New Zealand
18 Poland Road, Glenfield, Auckland, New Zealand

For more information about our titles go to www.randomhouse.co.nz

A catalogue record for this book is available from the National Library
of New Zealand

Random House International, Random House, 20 Vauxhall Bridge Road, London,
SW1V 2SA, United Kingdom; **Random House Australia Pty Ltd**, Level 3, 100
Pacific Highway, North Sydney 2060, Australia; **Random House South Africa Pty
Ltd**, Isle of Houghton, Corner Boundary Road and Carse O'Gowrie, Houghton
2198, South Africa; **Random House Publishers India Private Ltd**, 301 World Trade
Tower, Hotel Intercontinental Grand Complex, Barakhamba Lane, New Delhi 110
001, India

First published 2008

© 2008 Sarah-Kate Lynch

The moral rights of the author have been asserted

ISBN 978 186941 997 4

Random House New Zealand uses non-chlorine-bleached papers from sustainably
managed plantation forests.

Design: Elin Bruhn Termannsen
Cover photograph: Aaron McLean
Printed in Australia by Griffin Press

For anyone who ever had a bad day.
Or week. Or month.

CHAPTER ONE

The moment Whiffy O'Farrell threw a Victorian chamber pot into a Regency mirror I should have twigged that my days in antiques were numbered. Or my hours, to be more exact.

That, if nothing else, I should have seen coming.

Personally, I had nothing against poor Whiffy. He didn't smell very fresh, hence the nickname, but for a street person he really had rather lovely manners. Better than most non-street people, actually. Whenever he came into our west London shop — every couple of weeks or so, to look at our fob chains — he always accepted a cup of tea and a slice of whatever I was offering with the utmost charm.

I suppose it's possible that other antique shop owners were plying him with tea and cakes on a regular basis, so that's exactly what he expected from us. But I doubted it somehow, as no other antique shop I had been to bothered to offer tea and cakes. In our shop, though, it had become my habit to extend this courtesy to all our customers (or visitors, as many of them more correctly were). I felt it was our point of difference, it set us apart from the great mêlée of other, almost identical, shops in the city and I didn't see why Whiffy should miss out just because he usually ate from a rubbish bin.

More than once or twice I had seen him rifling for leftovers in the big black bin on the corner of Formosa Street and Warwick Avenue, just around the corner. He used the same thick fingers layered black with grime to excavate half-eaten Subway sandwiches as he did to drink delicately out of a fine bone-china cup, and I used to wonder what on earth must have happened to him to get him in such a state. Was there a wife somewhere, wondering why he'd gone out to buy tea bags and never come back? A daughter who passed him on the bus and turned the other way? A son who refused to have children of his own because his father had ended up a down-and-outer?

He was certainly down and out, there was no doubt about that, but he was steady on his feet and whatever he smelled of (and it was quite a ripe cocktail, let me tell you) did not seem to include alcohol. He wasn't a wino, I was sure, but on occasion he did mumble incoherently, like a drunk might, over the fob chains. When this happened, my partner Charlotte would 'tsk tsk' loudly and eventually shuffle him outside, holding her face away so she didn't breathe in the fumes. Afterwards, she'd race to the tiny loo at the back of the shop and wash her hands with what I thought was unnecessary vigour.

'Honestly, Florence,' she would scold me, her skinny fingers rubbed raw with L'Occitane. 'Must you encourage him to stay? It's an antiques shop, you know, not a soup kitchen.'

But when Charlotte wasn't there, I let Whiffy be. There was something about him that tugged at my heartstrings (filaments too easily plucked, my husband Harry told me once, fondly enough, although I had to look up filaments in the dictionary afterwards to make sure it was a good thing).

Whiffy would glance at me so gratefully as he elegantly lifted a forkful of Victoria sponge into his all but toothless mouth that I couldn't help but feel an ache and offer him a smile of encouragement. Then when he finished his cup of tea, he would wipe daintily at his matted beard with a filthy handkerchief and nod his appreciation before leaving the store — the aroma of living on a Maida Vale park bench wafting moodily behind him.

Well, I know people who live in fancy houses and smell only of the finest French perfumes who don't wipe their mouths or nod their appreciation of a good Victoria sponge. If you're the one who went to the bother of making it, you most certainly don't consider them to be cut from any finer cloth than Whiffy O'Farrell.

Unfortunately, the day the poor old boy lost it with the chamber pot, Charlotte was in attendance. She and I had owned the (possibly slightly faltering, now I come to mention it) antiques business on Warwick Place in Maida Vale's Little Venice for nearly ten years, after coming up with the idea over many bottles of Bulgarian red one night at dinner with our husbands, who at the time were both junior partners in the same City law firm.

Charlotte's husband, Martin, had gone on to become a senior partner in that same firm and they were very upwardly mobile. Harry, on the other hand, had abandoned the law in favour of writing unpublishable novels and we were very downwardly mobile. But happy. Or so I thought.

The point being that when I did think about it — which I possibly should have done a year or two sooner — Charlotte and I had started up Drake Dowling Antiques in the '90s, when we were both unquestionably on the same trajectory. But by the time Whiffy took to the reflective surfaces, we were heading in desperately different directions.

I still loved our shop as much as I ever had because it was so full of stories, of other people's histories. That's what antiques were to me, that's why I was interested in them in the first place. The shop was a repository for relics of varying strangers' pasts, a collection of little splinters of times gone by. We were the curators of these treasures, I figured, restoring and protecting them until someone else took them away and carried them into the future. And the someone elses always had stories to tell as well and nobody liked to hear these more than I did.

I liked the stories a bit more than the antiques, actually, although I did have a passion for the very fine bone china around which Whiffy's filthy fingers so gently curled when he visited. I loved all the china for its delicacy, its colour, its prettiness and its staying power, but it was the tea paraphernalia I truly adored: the teapots, cups, saucers, milk jugs and sugar bowls of yesteryear.

As our partnership progressed, however, Charlotte felt that there wasn't enough money in these small things; that we should concentrate on larger pieces of furniture and more priceless antiques so that we could 'grow the business' and 'focus on more lucrative markets'.

In short, Charlotte wanted to make more money. I couldn't really understand that, to be honest, because if anybody needed more money you would think it was Harry and me. Charlotte and Martin already had great pots of it. The Drakes had a beautifully appointed house in Hampstead that was impeccably kept; they drove a Range Rover and an Audi convertible, sent their three gorgeous daughters to expensive private schools, and dressed entirely in Nicole Farhi and Paul Smith.

Harry and I had a splendid but falling-down house that went weeks without seeing a Hoover, drove a tired old Golf or got the bus, had sent our only son Monty to the local comprehensive, and dressed entirely in whatever we could get our hands on that wasn't falling apart at the seams or speckled with chocolate.

Not that I'm complaining. Harry and I didn't need money, I had always believed. We had each other, we had Monty, and we had the splendid but falling-down house right there in Little Venice (a neighbourhood enthusiastically named after its two — count them, two — connecting waterways). It was worth a total fortune, the price of London real estate had gone ballistic in the twenty-odd years we'd owned it, but I would not dream of selling. It meant so much to me, that place. It was my own personal sliver of times gone by and anchored me to my adored grandmother, who had left it to me when she died.

Anyway, Charlotte had been fairly frosty towards me for quite some time before the Whiffy O'Farrell incident because I could not — or would not as she saw it — afford an injection of £30,000 to bankroll a trip to France to buy some of the bigger antiques that would 'grow the business'.

For a start, I didn't travel; for a finish, I liked English antiques. Let everyone else sell wrought iron garden chairs and borer-ridden armoires and pock-marked jardinières. Honestly, for a while there you couldn't move through Portobello or the Church Street markets without being sucked into a little piece of Provence. If you want a little piece of Provence, go there, that was my opinion. Don't carve the place up and start clogging London with it. Seriously, I didn't even care overly for Limoges and I told Charlotte that (or I jolly well meant to).

Either way the atmosphere between us had cooled ever since we'd first discussed the £30,000, which I found further perplexing because she knew I didn't have it to inject. And if I had found a spare £30,000 lying under the sofa or hidden in a brick behind the fireplace, I would have used it to put a new bathroom in our house and done something about our kitchen, which was extremely antique but not in a good way.

So Whiffy and I were having a robust cup of Irish Breakfast tea and an especially rich piece of fruitcake on this particular day when Charlotte arrived at the shop, the temperature plummeting as she stepped inside. Even the bell above the door — which she hated but I loved — sounded angry when it rang to herald her arrival. And it was usually such a happy little bell. At thirty-nine (the same age as me) Charlotte was very beautiful, but since she'd discovered Botox it had been harder to guess her mood from her face. Once upon a time she would come in with pinched lips and a ferocious frown and I'd know I was in trouble. More recently her outbursts had come as a shock because her face remained smooth and untroubled.

'What the hell is he doing here?' she demanded rudely as she bustled past the costume jewellery and beaded evening bags, and got wind, literally, of Whiffy.

His cup was halfway to his mouth but froze mid-air when she spoke, his gaze fixing on the wall behind the counter.

'We're just having a cup of tea,' I said chirpily, trying to hide my embarrassment at having her speak that way in front of him.

'Well, get him the hell out of here right now, it smells like a sewer,' Charlotte barked.

Whiffy stayed frozen and I considered doing the same but my cheeks were burning. Although I hated to make a fuss, I couldn't in all conscience hold my tongue.

'He's right here, Charlotte,' I said softly. 'And he's not deaf.' Although he could have been for all I knew.

'I'm sorry about this,' I apologised, just in case he wasn't.

'I don't care if he's deaf, blind or Jesus bloody Christ, Florence. Just get him out of here. You and all your charity cases. For heaven's sake, it's ridiculous!'

Her fury quite flabbergasted me. It's one thing to be pinched and frosty but to be furious?

'Charity cases?' I repeated.

'This is an antiques shop,' she snapped. 'I've tried explaining this to you before but you simply refuse to understand. It's a bloody business, Florence. We want people to come in here and buy antiques, not faff about all day drinking tea and chit-chatting about your latest cakey thing.'

She looked disdainfully at my latest cakey thing. She was very thin, Charlotte. Not much of a cake eater, actually. She preferred her food without icing, which is not something we had in common.

The bell above the shop door rang again at that point (definitely less angrily, I might point out) and Marguerite, another regular customer/visitor, wandered in. Marguerite didn't care for big priceless things that would 'grow the business' either. In fact, she didn't even care for teapots, sugar bowls or milk jugs, but she liked tea cups even more than I did and came in every couple of weeks to check for new stock.

'Morning, Florence,' she said. 'Anything new for me? I'm in the mood for a bit of Royal Grafton, I think.'

'Over here, with the Wedgwood,' I smiled and pointed,

trying not to let my agitation with Charlotte show. 'There's a tea set just in with the loveliest violet pattern.'

I turned back to my partner and in as hushed a tone as I could manage said, 'I make the cakes at home. I do it because I like to. And I buy the tea myself, so it doesn't cost you a thing.'

'But we're not a cake shop, Florence,' Charlotte snapped again. 'Wake up and smell the economics. You might be doing this for love and companionship or whatever but I want to be taken seriously as a businesswoman, as an antiques dealer. Do you get that? No, of course you don't.

'And as for you,' she turned to Whiffy, who was still frozen, and roughly plucked the cup and saucer (Royal Albert) out of his hands, grimacing at having to be so close to him, 'get back out on the streets where you belong, you filthy old devil.'

This was disgraceful behaviour and I could not let her get away with it. But before I could even start to object, all hell broke loose. It started when Charlotte gave Whiffy a decent shove with her elbow, so as to not touch him with her skin, I suppose. This jolted him out of his trance, during which time he caught sight of himself in the aforementioned Regency mirror hanging just behind me to my left. This seemed to give him a terrible fright. Perhaps he didn't know quite how much loo paper was stuck in his hair. Anyway, he opened his mouth in an awful sort of silent roar, then picked up the nearest thing to him, the chamber pot, and flung it at his own reflection.

The noise was incredible — the mirror shattering, the frame splitting, the chamber pot disintegrating — and it was not helped by Charlotte shrieking hysterical threats to call the police. I begged her to calm down as I scrambled for the dustpan and brush to pick up the broken shards of mirror and shattered chamber pot during which time Marguerite, bless her, somehow managed to get Whiffy out the door before Charlotte could even get to the phone.

Within two minutes, the shop was dead silent again, with nothing more than a distant car alarm filling the air between my white-faced partner and me.

'I can't do this any more, Florence,' Charlotte said flatly. 'I'm sorry to put it to you like this but it's been on my mind for a long time. I think it really would be best if you left.'

'If I left? What are you talking about?' I started to laugh, albeit nervously, but Charlotte didn't join in. Instead she fixed me with her steely glare, her perfect lips more pinched than ever.

'Are you *firing* me, Charlotte? You can't fire me. We're partners!'

'Partners? I want to buy and sell antiques for a profit but you are quite happy just sitting here drinking tea with the local tramps and whoever wanders in off the street. You are holding me back, Florence, you really are. The truth is, you don't care about the business — the profit, the trends, the stock — and I do. I truly do. I don't want you as a partner. I want out. No, I'm sorry, that's not true. I want you out.'

I can't tell you how shocked I was, not to mention hurt. Charlotte and I were friends, for a start, close friends, sort of. We didn't socialise as much as we used to because Martin was always working. And even when he wasn't, he and Harry were sort of at odds now that Harry was a writer not a lawyer. But I was godmother to their middle daughter Abigail, whom I loved to bits. I had also assumed that Charlotte appreciated the way I dealt with the customers. It wasn't her strength. She was good at buying the antiques, at the dealing. The profit *was* her motivation. But it wasn't mine, mine was the customers. And without customers we would never have sold anything to anyone, big or small. Didn't that make us good partners? Didn't that mean we shared the load?

Apparently not. The load, according to Charlotte, was not evenly distributed and she was shouldering too much of it, plus being stifled by my evil cake-making enterprise. Most buying and selling of antiques was being done on the internet these days anyway, she said, and I would know that if I showed more than the slightest bit of interest. My skills in terms of the partnership, she felt, had become more or less redundant. Well, not so much of the less, actually.

So, shortly after Whiffy O'Farrell threw the Victorian chamber pot into the Regency mirror, Charlotte offered me £30,000 to go away and leave her alone.

And despite being totally unprepared, having no other prospects, and not being legally obliged in any way to do so, I took it.

WHIFFY O'FARRELL

♥ ♥ ♥

People think that just because you look a certain way or smell a certain way or walk a certain way or talk a certain way or don't talk a certain way or lie on a park bench farting happily in the sun or should that be The Sun *a certain way that there's nothing inside you but they're wrong. So I don't know exactly who I was or why I'm here now or how my fingernails got so dirty; and I can't seem to reach into my brain to pull out any of the answers to the million questions I have rattling around inside my head. But I do know some things. I know there was a house and there were some little ones and I might have been one of them and there was an old man and a fob chain and I can picture them all separately but when I try to put them in a group they all fly off to different corners and I have to start again.*

Some days I think I know more about the past than others, but you know that doesn't really make me feel any better. And some days I know nothing at all and that makes me feel just the same.

They had fob chains in the antique store on Warwick Place and for a long time I used to go and look at them through the window until one day the dark-haired lady who works there came outside and asked me would I like a cup of tea and some cake. It had maybe been a long time since someone asked me that so I didn't really say anything as I seem to have lost the knack but I went in anyway and after I had looked at the fob chains I had some of the tea and some of the cake and it tasted very good and the dark-haired lady didn't ask me any questions or anything — just talked a bit about tea cups and then did some dusting.

Most people think I'm invisible so I'm inclined to think that myself but the dark-haired lady in the antiques shop saw me and that was a pretty nice feeling because it happened more than once with her. There was always tea and cake or biscuits or once a crumbly coconut thing that I didn't like as much which didn't mean it wasn't good because it was just not as good as the cakes.

The last time I was in the antiques shop I had some of her fruitcake and that was good too but then the blonde-haired lady who also works there started shouting and pushing at me and I don't like it when blonde-haired ladies shout and push at me. That is not a nice feeling.

I felt bad about the dark-haired lady because she stopped being at the antiques shop although that's good in a way because a nice lady like that shouldn't have to work with someone like the blonde-haired lady.

A nice lady like that should just make tea and cakes.

For a while I went back to looking at the fob chains through the window but now the antiques shop doesn't even have fob chains. Just great big cupboards and tables that look like they were built by monks.

CHAPTER TWO

Rotten things tend to happen in threes in my family. They always have.

'Oh, Florence, you can't truly believe that!' Harry had been known to exclaim when I aired this theory. Things, rotten or otherwise, happened whenever they happened for a variety of reasons, according to him, and couldn't really be corralled neatly into groups just to suit me. Rotten things could come in twos or fives or tens, according to Harry. 'Or even singles, Floss. It just depends when you start counting them and when you stop.'

He's entitled to his opinion, of course he is, we all are, but after nearly forty years on the planet my own personal tragedies had a rhythm to them that I think I understood pretty jolly well.

Consider this: in the space of just one awful month not long after I turned sixteen, our cat was run over by a drunken cyclist; our budgie pecked open his door and flew the coop, never to be seen again; and the tortoise who'd lived at the bottom of our garden since 1972 moved next door and wouldn't come back.

Shortly afterwards I came down with a terrible flu, which was followed by chicken pox and then, finally, appendicitis.

No sooner had I recovered from that spectacularly awful roll than I lost three grandparents in the space of two weeks.

Pets, health, grandparents: sometimes even our threes happened in threes.

So when I was fired from a job where I was theoretically my own boss, which in anyone's book definitely counted as a rotten thing, I immediately jumped to the conclusion that this was the first in a hat trick of horribleness.

The question was, what would come next?

What came immediately, which could have been a second rotten thing of the most truly rotten variety, was a fast-moving white van (is there any other sort?). I had left the shop, Charlotte's cheque in my hand, somewhat in a daze, and was looking across the road thinking how much I didn't want to go home and sit in our empty house. Harry was at a creative writing workshop in Aldeburgh and our nineteen-year-old son Monty was away in Australia doing fun things during his gap year, which was thankfully about to come to an end. Never had I missed him more.

The only one at home would be Sparky, the world's droopiest terrier. Something terribly sad had clearly happened to Sparky before we got him and he had never really cheered up. Had we known he lacked so much as a single spark, we might have rethought his name but Monty had always wanted a dog called Sparky so when we finally relented and got him one, Sparky it was — but sparky he wasn't. He was the Eeyore of the dog world: his eyes deep pools of gloom and his brow permanently knitted in sorrow. If you felt just the tiniest bit sorry for yourself, Sparky was perfect company because he liked nothing more than cuddling up to you as you sobbed delicately into his soft grey coat. If you had lost the will to live and required encouragement to carry on, though, his was not the face you wanted to peer into.

All this must have been going through my mind as I stepped thoughtlessly into the path of the fast-moving white van. With a screech of brakes it swerved dramatically across the lane, only just avoiding me, the driver honking his fury, stopping for a split second then speeding off again, a cloud of profanities issuing out the windows on both sides.

I stepped back on to the footpath, my heart knocking against my ribs, my breath coming in short panicky bursts. I couldn't think what to do. I just knew I didn't want Charlotte coming out the door, which until minutes before had been half mine, to find me clinging to a lamppost hyperventilating and sweating profusely. There was no dignity in that.

As the up-tempo beat of a girl band pop song trickled into my consciousness followed by the heady aroma of freshly poured beer, I turned to look through the open doors of the Warwick Castle, the pub right next to our shop. I would maintain my dignity in there, I decided, although I suppose that's not really what pubs are for.

With a slightly trembling voice, I ordered a gin and tonic from the tattooed barman and avoided the eye of the middle-aged midday tippler already three sheets to the wind beside me.

Grabbing my drink I moved into the sunny little annexe next to the main bar. To my surprise there, under the Pale & Burton Ales mirror, sat Marguerite.

She was perched at a tiny table bearing a pot of tea and two cups. I didn't know you could even get tea at the Warwick. I had certainly never seen any of the Sunday lunch crowd, who spilled out onto the pavement and yabbered loudly during the summer months, swilling tea. They favoured pints of light and bitter and long-winded stories about football matches going wrong, as far as I could tell.

Marguerite waved as though she had been expecting me. There was really nothing for it but to join her.

'I just about got run over by a van,' I told her, my hand shaking as I pulled back my chair. 'Honestly, I'm all of a twitter. It's turning into the most horrendous day. I'm so sorry about what happened in the shop and I can't thank you enough for what you did with Whiffy. Oh, that's what we call him, the chamber-pot man. Actually, it's mean now I come to think of it but he's never told me his name and it's not because I haven't asked. And he is whiffy. Plus Sinead, our lovely cleaning lady — well, girl really — at the shop, thought he looked like an O'Farrell who'd lived across the road from her when she was little. But still. Yes, the shop. Look, Marguerite, you'll have to forgive Charlotte, she's not always like that, she's just under a lot of pressure right now. Of course, that doesn't give her the right to . . . Well, anyway, it doesn't matter as it turns out. I'm no longer . . . We're no longer. Yes. Well. I hardly ever come in here. Isn't this nice? Just the one rotten thing so far then.'

I was talking utter nonsense, I did that sometimes when my nerves were jangled, but Marguerite didn't seem to mind. She simply pushed a cup of tea towards me. 'This is for you,' she said, smiling.

'For me?' I started to protest but she wouldn't hear of it so instead I abandoned my gin and tonic and took a sip. I didn't even really like gin and tonic, I was desperate for a cup of tea in fact, now that one was being thrust in front of me. I then told her, in a somewhat calmer fashion, what had transpired with Charlotte after she and Whiffy had left. To my embarrassment I even snivelled a little bit. That could have been the near miss with the van or it could have been the firing. It all just seemed so sordid. Why had Charlotte treated me like that? Why had I let her? Why couldn't van drivers keep to 30mph in a narrow lane?

I didn't really know Marguerite very well and as I blathered on it struck me that she had quite a peculiar manner about her that I'd never noticed before. As I told her my story of woe, she simply smiled at me in an almost trance-like fashion. Then she took my tea cup away before I'd quite finished with it and started swishing and swirling and pouring what was left of the amber liquid back into the saucer. I was mortified but of course far too polite to say anything. Anything about that, I mean. I didn't seem to have any trouble burbling on about antiques and careers and husbands and sons and university fees and electricity bills.

'But Florence,' Marguerite put her hand on my arm, mid-burble, to get my attention, 'I just have to tell you that this is going to be the best thing that ever happened to you!'

'I beg your pardon?'

Marguerite was squirming in her chair and buzzing with an excitement that seemed totally out of place. She didn't look like a drug addict but I suppose you never know.

Seeing the look on my face, she made a visible attempt to collect herself. 'Look, it's all here in your leaves,' she said, her fervour instantly gaining momentum again as she showed me the inside of the tea cup with the tea leaves splayed around in a haphazard fashion. 'Of course, it's not the best cup for reading, you really want a much finer one, more fluted, and not too heavily patterned. The violets you just pointed out next door would actually work quite well. But anyway this should do nicely in the meantime.'

'You read tea leaves?' I asked, trying to stifle my disbelief.

'Yes, I do,' she replied. 'It's my little secret. Actually, I've noticed signs of change in your leaves at the shop but I've never had the chance to look this closely. Most people's leaves will read change in some form or other but for you it's big changes, and today I can see exactly which ones.'

'You can?' I was too astonished to be entirely sceptical.

'I can.' She was so pleased I couldn't help but feel pleased too, even though she was possibly quite mad and in need of locking up. She didn't look mad though. She was always delightfully put together, Marguerite. Even when she was pregnant with twins she'd looked like a supermodel. The babies were at home with a nanny today, I supposed, and Marguerite looked as stunning as ever. Her long blonde hair hung loose in rich curls and she was wearing a pink linen coat over a floaty floral dress. She looked less mad than I did. And infinitely better dressed.

'What exactly do you see?' I asked her, on those grounds. 'Do you see Charlotte giving me the heave-ho?'

'Well, not exactly. Look, I'll show you.' She tipped the cup in my direction again and pointed at one of the blobs of dregs. 'That's a house,' she said. I agreed that it was a rectangular sort of a blob not completely un-house-shaped. 'A tall house, three storeys maybe,' she continued. 'I often see generic houses but this is a particular house. There are enormous trees on either side of it. And there's an over-sized door; see, it takes up nearly all three storeys?' She twisted the cup slightly. 'Now the house and the door are one thing but look here, Florence. There's a hammer, can you see it?'

If I squinted, I almost could. I nodded and she twisted the cup again.

'And here — oh, it's so exciting, Florence — there's a teapot; see the spout? It's perfectly clear. And next to it, can you pick the rose?'

I thought perhaps I could see the spout but the rose was beyond me. In fact, I had already lost the hammer. That was quite a lot of things to have in one tea cup, I felt.

'But what does it all mean?' I asked her.

'This is what it means: there is a house, your house I think. It has a big tree outside or a forest nearby perhaps and it is close to a lake. No, that can't be right, you do live in London, I assume? It won't be a forest or a lake. Are you near a body of water? No, I suppose not.' She looked thoughtfully out the open doors of the pub, across the top of the wine barrels and the jaunty pots of red geraniums on the footpath, a frown crossing her lovely face. 'Actually, it's a lot like that house right over there,' she said, pointing across the street. 'The one with the big ashes in the back garden and that other splendid tree in the front. How odd. The Grand Junction where the two canals meet is just over there, isn't it? Hm, maybe I have my wires crossed.'

'But that's where I live, Marguerite,' I said, flummoxed.

'What do you mean? Where?'

'In that house right across the street.'

'You do? That one right there?'

'I do. That one right there.'

'With the ash trees in the back and the whatever-it-is in the front?'

'It's called a tree of heaven,' I said. I'd loved that tree ever since my grandmother first told me its name. How wildly romantic, we had decided, for a tree so angelically named to be growing right there in front of her — now my — house.

'Gosh,' exclaimed Marguerite, 'how marvellous!'

'Well, don't marvel too much because unless I find another job in the next five minutes someone else will be living there and I and my unsuspecting family will be in the poorhouse drinking bowls of watery gruel,' I said, fervently hoping that poorhouses no longer existed or if they did, the food had improved since Oliver Twist's days.

'Don't be silly,' she said, although I didn't particularly think I was being the silly one. She was reading tea leaves after all. It was spooky she'd picked my house, mind you — unless she already knew I lived there, but I couldn't recall ever mentioning it. I rarely told people where we lived because they assumed we were rich and invited us to places I didn't have the clothes for.

'Go on, then,' I said, momentarily encouraged.

'Well, in the light of what's just happened,' she continued, 'I believe the tea leaves are saying that the antiques door has closed for you, Florence, but that doesn't matter because your heart was never really in antiques.'

I had long suspected this but then sort of forgotten about it, although I supposed that was what Charlotte had been saying. I was just not the ambitious type, Harry was always telling me that. The truth was, I'd been happy enough to trot across the street and work in the shop so had never bothered to consider doing anything else. But what was wrong with that? Happy enough is happier than most people ever managed.

'Your heart's like mine, I suspect,' Marguerite was saying. 'It's in tea. The door that is now opening for you is the teapot door. No, don't look like that, Florence. It will all make sense in a moment.'

Now, I liked a cup of tea as much as the next person, possibly more because I was fussy about the cup, but I couldn't picture what door a teapot could open that I would be interested in walking through.

'The hammer is significant here,' Marguerite continued, 'because it means strength but it can also mean building or construction. In conjunction with the house, the over-sized door and the teapot, do you know what I think you are going to do?'

'Please, be my guest,' I urged her. Perhaps there was a future for me in demolishing teapots.

'I believe you are going to turn that house across the road with the big ashes and the tree of heaven into your very own tearoom, Florence. I think you are going to make a career out of giving people tea and cakes which is what you have been so good at doing anyway. It's just you never considered it work.'

Well, maybe my heart wasn't in antiques and maybe I did love tea and cakes but to make a career of it? In my own back yard, so to speak? That was loony, even I could see that, and Harry and Monty would agree, I was sure. Sparky might even raise an eyebrow.

'There's just one thing that's puzzling me,' Marguerite continued before I could express my doubt. 'The rose. Generally roses are a reference to the heart, which in a career sense could mean following your heart. But I also get the very strong sense that in this case, the rose means a rose. Do roses have any specific meaning for you, Florence? Are you a gardener?'

No, I wasn't. I couldn't keep a rubber tree alive and had certainly never in all my life grown a rose. I couldn't even remember ever being sent any. Roses had no specific meaning for me whatsoever. None.

I was just about to tell Marguerite this when I felt a funny sort of burr of awareness: a clue that I was just about to get something. It started in my toes and crept up my legs, into my middle, shuddered through my shoulders and ended up humming behind my eyes, which were fixed on my house across the road.

I may have been a little confused about where my heart wasn't, but I knew where it was: in that house. I'd spent the happiest times of my childhood in that house; I'd brought our precious son Monty up in that house, watched him grow into the best sort of boy a mother could possibly hope for in that house; but my heart had been there long before Harry or Monty.

It was, after all, where my adored grandmother lived, the one who loved me so much she left the house to me in the first place.

Her name, of course, was Rose.

MARGUERITE

♥ ♥ ♥

I'm told I'm the last person you'd expect to be able to read tea leaves, but there you have it.

My mother always had the knack, and her mother, and apparently her mother too. We're not at all gypsy-like, which is what people seem to expect, although I do remember Mother having a skirt with a sort of handkerchief hemline at one stage. Of course, it came from Yves St Laurent and cost a bomb.

Tim, my husband, rolls his eyes whenever he sees me peering into someone's fine bone china but he has experienced enough in our life together that I have seen beforehand to know that there is definitely something in it. The leaves told me where to find him, after all.

I'm a merchant banker, or was until I stopped to have our twins Lily and Georgina. I've missed it enormously since I've been at home with the girls. That's why I love going into Drake Dowling to have a cup of tea with Florence, to chat with whoever else is in there and check out the cups.

The best cup for a good reading is the finest china; the best shape the classic one that curves out gently from the base, letting the tea leaves rise unrestricted up the sides. White or cream or pale is better, and the less ornamentation on the inside the clearer the picture.

The cups at the Warwick Castle weren't perfect, to be honest, being slightly chipped and of the catering variety, but still, I saw

Florence's future as clearly as I'd ever seen anything and it was starting almost right away.

I was terribly excited about that, as I never thought she was right for antiques, nor to work with someone like Charlotte, who is a hard-headed businesswoman and has a great future in a major auction house, actually, which is probably more up her alley than a back-street antiques shop. Anyway, I felt in my heart that Florence's tearoom was a fait accompli, I truly did, especially when she told me about her grandmother. That made it a text-book reading. I've only ever had one or two others quite as clear so it was pretty thrilling.

There was one black cloud though, which I didn't mention to Florence as she'd already had such a blow that day. To the left of the handle of the cup, before the house, which meant timing-wise its impact would probably be felt sooner, was a heart. Or, to be more accurate, two parts of a heart, split down the middle.

You don't need any special knack to work out what that means.

CHAPTER THREE

Until I met Harry, my grandmother Rose was the love of my life.

My mother's mother, she had been the first to go in that awful grandparent trifecta of my teens and I was so heartbroken I wept into my scratchy hessian pillowcase non-stop for weeks. Everyone was terribly understanding, assuming it was the shock of losing three of them in such a short time that was crippling me so badly, but to be honest, I could not really drum up much grief for my paternal grandparents after losing Rose. I spent it all on her. Gorgeous, lovely, precious, sweet, adorable her.

Don't get me wrong, Poppa Phil and Nanny Mary, my father's parents, were perfectly lovely, despite the smell of mothballs (her) and terrifying nasal hair (him), but Rose was something else. I adored everything about her. She smelt of freshly laundered linen sheets and jasmine, never had a hair out of place, was always spot on time, introduced me to scones and clotted cream, and was mine, all mine, preferring me to my cute redheaded younger sister Poppy — which never happened — and electing herself my living guardian angel.

And I needed a guardian angel, believe me, or felt like I did, which is probably the same. A lot of the time, even when I was little, I thought my parents had brought the wrong baby back from the hospital; that I'd been swapped for someone else's more conservative bundle. They were hippies, my parents, not that there's anything wrong with that, but even as a toddler I was pretty square, so I found them a bit embarrassing really and vice versa, I'm sure.

As with many young folk coming of age in the 1950s and '60s, Mum and Dad had started out perfectly middle class. She had trained to be a nurse and he was at university studying accountancy when they met, although they keep that pretty quiet because it seemed too middle of the road, I suppose. It was Mum who first discovered reefers and free love at some event smelling heavily of patchouli oil, from what I can gather, and Dad followed slavishly behind her. Like many reformed people, they took to being born-again hippies with a verve that born-the-first-time ones often lacked. My mother's armpit hair was so long I'm sure she took pills to hurry it along. And my father never wore underpants and didn't notice if his harem pants had holes in them.

I was a total throwback. I didn't mean to be. It just turned out that way.

They begged me to call them Beth and Archie but all I ever wanted was Mummy and Daddy.

They dressed me in hemp and gave me wooden blocks to play with; I wanted pink frills and Barbie dolls. They loved acting out politically correct fairy tales and baking their own cement-like five-grain loaf; I liked *The Brady Bunch* and white bread. I dreamed of getting married and wearing a one-piece in the summer; they didn't believe in marriage (although they were themselves married — the photos are hilarious) and loved any excuse to get their kit off and parade around in the nude.

When Poppy came along, she proved to be their perfect child. This could have caused some resentment on my part except that Poppy was and continues to be the most adorable creature in the world. Plus, her arrival got me off the hook. I had been a major disappointment to my mother by weaning myself off the breast when I was seven months old — a crime tantamount to eating a Wimpy hamburger and enjoying it in her world — but pliable Poppy kept suckling away until she was four. A bit beyond the pale, if you ask me, but no one did.

So, my parents, with their philosophy of knit-your-own-peanut-butter-and-wear-a-poncho-while-you're-doing-it, thought (in a loving way of course) that I was something of an oddity — but my grandmother, Rose, did not. She got me. She just plain old got me and you are so lucky to have that as a child, I think: an adult from the grown-up world who thoroughly understands who you are and assures you that it's perfectly all right to be that way. Take my name, for example. My parents had christened me Florence thinking I had been conceived in that most romantic of Italian cities. It was quite a way-out thing to do in those days although they had to constantly explain that I was named after a shagging marathon in the Hotel Caravaggio on Piazza Indipendenza, not some dusty old maiden aunt. Anyway, when I was six months old they were reminded by the friends with whom they'd hooked up in Italy that they'd actually missed their first connection. They subsequently realised my beginnings were most likely formed in the ladies' loo at Luton Airport. As a result of this blunder, they veered away from Florence and tended to call me Flower or Effie, two names I never really liked even though obviously they were both a lot better than Ladies' Loo at Luton Airport (depressingly likely to be shortened to Lula and loved by one and all if given half the chance).

When I was three, I told Grandma Rose that I did not like being called Flower or Effie. I liked being called Florence because that was my name. Grandma agreed it was the better choice and said that as we were on the subject, she didn't particularly care for Grandma and would I be ever so kind as to call her Rose. It was the first real conversation of my life.

This must have irritated my poor mother enormously, given that I wouldn't call her Beth. But in my eyes Rose could do no wrong.

It was Rose who took me to Hamleys to buy toys because my parents didn't believe in them; Rose who bought me a pair of bespoke red Mary-Janes after Mum gave me orthopaedic brown sandals for my birthday; Rose who let me bake cakes with white flour (outlawed in our house) from her enormous supply of recipe books; Rose who let me play tea parties with black tea instead of garden clippings in the front room with her best china.

In my teens I would visit her as often as I could in the house across the road from the Warwick Castle. I lived with my parents in a ramshackle house in Primrose Hill that was painted psychedelic colours and furnished largely with beanbags. We lived on mung beans and made our own yoghurt but unlike real proper hippies, we didn't have to, we chose to. Dad may have kept his accountancy background a secret but he obviously had some skill and his fair share of luck because he made a quiet killing playing the stock market.

I mean we had central heating and new underwear and good haircuts and insurance. There was a compost heap out the back and a vegetable garden but that's about as self-sufficient as we got. And I say the house was ramshackle but it more had the appearance of being ramshackle. It needed attention on the outside (the windowsills flaked paint and ivy grew wild and fierce) but inside everything was in perfect working order and should it ever fail to be, someone was brought in quick smart to fix it.

But the house was busy, in more ways than one. Bright colours hummed from the walls, Indian cotton cushions were strewn from wall to wall, unannounced visitors dropped in constantly, music pounded from the stereo. It was modern and edgy and loose. Poppy thrived. She was a little girl who went with the flow. I, on the other hand, went to Rose's.

Her house was the opposite of my parents'. It was quiet and structured, even to look at. It was three storeys, as Marguerite had seen in the tea leaves, plastered brick that was painted a calm creamy colour. Georgian, with large sash windows, a delightfully overgrown garden at the back and a cobbled courtyard at the front. The only thing that kept it from being symmetrical — I loved symmetry, was obsessed by it, to my parents' further shame — was a boxy twentieth-century addition at the ground level on the Warwick Place side.

From the front it looked out on the pretty blue Westbourne Terrace Road Bridge and the sparkling (as I always thought of it) expanse of water that is the junction where Regent's Canal meets the Grand Union Canal. This was my favourite view in all the world.

Little Venice, nestled into the elbow of Maida Vale and Paddington, wasn't really anything like big Venice but those two waterways with their collection of colourful canal boats and cobbled walkways did give it a charm you could not find anywhere else in the city.

Regent's Canal curled from our junction to the Thames at Limehouse, while the Grand Union meandered all the way to Birmingham in the north, I believed. There, right in front of our house, the two met in a large pool with Browning's Island in the middle. The poet Robert Browning had lived in the area and was rumoured to have given Little Venice its name, which certainly made sense given the poetic license employed.

Once upon a time the canals had provided the city with an important industrial transport route but then fast moving white vans took over, I suppose, although officially the railway got there first. Boats were now just a delightful decorative addition. Anyway, my great-grandfather had bought the house in the 1920s when the elegant eighteenth-century mansions on either side of the flagging canal were going for a song. A doctor, he'd built the boxy extension that housed his surgery and my grandfather, also a doctor, used it for the same purpose although had 'modernised' it sometime in the '60s.

My grandfather and Rose must have rattled around in such a big place but it was an oasis of off-white and peace compared to my hectic home life and I loved it. Everything was in its place and the place never changed. When I came to stay, Rose would always make a big fuss about meals because meal times were not recognised at home, apparently being a contrived archaic structure. This was the cause of much sourness between my parents and Rose and me, for that matter.

At Rose's we had dinner in the dining room at seven, breakfast in the kitchen at eight, lunch in the garden — weather permitting — at half-past twelve and if we didn't bake something ourselves for afternoon tea at three, which we usually did, we would go out for this most refined of eating opportunities.

We went to the Ritz, to Simpsons of Picadilly, to Fortnum and Mason, to Harrods. On my tenth birthday Rose took me to Claridge's, for a silver tray stacked high with tiny bite-sized morsels accompanied by bottomless pots of tea, poured with unerring politeness by unobtrusive yet attentive staff. The Art Deco glamour and seductive ambience of Claridge's seemed to me the height of grown-up sophistication.

We took tea at the Dorchester for my eleventh birthday, at the Savoy for my twelfth, then went back to Claridge's to see if it really was our favourite for my thirteenth (it was, so we went there for my fourteenth and fifteenth too).

It was a treat that I utterly treasured but I treasured having tea at home with Rose too. When my grandfather, Cecil, was alive, Rose and I would wait for him to join us in the sitting room, spying out the upstairs window at his patients as they came and went, guessing what was wrong with them. The slings and crutches were easy to spot but gentlemen who sprang up the front steps two at a time or ladies who skipped under the tree of heaven and across the road afterwards had us guessing for hours.

'It could be leprosy, you know,' Rose would suggest in her gentle voice. 'The way she's hiding inside that great big coat.'

'Or scarlet fever,' I would counter. I loved the idea of scarlet fever. 'She might be going blind and deaf like Helen Keller did after she got scarlet fever. Any minute now it will hit her, I expect.'

At three on the dot, my grandfather would walk in and Rose would pour his tea and arrange a plate of homemade goodies for him, always including a couple of Rich Tea biscuits, the only things he ever actually touched. My mother had been an only child and a wilful one who had distanced herself somewhat so in their later years my grandparents mostly had just each other. Although I can barely remember Cecil saying a word, I remember the way he looked at Rose and that told me everything.

When he died, pre-dating the grandparent trifecta by nearly a decade, my grandmother retained the composure for which I loved her so dearly. She grieved, but delicately. Not for her the weeping and wailing and Buddhist chants, the likes of which were going on at Primrose Hill even though Mum barely spoke to her father while he was alive. No, Rose suffered in silence. Even as a six-year-old I could spot the pain, the loneliness she felt, but her sadness did not overwhelm her or anyone else.

One thing did surprise me in the wake of Grandad's departure though. Rose had the most beautiful collection of china, mostly Royal Doulton, about which she was justifiably proud, much of it chosen and bought for her by my grandfather. But from the day of his funeral onward, she mixed the cups and saucers from different sets, quietly insisted on it. Should a cup end up accidentally with its true partner, she would lean across and switch the saucer. I asked her why she did this once and she just smiled and gave a little continental shrug.

This mismatching habit of hers said a lot about her because it was a cheeky kink in her otherwise silky smooth armour. She was conservative with a twist, Rose, as I suppose was I. In truth it probably kept us from being dead boring. Mum and Dad and Poppy, on the other hand, would rather gouge out their eyes with macramé hooks than admit to a single ounce of conservative. For them it was pretty much all about the twist. Mum and Dad's twists were quite deliberate, of course, because they were really still rebelling against their upbringing but Poppy's twist came naturally.

Not that they are terrible people; heavens, far from it. They are delightful people. Truly delightful. Everybody loves them, and I do too, deeply. We are, and always have been in many respects, very close.

Less close, I suppose, since they all upped stumps and moved to Tannington Hall, a Tudor farmhouse in Suffolk, where Mum and Dad talked about growing organic herb crops and Poppy helped. Dad remained embarrassed about his prosperity but he seemed able to make money almost by accident, investing in things everyone (including him) thought were totally mad only to find them the new best thing since sliced bread in five years' time. The point being that he had no real need to actually farm organic herbs so talking was as far as he would ever go and in the meantime they loved it in the country.

The three of them formed a perfect loopy little unit who seemed never to tire of each other's company nor lengthy discussions on the pointlessness of vegetarian pork scratchings. Look, if you've always dreamed of having a family who will endlessly discuss labial piercing or placenta pie over the dinner table, they are probably perfect. If you're gagging to express every single feeling, even the ones so small as to hardly count, they are just the ticket. If you like to shock, bingo! My parents love being shocked. The best thing a daughter could do, in their eyes, is streak across the cricket pitch at Lords or run away and join the circus. My school friend Bettina Malone did both; the former after one too many snakebites at the Washington pub and the latter after falling for the juggling teacher at an extra-curricular gym class. My mother cried tears of actual envy. There was I studying for A levels instead of taking to the hills in a Humber 80 decorated like a clown's head. How could I?

As an obedient teenager I felt like a letdown where my parents were concerned but I knew I was the light of Rose's life, which made everything all right. I just wish I'd had some idea that she was going to leave me so swiftly, cancer claiming all three grandparents in that one fell swoop. (Actually, we did not call it cancer. Despite the fact that my parents embraced everything far more than anybody ever really needed to, the word was never again spoken in our house after the funerals were done and dusted. It was referred to as 'the measles'. And even then it was mentioned only in a whisper.)

In the months before Rose died I was busy being a girlie swot, poring over my schoolbooks and spending my remaining waking hours being madly in love with my boyfriend Harry, with whom I was not having sex, despite my parents' insistence that I should.

For my sixteenth birthday, just months before she died, before we even knew she was ill, I begged Rose to eschew our traditional Claridge's afternoon tea in favour of going to see *Indiana Jones and the Temple of Doom* at the Odeon in Leicester Square. Afterwards, I chewed my way through a spectacularly overdone piece of indistinguishable meat at the Angus Steak House around the corner.

It's not easy being the carnivorous daughter of strict vege-tarians, I probably went slightly too far in the other direction. I think Rose liked the odd lamb cutlet but that was probably as meaty as she got and it is a credit to her that she handled this birthday fiasco as though it were also her idea of a perfect way to spend the day. I don't recall her actually swallowing so much as a morsel of steak (if that's what it was) but she had a lot of very nice things to say about Harrison Ford.

When she died I tortured myself about wasting that last birthday treat. How could I have been so selfish? We could have had cucumber sandwiches and scones and bite-sized pastries on those delicate Claridge's plates one more time but instead

I was drooling over Harrison bloody Ford. I've loathed him ever since. I nearly had a bloody aneurism when he dumped his wife for Ally McBeal.

As for being left Rose's house: that made me feel sick, utterly sick. Just thinking of it being there without her in it filled me with anguish. The memories of all the wonderful times we'd shared there together were just too awful to contemplate, I couldn't bear them, so I told Dad to get rid of the place, to sell it, to give it away; a command he completely ignored. There's nothing a pretend hippy likes more than collecting property in parts of London destined to become fashionable, after all.

The place was rented out for years and I couldn't stand to even drive past for many of them. One day, though, I woke up after a particularly nonsensical yet stirring dream involving the giant Disneyland tea cups and Rose and a mountain of chocolate and felt the need to revisit it. I walked Monty over from Notting Hill in the push chair and sat on the stone wall by the boater facilities on the Delamere Terrace side of the canal where I had a perfect view of the window from which we used to spy on the patients. I still missed Rose dreadfully and thought about her every day. Sometimes I even caught the odd whiff of her delicate fragrance on a passing stranger or saw a silver chignon being patted into place across the room and that teenage sadness at losing her claimed me just as fiercely once again.

That spring afternoon though, I looked up and saw the two of us there, pointing out the window and making up stories. I could almost feel the crumbs of a coffee cake caught in the corner of my mouth, and I was suddenly overwhelmed with the happiness I'd felt sitting on her Sanderson sofa, helping myself to cream from one of her delicate jugs and wondering aloud if the lady with the enormous bosoms and thick ankles had scurvy or was pregnant with quintuplets.

That spring afternoon, for reasons I couldn't fathom then nor now, the memory wasn't painful at all, it was gloriously cheerful. It was as though someone had flicked a switch in my emotional fuse box. She was gone and I could never bring her back, sad — but she'd been there in the first place and nobody could erase the memory of her, wonderful. Time might take my youth and add a husband and a child and a fairly ho-hum career (at that stage in part-time reception and part-time shop assisting) but nothing, nobody could take away the times Rose and I had spent together. They were there for eternity. I don't know why this hadn't occurred to me before, maybe I was just growing up, maybe that's how grief works, but I felt the weight of my sadness lighten as I sat there while Monty chewed on a rusk and cooed at the passing birds and Rose's image faded from the upstairs window but stayed crisp and clear just like the spring day itself in my mind.

I went straight home and suggested to Harry that we sell our Notting Hill flat and move to the big house in Little Venice. From that day on remembrances of Rose were never sad affairs. I took every precious occasion I could remember and instead of squashing them in a box to save myself the pain of not having her with me still, I strung them up next to each other in my mind, like Christmas lights, so on darker days I could turn them on and still feel that she was right there with me.

The day I was booted out of my own business was obviously one such dark day.

I'd lost a job, a friend, a mirror, and a chamber pot in the time it took to brew a decent pot of tea. Days did not get much darker.

Or so I thought.

ROSE

To my darling Florence
I found this the other day when I was doing a spring clean of
the kitchen cupboards. How it got separated from my old recipe
book I can't imagine, but it strikes me as the sort of treat you
would just adore. I can remember making this with my own
grandmother, God rest her soul. Goodness knows where we got
the eggs and sugar but I remember the smell of that cake coming
out of the oven as though it were yesterday. It must be the tea, I
think. I could have waited till I see you next week to give it to
you but just found it and thought I'd pop it in the post as you
no doubt need cheering up while studying for your exams, you
clever girl.

Give my love to the family and Harry.
Rose

SULTANA CAKE

1 pkt sultanas
½lb butter chopped into pieces
3 eggs
¾ cup sugar
2 cups flour
3 small tsp baking powder

1 tsp vanilla essence
3 tbsp sherry (optional)
1–2 tbsp brown sugar (optional)

Cover sultanas with water or if you have cold Irish Breakfast tea left in the pot use that for extra flavour. Bring to the boil on the stove and simmer for five minutes.

Strain off the water/tea and add the butter, letting it melt. Meanwhile beat eggs and sugar in a large bowl till thick.

Add sultanas and melted butter to egg mix.

Sift in flour and baking powder, then add essence. Mix and put in a well greased or lined eight-inch round tin.

Bake for the first couple of minutes at 350°F then reduce heat to 300°F and cook for up to 1½ hours, checking after 1¼.

On removal from the oven, gently drizzle the sherry over the hot cake and rub in the brown sugar, which makes for an extra delicious crust.

CHAPTER FOUR

At home after the dreadful business with Charlotte and my strange experience with Marguerite, I didn't quite know what to do with myself so opted in the end for collapsing on our big squashy brass bed, Sparky slumped pathetically beside me as I tried to conjure up one of my happy Rose moments.

I lay there, eyes closed, trying once again to recall the two of us spotting ailments from the front-room window. I could see her, I could see me, I could see the Sanderson sofa, and I could see the courtyard, but it wasn't full of departing patients in flares getting into their Triumph 2000s, as it had been all those years ago. Instead it was planted with pale yellow roses and other flowering shrubs. There were tables dotted around these little garden areas and they were covered in pretty linen tablecloths. On top of the tables were tiered plates heaving with chocolate éclairs, fruit tarts, sponge cakes, shortbread, scones, tiny savouries and crustless sandwiches, plus teapots and cups and milk jugs of every description. Around the tables were strangely faceless people, one of whom was dressed in a Vivienne Westwood top I had seen in a *Vogue* magazine the day before. They were modern healthy people, not '70s sick people, and they were having a jolly good time. I could almost hear the clatter of teaspoons against cups; forks against cake remains.

This most certainly wasn't the past I was looking into. So what was it?

I felt that odd burr of awareness shimmying up my body again, stopping behind my eyes, which instantly sprang open. I sat up and pushed the mournful dog away from me. Those people in my mind were having tea in my front garden. More correctly, they were being *served* tea in my front garden. To all intents and purposes, they were indeed treating my front garden like a tearoom. Could there actually be something in what Marguerite had seen in the tea leaves?

It was ludicrous, of course it was.

But it also made a strange sort of sense.

How hard would it be to turn this house I loved so much into a tearoom? I wondered, feeling a little tremor of excitement. Probably not as hard as a normal house because this one was already slightly higgledy-piggledy, thanks to part of it spending eighty years as a doctor's surgery.

Our family kitchen was on the first floor with the formal sitting room, which is where Harry and I spent most our time when we were both there, as had Cecil and Rose.

But on the ground floor where the doctor's rooms had been, there was a kitchenette, a small bathroom and two large rooms, one of which Monty used mostly as a TV room and the other Harry and I used as an office. The backyard was a delightfully (I thought) overgrown jungle but it had its own access out to Warwick Place. Rose had used this to come and go during surgery hours and I had used it to go to work when I had a job, which was up until that very day, or when I was walking anywhere via the lane as opposed to using the car, which was parked in the front. What it meant was that there were two separate entrances to our house. One at the front that patients, or customers, say, could use. And one at the back for us.

In my grandfather's day the front courtyard had been cobbled and left neat and empty for the Triumph 2000s, but when the house was rented out (and indeed when we moved in) weeds were the dominating feature. It was still vaguely cobbled if you looked close enough but we never used it for anything. We just ignored it. Poppy couldn't bear this wanton neglect and over one lentil-casserole-fuelled weekend planted wildflowers around the edges and between the cobbles. After that we continued to ignore it but it looked a lot prettier, even though people in nice clothes often looked at it balefully and shook their heads when they walked by.

It's just that Harry and I were both hopeless gardeners. I killed things just by thinking about them and he completely didn't care. We were both wildly impractical when it came to things around the house. I cooked but that was about it and Harry could clean, but sort of didn't, and never even pretended to be handy, couldn't straighten a picture on the wall, let alone fix a rattly doorknob or unstick a stubborn window.

These chores were either left undone or tackled by my father who did pretend to be handy, even though he also wasn't. As a result, the house, while generally ultimately clean because eventually I would dust and vacuum, was otherwise a bit shabby. Wallpaper curled out cutely from the walls in various places up the two stairwells, the carpet was frayed in popular parts of the house, the bathroom was not at all *House & Garden*, the kitchen cupboards needed painting and the oven replacing (not the least because it was brown). On one hand it was in need of major redecorating; but on the other hand, that wallpaper, the carpet and the once-upon-a-time ivory paintwork in the kitchen was what I had known and loved since seeking refuge from the fresh purple and oranges of Primrose Hill.

When Monty was about fourteen I had let him paint his bedroom in black and white stripes, which was really the extent of any renovating. The black was now more of a dark grey and the white was a little grubby in patches but he'd done a good job, better than his father or I would have done. I'd been so impressed that he'd known just what he wanted and that it was something out of the ordinary. He really was a treasure, my boy.

At the thought of him, I pushed myself off the bed and went downstairs to check my email.

Monty had been in Australia for more than nine months and was due back in the next few weeks. I'd been missing him desperately but was under strict instructions never to admit it. 'If you turn into one of those creeps who says your son is your best friend, I will kill you,' Monty had told me himself before he left. 'You should have a best friend your own age.'

And really, he wasn't my best friend. Harry was. But Monty was my best everything else.

At the risk of sounding like the sort of woman other mothers would like to clock over the head with a frozen chicken, he was the dream child. It started with an easy pregnancy in my then twenty-year-old body, which sprang back into shape as if by magic, then continued as we watched in wonder while our little treasure fed better than most, slept more than most, and lavished his glorious smile on anyone who had the good fortune to come anywhere near him.

Monty was everyone's favourite toddler, schoolboy, teenager, everything. He didn't even get spotty. Or smelly. Or angry. I know people always think their own children are the bee's knees, even the hideous ones who set sparrows on fire in their spare time and grow Mohawk hairdos, but Monty truly was head and shoulders above the lot of them. Practically every school report he ever got said almost exactly that.

Of course it had been a loathsome wrench to let him go all the way across the world to where the streets were thick with crocodiles and those silly hats with corks hanging off them but he was a sensible boy, a trustworthy boy, a good boy. He was master of his own destiny, I kept reminding myself. As Rose had believed in me, I believed in Monty. He had a very sure sense of himself, our son. If he wanted to go and discover himself on the other side of the world even though he was only eighteen, then it was the right thing for him to do and no one should stand in his way, not even me. Much. After the initial outburst.

So I lay in bed and sobbed my heart out for a week after he left but at least the pillowcases weren't hessian and eventually Sparky got so depressed on my behalf I felt obliged to get up and get on with my life.

To begin with, Monty emailed nearly every day — in fact I worried he wasn't having enough of an adventure — but as he'd moved about Australia, bartending in Darwin, gardening in Perth, valeting in Sydney (a boy who had never picked up a towel in his life? I never said he was *perfect*), the correspondence had dropped off. In recent months we were lucky if we got more than a couple of lines a week. He was somewhere near the New South Wales/Queensland border working at a health spa set in the rainforest. His access to email was limited, he'd told us, but he was having the time of his life.

That's the best you can hope for your children, I kept reminding myself: that they are having the time of their life as often as they can manage it.

I switched on the computer and sure enough, there was nothing from him, just a bunch of irritating jokes from my mother who had embraced the computer age with all her tie-dyed might and drove me potty sending long lists of why cucumbers were better than men and the like.

I was contemplating telling her just what to do with her latest cucumbers when I heard the front door open and the sound of the Grand Junction filter in.

'Floss?' It was Harry, calling out in a strange tone, sort of half-heartedly as though he didn't really want me to answer. 'Floss, are you home?'

What was Harry doing here? He wasn't due back from Aldeburgh for another two days. I blinked at the computer screen, Monty's name glaringly absent from my inbox, and I knew as sure as I know that white chocolate is not really actually chocolate and shouldn't even be called by that name that rotten thing number two was heading my way.

'Floss?' Harry called out again in the same odd voice.

I could tell from the noise of cars crossing the bridge and a police siren wailing in the background that he was still standing inside the open front door.

Monty, I thought, my heart clenching like a fist. Something had happened to our son.

Suddenly losing my stupid job seemed utterly meaningless. That blow had been vicious but other than stepping dazedly into the path of oncoming traffic I had emerged unscathed. That was only my career. This was far more brutal. My blood turned to lead, slowed in my veins, dragging my weight down, rooting me to my chair. I tried to move. I tried to keep breathing. I managed a strangled squeak.

I heard the front door being pushed shut, Harry's boots on the worn floorboards, one step muffled as he crossed the worn hall runner, then felt a rush of cold air as he opened the door to the office.

'Floss, here you are. Didn't you hear me calling you?'

I had loved Harry Dowling from the first day I saw him, waiting for the 268 bus. We were both fourteen at the time: me just turned, him eleven months into it. He was tall and as good-looking as boys that age got, but not in a way that he was aware of, which made him far less intimidating to a shy girl like myself who could nonetheless recognise his potential. He was standing by the kerb wearing a nerdy scarf wound around his neck and had a long dark fringe that he seemed to hide behind, although it couldn't disguise the wicked dimple on his left cheek that appeared when he smiled. Which he did, that morning, cutely at me and I felt the world stop spinning. For a moment there was only the two of us in the universe.

It sounds silly but it's true. Or that's how I remember it. And I certainly never felt the same ever again. It only ever happened to you once, I imagined. Or did it happen the first time and then you stopped expecting it? I didn't know because I never so much as looked at another bloke after I met Harry: even when Eddie Carmichael, the captain of the first XV, confessed his undying passion for me after three glasses of rum punch at a toga party during our sixth form year. And he was gorgeous, Eddie Carmichael. But, no, I only ever had eyes for Harry.

Right from the word go, when we started going out together, about seven minutes after I spotted him, I remember thinking how lucky I was that no one else had snapped him up before me. I was not what you would consider a catch at that time, being tall myself and gangly for a fourteen-year-old, but Harry was a catch, anyone could see that. Good-looking, kind, witty people are few and far between in the teenage world, in any world. The very fact that he chose me over all the short, blonde strumpets waiting for the 268, and there was a surprising number of them, just added to my good fortune. And as the years passed, as we got engaged, then married, moved into a flat, had Monty, moved into our house, I never lost that feeling of being lucky to have found him. Not many people have this, I used to think. And by 'this' I meant not just the happiness but the recognition of the happiness, which is an entirely different thing because sometimes you can be happy and not even know it. Usually, when I looked at Harry, I knew it, and I felt quite simply and beautifully blessed.

Not today though. Harry's face was pale and his fists were clenched at his sides. Something was deeply not right. It was not a time to feel blessed. It was a time to feel terrified. My innards, often one step ahead of me, turned to jelly.

'Is it Monty?' I asked, taking in a huge gulp of air, pushing my chair back against the wall, preparing my body for the physical pain that was already tingling at my edges. 'What's happened? Is he hurt? Is he dead?'

'Floss, please, it's nothing like that,' Harry said, his voice more sure now, more serious. Harry never squeaked. 'It's not Monty. He's fine. Truly. It's not him. Florence, look at me.' I looked. 'It is not Monty. This is not about him. It's just . . . well, it's about me, actually. Florence . . . we need to talk.'

You don't have to watch many movies to know that 'we need to talk' does not bode at all well for the future but I was so busy feeling relief, that good old whisky chaser of an emotion, flood through me that I did not pick up on this vital clue.

'You're sure? He's really OK? Oh, Harry, please tell me he is OK.'

'I have told you that. I am sure. He's really OK. It's not Monty. He is fine, honestly Florence. It's not Monty.'

Well, if it wasn't something awful about our son, how bad could it be, I remember thinking, as my heart popped back to its original plumpness and my blood lightened and started flowing normally around my body again.

And Harry was right, I thought, as I followed him up to the kitchen, we did need to talk. I needed to tell him that I had just made a whopping £30,000 but that the news wasn't all good. Would he be angry? I doubted it. He had always been so grateful that I had encouraged him to give up law, which he hated but was good at, and take up writing, which he loved but which had so far to earn him a penny. But we'd needed my income from the business, paltry as it sometimes was, to pay the bills and without it we'd need to think of a way to get some cash flowing. Could he write a novel that perhaps had more appeal to a bigger audience, or in the first place a publisher? That was maybe a bit more John Grisham/Dan Brown than Booker Prize? This had been suggested, I think, in one or two of his many rejection letters but I always sided with Harry because I believed in him. I always had. I didn't really care about money, I realised, as I filled the kettle with water and warmed the teapot. We could live on baked beans and London smog as long as Monty was all right.

I think I even managed a feeble smile as we settled on either side of the old pine table his gran had given us when we married and he reached for my hands, cupping them in his.

I had forgotten by now that there was still something Harry

had come home early from his course to tell me, so thrilled was I that our son was alive and well and probably only scraping kangaroo carcasses off the front fender of an SUV not lying underneath it in a pool of blood.

'The thing is, Charlotte fired me,' I told him before he had a chance to speak. 'Whiffy threw a chamberpot at the Regency mirror behind the counter and smashed it and she said she'd had enough of me and that I was keeping her from growing the business and she didn't want me for a partner any more. She offered me £30,000 to go away and I took it, Harry, and I thought for a bit that it was the first rotten thing — which I know you don't believe in but still — and I know I should have consulted you but the thing is I don't really think it was a choice if you know what I mean, especially not the way Charlotte put it. Then suddenly it didn't seem quite so dreadful anyway because Marguerite saw this amazing opportunity in a tea cup at the Warwick Castle.'

Harry's jaw was hanging open and he was looking at me in a most peculiar fashion.

'I know it's not exactly a fortune,' I rambled on, 'but still, it is a lump sum and where else are we going to find one of those? What I'm thinking is — after talking to Marguerite and it might seem loony at first but actually it isn't — that we could use the money to turn downstairs into, wait for it, Harry: a tearoom! Yes, it's a little bit out of the blue but as one door closes another one opens and the pipes and what have you must already be there, the space is definitely there, plus we could have tables and chairs in the courtyard and now that I have had a moment to think about it, I can't imagine a better way to spend my day than . . .'

Still, Harry was staring at me, a look of horror, I suppose you could call it, claiming his face.

'It's not the worst idea in the world,' I suggested. 'Is it?' Perhaps it was. I hadn't really thought about it that much at all, obviously. It had just sort of made sense. At the time. Or shortly afterwards. Now I wasn't so sure.

'You might have to work a bit somewhere, Harry, but not for long,' I ploughed on, witlessly. 'And I'm sure the tearoom would make money as long as we don't spend more than we have and don't expect it to happen overnight. But there's nowhere else decent for miles, or nowhere sort of quaint, unless you count the barge across the bridge and that's tiny and does eggs and sausages and I mean to do proper tea on cake stands and everything, like Claridge's but, you know, smaller, not the food but the place and with a bit of a twist.'

No, it wasn't horror on Harry's face. It was worse. It was misery.

'It's only a tearoom, Harry,' I said, getting a giant case of the speed wobbles. 'Not even that. It's only an idea about a tearoom.'

Misery was not a natural state for Harry. He was a calm, steady, contented person. Usually he sailed straight through the likes of grief and stress, was never tossed about by their peaks and troughs. Even his decision to abandon his job had been remarkably free of angst or drama. Stoic was the word, I suppose. Now though, with his face all drawn in, his eyes so dark and sorrowful, he seemed oddly unfamiliar to me. A miserable stranger.

'I can't think of any other way to do this, Floss,' he said.

I had no idea what was coming. Any other way to do what?

'The thing is that I've been putting it off for quite a while now,' he continued, 'and if I could, I would put it off forever, especially after what's happened to you today. I mean the timing is just appalling. Truly appalling. I can't believe it, really, but I can't put it off any longer. It's not fair to you or me or . . .'

What in heaven's name was he on about? I couldn't work out how this was connected to the chamber pot or the money or my job. That cup of tea I'd had at the Warwick earlier, however, swirled clever and dark in my murky depths.

'The thing is,' Harry said, 'there's someone else.'

Now it was my jaw that dropped open. Was this a joke? 'We need to talk' followed so quickly by 'There's someone else.' You'd think even a nitwit like me would start getting the gist of things about now but still, I remained bewildered.

'There's someone else, Florence,' Harry said again. 'And I'm afraid it's not what you'd expect. Not who.'

Well it wouldn't be, would it; I wasn't expecting anything at all. Anyone.

'What are you telling me?' I asked dimly.

'It's a man,' Harry said softly. 'He is a man.'

A *man*? I was lost, totally lost, all coherent thought swirling about with that cup of Twinings' finest.

'What?' I asked again, feeling Harry's hands growing clammy on top of mine, reminding me mine were still there, his own bigger ones cloaking them. 'A what?'

'His name is Charles, he's a doctor at the Whittington Hospital. I'm so sorry, Floss. I love you with all my heart, you know I do, but this is different. I just can't keep on . . . I don't want to hurt you, you must know that, it's the last thing I would ever want to do but it's time I . . . Oh God, Floss, I'm just so sorry.'

I can be slow at times. I used to blame my mother for smoking pot when she was pregnant with me, although she claims she cut down for the duration and never once took magic mushrooms.

Then as I got older I realised it was a panic issue. My parents don't believe in panic — actually catching fire on one occasion failed to so much as ruffle my father — but I think I was born with a massive panic gene. Because of faulty wiring and a lack of guidance, however, it tended to trip up. My body seemed to physically react to trauma in a flash. It just took my brain a while to catch up.

So as the contents of my stomach were lurching hysterically inside me across the table from Harry who apparently had someone else, my muddled mind continued to grapple with the meaning of his words. Why is he talking about this doctor, I thought? Was there something wrong with him?

'What's the matter?' I asked, the Twining's rising yet again. 'Oh, please tell me it's not the "measles". I couldn't bear it.'

Harry looked more stricken than ever as he shook his head. After twenty years of marriage he knew enough about my faulty wiring to know when I was getting something and when I was not. And I was definitely on delay.

'Floss, listen to me,' he said, squeezing my hands even tighter, pulling me into his safe, solid sanity the way he always had.

'I'm not sick. I'm perfectly healthy. I'm just gay.'

I'm just gay.

Three words you never want to hear your husband say, by the way, and a reason to panic if ever there was one.

Indeed, my fingers and toes were tingling, my hearing was coming and going, I felt bile rising in my throat, and I was as cold as a stone. But that was as panicked as I got because it turns out that panicking isn't what you do when the love of your life tells you he's changed his colours.

Instead, you die.

It's as simple as that. The bit of you that for all those years has been his loving wife and a devoted mother to your darling son, which, by the way you realise in that exact moment is most of you, just shrivels up and dies. In an instant. It is terrifying. Far more terrifying than panic, which you know from experience will pass. This feels permanent. Like death.

But how could he be gay? I heard a voice that sounded like me only much more frightened asking. When had he had the chance? We had grown up together, for heaven's sake, were growing old together, I knew him like the back of my hand. How could I possibly have missed the fact that he preferred men?

'But you have terrible taste in clothes,' I said, utterly confused. He didn't even use any product in his hair. He hated musicals. And Kylie. I knew these were the ridiculously stereotypical gay traits found pretty much only in *Will & Grace* reruns but I was caught off guard, I'd not had the chance to do any research.

'I'm so sorry, Floss,' was all he could say as tears started rolling down his face. 'I'm so, so sorry. I know you probably won't ever forgive me but that doesn't mean I'm not sorry.'

It occurred to me that I had never seen him cry before or if I had it was so long ago I couldn't remember. Gay for five minutes and a great big sissy already? Who was this man?

I stood up and hit him across the head with a bunch of bananas.

Never mind panic. Never mind death. Part of me was suffering from bits of both but the rest of me was alive and, as it turns out, bloody furious.

I won't embarrass myself by recounting exactly what transpired next but it did involve a lot of fruit (some of it past its best), a selection of my mother-in-law's fine bone china (how could I?) and a lamp stand with a butterfly shade which I've always loved to bits so I can't imagine why I smashed it against the kitchen counter and held the jagged end against Harry's throat, then against my own, then back against his.

Well, yes, I can. I was devastated. I'd always thought devastation was a word that only truly applied to victims of natural disaster like those tsunami survivors you see on the news, the ones whose villages have been washed away taking their houses, their families, the lives they thought they were going to lead with them. I'd seen pictures of these broken mortals weeping inconsolably next to piles of sticks and rags that used to be their homes, and had thought that was devastation. They were devastated.

In fact, that was exactly how I now felt. Like an enormous wave had appeared out of nowhere without the slightest bit of warning and swept away my future.

My husband didn't love me any more, that was my tsunami. No, it was worse than that. My husband did love me, he just loved someone else more, in a different way, a better way. Better for him, anyway.

And I'd thought we were blessed.

HARRY

♥ ♥ ♥

I could tell sitting across the fruit bowl from her that it hadn't sunk in about Charles but for heaven's sake, what is the right way to tell the only woman you have ever loved that you're about to ruin her life? It was not a language with which I was familiar. If there had been any other way . . .

As it was, as we sat there, I cursed myself for not spending more time working out the correct phrasing, preparing her better, but in all honesty, I had already gone over it a thousand times in my mind, and in the end I think I knew that the words weren't going to make much difference to the final outcome. Pretty peculiar really, considering words are what I'm all about. As a lawyer, it's getting the words exactly right that counts and I suppose that's true of writers, too, although obviously I have not yet perfected that craft and quite frankly probably never will.

On the other hand, who wants to be good at leaving their wife? Especially a wife as wonderful as Florence? I was bound to botch it up, there was probably no way around that. Even knowing her as well as I did, though, I couldn't have picked that she would translate me telling her about Charles into me dying of some awful disease, although she always had quite an aptitude for ferreting out the worst possible scenario. Once she'd worked that much out, she told me years ago, she could relax because it might not be so bad in the end.

Is it worse, the truth, I remember thinking as I tried to tell her about Charles? For her, anyway? When she gets it, when she finally gets it, will she wish I was dying; will she wish I was dead?

The look on her face when it did sink in broke my heart. That beautiful face. Those big brown eyes. That thick, dark hair that drives her mad because there's so bloody much of it but has strangers turning to watch it swing across her shoulders as she walks down the street.

What kind of a man can walk away from this, I asked myself, as I watched those eyes widen, a light come on, then go out in them. She seemed to sag to half her normal size. It crushed her. What kind of a man does that?

I suppose I had not known myself what kind of a man I really was until I met Charles. Even then I denied it as long as I could possibly manage. I'd always known I had more than a passing interest in that sort of thing but I thought this was probably on the acceptable side of normal. Besides, I was madly in love with my wife. I had been ever since she noticed me at the bus stop I'd been staking out for weeks, after first noticing her buying crisps at the corner shop. We were little more than children, really, now that I look back on it. When Monty was fourteen I used to spy on him watching cartoons on TV and think, I met the woman I married when I was his age. What did I know then?

Well, I knew I loved her and nothing will ever change that. But meeting Charles was different and nothing could change that either. Meeting Charles just made the rest of my life feel wrong. No, worse than that, it made it feel like a lie. And I may be many things but I have tried, especially where Florence has been concerned, especially at home, never to be a liar.

To be honest, the blow to the side of the head with the bananas felt good and I don't even like bananas. But I deserved them. I deserved worse, much worse, but I also deserved better, and so did Florence.

CHAPTER FIVE

How does one get over something like that? The husband being gay thing, I mean, not the deadly assault with bananas.

And by 'get over' I'm not talking in a long term 'how does one survive in a world without one's previously heterosexual other half' sense. I'm talking in a 'how does one live through the very immediate seconds, minutes, hours, that keep ticking by after the world has been turned upside down' sense.

How do you survive those? How do you get over that?

Well, the answer is simple. You don't. Not exactly. There is the aforementioned bit of you that dies, then there's a bit that wishes the rest would follow or that it had never been born in the first place, then there is whatever's left over. This bit, rather astonishingly, can have quite a lot of pep. This is the bit that attacks your husband with rotting bananas, that tries to pull at his clothes, that tears at your hair and beats at your breast. The dead and the wanting-to-be-dead or never-born bits are unbearably sad but the banana bit is angry.

Although it wasn't Harry's being gay that made me furious. It's true. In the immediate aftermath of his bombshell, I believed I loved him too much for a tiny little thing like sexual persuasion to get in the way. In the fullness of time, I saw this to be completely untrue but for a few minutes there, after the bananas but before the lamp stand, I believed we could somehow work around it. But when I told Harry this he did not smile and look relieved as I imagined he might, he got that same miserable look on his face and I realised that there was more, that there was something else I was not getting. That's when it occurred to me that being gay and meeting Charles from the Whittington combined with all that repetitive talk of being so sorry and endlessly begging my forgiveness was just a lead up to the real bombshell: Harry was leaving me.

Yes, leaving me. He was moving into a bedsit in Lancaster Gate, he told me, until he had 'sorted out' his position with Charles. He'd already signed the lease.

I couldn't have felt more ambushed if he'd jumped out from behind a tree wearing a chamois leather loincloth (not out of the question in the new circumstances) and pointing a bow and arrow at me.

It was unfair enough that this was happening in the first place but it was worse that I'd had no warning. This is the thing no one prepares you for where disasters are concerned. There is no ominous black cloud, no spooky chill, no neon sign that flashes: Stop! Please! Go back to bed! There's something really, really dreadful waiting to happen around the corner! I beg of you, do not continue!

If only. Instead I'd kissed my husband goodbye just two days before as he'd headed for Aldeburgh and carried on innocently as usual. But now I had this, this, *this* being dumped on me from a great height. Bloody Harry had spent I don't know how long thrashing out his plans, coming to his conclusions, making all his decisions, but I was totally new to the lot of it and the shock had me in pieces.

As we sat there at the kitchen table, or I chased him around it, or I collapsed on the floor against the creaky dishwasher, I kept forgetting what was going on. My mind would race ahead to being a lonely old maid and I'd see myself sitting in a wheelchair (for some reason) dressed in black with lipstick à la *Whatever Happened to Baby Jane?* smeared all over my face and my mind would get stuck in this desolate future while Harry stood on the other side of the room, burbling on about being true to himself and doing what's best for everyone.

Then I'd switch back to the moment, to him, only to lose myself instantly to the past. I had been with Harry for twenty-five years. Was it all bollocks? Had our sex life been abnormal? I didn't know. I'd only ever slept with him. And it's not like he'd ever tried to take me from behind or insisted on a Swedish strap-on or whatever the hell they're called so I don't know how I was supposed to fathom that he was bloody well gay.

He was loving, he was affectionate, he was engaged in me, in us, in our life. How had this happened? Where had it happened?

'At the gym,' he told me. 'I met him at the gym.'

You know, it's not until you absolutely lose your dignity that you realise just how much you need it in the first place. I cringe when I think of what happened that day, for many reasons, but mostly because Harry and I had never been ones to row. We had the odd grumpy silence, made the odd snarky comment, but we just weren't shouters or screamers. But I shouted and screamed at him then with a venom I had not known I was capable of. I told him his mother was an alcoholic and his father a bully (almost true but never previously mentioned); I told him he was a turgid writer without a glimmer of talent (same); I told him he hitched his trousers up too high and shouldn't wear thick white socks with his sneakers (I had mentioned the socks before). I went on.

I know now that Harry could not help who he was and how difficult it must have been for him to confront the truth and therefore me. He loved me, I know he did, and still does, and he truly did not want to hurt me. Ultimately he cared about that less than he cared about being true to himself, though, which is fine. Really. I mean for him, especially, but eventually even for me, fine. Who wants to live a lie? Who wants to make someone else live one?

Not me. Although that afternoon I could see none of this. All I could see was the life I thought I was so happily living whooshing away from me like those filthy, brown tsunami floodwaters. And as I was caught up in this hateful torrent and dragged downwards, the survival mechanism that kicked in was not one of grace and serenity and understanding but one of ferocious anger and bitterness and over-ripe fruit.

Worse, as Harry escaped the house, his ear caked with squashed banana, so many things still unsaid, I knew that I was right about the rotten things, that I was two really big ones down but still had one to go and it was bound to be a pearler. The universe had at least one more crappy treat in store for me and I had better gird my loins in preparation — especially as my loins were unlikely to get much other activity in the immediate future.

I had spent half my life being Mrs Harry Dowling and now I was to be what? Who?

I didn't even have a job.

Sparky was beside himself with sympathy, which frankly

just made me want to go outside and shoot my face off. His too.

I didn't know what to do with myself as I sat in the kitchen, the debris of our broken marriage splattered and shattered around me. I couldn't even think who to turn to, other than Harry, who was too busy leaving me, or Monty, who was still on the other side of the world.

Monty!

What were we going to tell him? How? I leapt to my feet and ran downstairs to the front door to see if Harry was still lurking outside somewhere, picking sludge from his hair, but when I pulled the door open, a ruddy-faced man with low-slung work-pants and a huge beer belly was standing on the doorstep grinning at me.

'Afternoon, missus. Stanley Morris, plumber,' he said, holding out the hand that wasn't carrying his tool kit and looking over my shoulder down the hall. 'I'm here about your leaky tap. Kitchen down the back, is it?'

My leaky tap. I had rung the plumber about a month before to come and fix it but had given up hope that anyone would ever show. Yet here he was. Now. Just after my heart had been ripped out of my chest and jumped on by the man I trusted most in the whole wide world.

Yet, the tap was indeed leaky. Life went on.

I remember my mother saying something to the same effect after the grandparent trifecta. She was smoking a joint and gazing out the window as the rubbish truck collected the next door neighbour's rubbish.

'It's so hard to believe that everything is just carrying on as usual,' she said dreamily, her rings and bracelets jangling as she ran her fingers through her long, wiry grey hair. 'We all think we are so important, but we're not, are we? We can live, or die, and it makes no difference to the garbage man. There's still the same amount of garbage in the world, with or without us.'

'But *we* compost and recycle,' I pointed out. It was a sore point: the compost bin was alive with a kingdom of tiny flying insects and it was my job to fill it. 'So it would really make no difference to the garbage man if we lived or died because he doesn't collect our garbage anyway.'

My mother looked at me, disappointedly I suspect, then went back to gazing out the window.

She *was* talking rubbish about the garbage man, but I remember silently agreeing that it didn't seem right that one still had to do one's homework and walk the dog and dry the dishes and change the loo roll when such a great gaping hole had been left in one's universe by the death of a much treasured loved one.

Now, all these years later, here was my husband leaving me for another man one minute and Stanley Morris wanting to fix my leaky tap the next. And despite everything that had just happened, I really did want the tap fixed because every time I turned it on a jet of water shot out and got me square in the eye, no matter where my eye happened to be at the time, and no matter what the marital status of the body in which the eye belonged.

'Upstairs,' I said weakly to Stanley Morris, then followed his somewhat jiggly backside up to the kitchen. He could have hitched his pants up higher, frankly, but he kept up a friendly patter as we climbed.

'Lovely old place you've got here,' he said. 'Used to be a doctor's surgery, am I right? I used to come here when I was a lad, I think. We lived just around the corner in St John's Wood. You know them council flats in Lisson Grove? Yeah, grew up there, I did. She still lives there, my old mum. Eighty-seven and not showing any signs of going anywhere else in a hurry either, God bless her. There was a doctor closer to us than this, of course, right across the road, but my old mum didn't care for him. Said he had cold hands. Funny, innit, what they object to, the old ones, not that she was so old then but you can't tell a young 'un that, can you? Or you can try but you won't get very far. Now, let's see what we have here.'

Standing at the kitchen counter, Stanley Morris paused to push a broken bread and butter plate out of his way with the side of his foot and wiped away some squashed banana with a J-cloth. I stared in embarrassment at the hideous mess strewn around us. It looked like a chimpanzee's tea party gone horribly wrong, but Stanley Morris seemed to take it in his stride.

He turned the tap on and the jet of water hit him straight in the eye.

'I see what you mean,' he said jovially. 'Cor, this is an old model, this mixer, but that's not all bad, that is. You can still get replacement parts for the likes of this. The new ones? Nah, you've got to be joking. Cheaper to put a new one in than repair the old one, even if it's brand spanking new. Makes you sick, doesn't it? Makes me sick.'

As Stanley Morris continued to prattle on I quietly swept up the broken crockery and pieces of lamp shade, which reminded me of the chamber pot and the fact that I had been fired earlier — surely not the same day? It seemed a lifetime ago.

'Beautiful part of London this, I reckon,' Stanley chattered. 'My old man's old man worked the canal boats back in the dark ages. Hard to imagine everything being delivered by water though, innit? I ain't been to the real Venice myself but my daughter has. She saw all sorts of things being delivered in them boats. Wotcha call 'em? Gondolas, yeah, gondolas:

tables and chairs, cabbages, bottles of water, birds in cages, you name it.'

He opened the door beneath the sink and, huffing, got down on his hands and knees to peer in.

'Never been anywhere in Italy me,' he continued, his voice echoing around my kitchen cupboards as he rattled around with his spanner. 'Probably wouldn't bother with Venice anyway. All that walking. Not a single car. But Rome, I could handle that. The Colosseum, Trevi Fountain, Spanish Steps. My daughter's been there, too. Says you can get a good cup of tea at the bottom of the Spanish Steps but you'd better make the most of it because it's the only one you'll find in the whole of Europe.'

He turned over and lay on his back, his torso and legs sticking out into the kitchen. His belly didn't look anywhere near so beery lying down. It looked like the belly of a man who loved his mum and his daughter and was not fazed by smashed crockery and squashed banana.

I felt an inexplicable rush of warmth for Stanley Morris.

'My husband's just told me he's leaving me for another man,' I told the bottom two-thirds of him.

His spanner stopped rattling. He scooted out from under the sink.

'You all right then?' he asked. He didn't seem embarrassed. Or even surprised. Maybe it happened more often than I imagined.

I shook my head. I was not all right.

'Come as a shock, did it?'

I nodded. It had come as a shock. 'We've been together since we were kids,' I said. 'We've been married for twenty years. I had no idea. I thought we were happy.'

Stanley Morris nodded, sighed, then used his spanner to

scratch a spot on his back in between his shoulder blades.

'I know just how you feel,' he said. 'My missus left me without a word of warning and all. There was me thinking we was enjoying perfect marital bliss and there was her thinking she'd rather live in a tiny little flat on her own in Hounslow freezing to death and working at the local William Hill.'

He shook his head and got up.

'Uff. My knees, I tell you.'

'I don't know what to do,' I told Stanley Morris, even though he was just the plumber.

'Not much you can do,' he said, turning on the tap. No jet of water. 'There we go. It gets better, that's all I can tell you, although you couldn't be blamed for not believing me. Know what my old mum told me when my missus run off? "It's not an arm or a leg, Stan," she said. Not an arm or a leg. Thought she was being bloody miserable at the time but the old girl was right. It don't kill you. Life does go on.'

Just having him in my kitchen was the surest sign of this I could ever concoct.

'We have a son,' I said. 'I just don't know what . . .'

'How old is he then, your boy?' Stanley Morris asked as he started to pack away his tools.

'Nineteen.'

'Well, there you go. Old enough to understand it's not an arm or a leg,' he said with great confidence as he closed his tool box. 'My Lizzie was fine. She was about the same age as that, maybe a year or two older, and she was fine. A bit down on her mum for a while but at the end of the day, she's still her mum.' He checked his watch. 'Here, look at that. I've got a rendezvous with a blocked drain in Hammersmith in about half an hour but I could murder a cup of tea in the meantime.'

He was doing this for me — a complete stranger — I knew

70

he was. And I was pathetically grateful.

'I'll put the kettle on,' I said, brushing fragments of a gravy boat off a kitchen chair. 'I've got Earl Grey or Fortnum's Royal Blend. Do you have a preference?'

'Now there's a woman after my own heart,' Stanley said, picking up the handle of the gravy boat and dropping it in the rubbish bin. 'Find Earl Grey a bit delicate at this stage in the day so I'll take t'other, thank you kindly. Like your tea then, Mrs Dowling?'

'Please, call me Florence,' I said, getting Rose's favourite cups out, switching the saucers and choosing a tea cosy that looked like a bunch of grapes that Poppy had knitted for me years before. 'And yes, I do like my tea. In fact, I'm thinking of converting downstairs into a tearoom. What do you think of that for an idea?'

I don't know what possessed me to come out with this because I wasn't thinking about it at all or, if I was, I shouldn't have been.

'I think that's brilliant, that is,' said Stanley Morris with great enthusiasm. 'What's more, you'll be needing a plumber.'

STANLEY MORRIS

♥ ♥ ♥

I knew the moment I clapped eyes on Mrs Dowling, or Florence as she asked me to call her, that she'd just had one hell of a shock. I suppose I looked just like that when Beryl bunked off on me and all. Still, if there's one thing I have learned it's that if you carry on as though nothing strange is happening, it usually stops being strange.

You get used to walking into disasters in my line of work, plumbing ones and otherwise. People can get all gussied up and pretend they're one thing or another when they go out in the world, after all, but catch them at home and that's pretty much the way they really are.

I felt right sorry for her, I can tell you that. Her husband coming out, as they say, and that tap of hers leaking all over the show. She was such a nice lady too, polite and helpful, despite what had just gone on. She told me over a cuppa and a slice of lemon cake that she'd just lost her job and all. On the same day. Ouch, that's got to hurt, dunnit?

But I thought right away she could have been on to something with that tearoom idea. My sister Marion lives up in Ely, it's the place with the nice cathedral near Cambridge. Anyway, there's this tearoom there, Peacock's, right on the river. Some lawyer chap got fed up with spending half his life in the Ely police station so turned his downstairs into a tearooms and it's packed to the gunnels every weekend and most days during the week.

Sounds a bit like what Florence wanted to do with her place in Little Venice. Corker spot for it.

There's not a lot of good places for a cuppa around that neck of the woods, truth be told. Starbucks on every bleeding corner in the West End but try getting a good cup of tea and a slice of something baked by human hand and you may as well just go home. Not that I have anything baked by human hand at my place but I certainly can manage a good cup of tea and there's nothing wrong with a HobNob.

Anyway, I said I'd keep in touch with Florence because I thought she was on to something and as I say, she would need a plumber. I also thought she might need a shoulder to cry on and happens I've got very reliable shoulders.

CHAPTER SIX

When I woke up the day after Harry left me and Stanley Morris fixed the tap, I had a few glorious ordinary moments before remembering my life had turned to custard.

I rolled over in the bed, all warm and toastily contented the way you are when you've slept badly most the night but deeply in the end. I saw with half-closed eyes through the gap in the curtains that it was a sunny day. I smiled and stretched out in the bed, my foot hitting a foreign object: Sparky. Lurch. What was he doing there? Lurch. Where was Harry? Lurch. What had happened to my life as a gainfully employed happily married mother of one? Lurch, lurch, lurch.

I would have given anything then to disappear back into that bliss of not knowing. I understood, for the first time perhaps, how drugs or drink or anything else you might end up in rehab for would help dull the pain of reality. I felt so wretched once real life overwhelmed me with its new hideousness that

I would have swallowed anything at all if I thought it might make me feel even the tiniest bit better.

But there was nothing to swallow, not in my room anyway, unless you counted Panadol. And there were only two of them and they both had fluff on them from being under the bed for at least a year.

I rolled over again, chilled now, and lay there wishing that I was dead, although I could never do that to Monty, so I wished that Harry was dead instead, then realised that would hurt Monty too. Instead, I wished that Harry wasn't gay, that things were the way they always had been, that I did not feel so horribly bloody scared. I wished that it was night-time so I could go to sleep and wake up and have those few innocent moments again. And I wished that wishing got you somewhere other than where you started off in the first place.

Then I thought of little Edith, another regular customer/ visitor at the shop I had half owned until the day before. I stopped thinking about her for a few moments to revisit the minor horror of being dumped by my business partner just hours before being dumped by my husband then, finding that too unspeakably awful, thought of Edith again instead.

I'd initially met her when she came in to talk about selling some of her gorgeous Spode china after her husband Arthur died. They'd been married more than fifty years and never spent a single night apart, she told me that first day, as two tiny contained tears rolled down her small, perfectly made-up face.

'The mornings are the worst,' she'd confessed in little more than a whisper as I attempted to comfort her with some ever-so-slightly undercooked gingernuts. 'There's this little pocket of time between waking up and realising what has happened where everything is just fine. And then I remember.'

75

I'd felt sorry enough for her at the time, now I saw how truly excruciatingly cruel that was — to get a little island holiday from your grief just makes it feel worse when you come back home. And I was grieving, I recognised that. No one had actually died but the future I assumed I was going to have was certainly dead and buried. Even if Harry became un-gay we could never erase the fact that for a while at least he thought he was and there had been a Charles from the Whittington on the scene.

I looked at the phone on the bedside table and thought of ringing Poppy. But just imagining saying what I had to say made me feel so ill I couldn't contemplate it further. Then I remembered she was on a face-reading seminar in Framlingham or some such so I wouldn't be able to get in touch with her anyway. She and my parents didn't believe in mobile phones because of the possibility of catching measles of the brain.

I thought then about ringing Mum or Dad but I just wasn't the sort of daughter that easily confided her tragedies. Not that I'd had any real tragedies as an adult to confide. Or as a child, now I came to think of it. Other than Rose dying when I was sixteen and my ovaries being a bit of a disappointment, my life had been a delight. I'd been lucky.

Until now.

Now I was one job down, one husband down, and one rotten thing away from who knew what?

On top of that, I had no one to talk to. What had happened to my friends, my life outside being a wife and mother? When had I stopped making an effort to keep in touch with the outside world? When had I become so wrapped up in myself, in ourselves? Why was this only occuring to me now?

I cried for a while then. Well, till lunchtime actually, Sparky curled up on top of the duvet, his wagging tail slapping against my hip as he lapped up my unhappiness.

I cried all afternoon too, but I did that in front of the television watching *Countdown* and *Deal or No Deal*. I tried to drink a cup of tea but felt sick to the pit of my stomach. I had not known that despair was a physical sensation but my body surrendered to it. My innards felt sticky: thick and black, like tar. Everything about me felt poisoned by my misfortune.

It was pretty standard being-dumped-by-your-husband-and-losing-your-marbles fare, I suppose. The hours passed. I didn't get out of my pyjamas, I didn't brush my hair, I didn't eat. About twenty-four hours after he left me Harry rang to see if I was all right, which plucked my useless bloody heart filaments so sharply I thought they were going to snap. I cried so much then I could barely get out a word and when he offered to come over the thought of being in his arms again lifted me for one wonderful moment above my cloud of misery. But when I asked him if he was still gay his answer was yes, so I told him to stick it up his arse along with everything else and there I was in the cloud again. I'm not even sure what I meant about the arse sticking but as I say I had not done much research.

He rang again and again after that but mostly I ignored the phone messages. I stayed in my mousy pyjamas, weeping and wondering how it was that I had poured all my love and energy into a man I didn't even know. Worse, he was the only person I wanted to talk to. No, worse even than that, he was the only person I *had* to talk to. And now I no longer had him.

My best friend from school — sweet, sensible Caroline — had moved to Wales with her husband and three sons a few years earlier: why had I let that friendship fizzle out? At first I had made an effort to at least answer her calls but I'd never been to stay with her, no matter how often she begged me to. And now I couldn't even remember if I'd sent her a Christmas card.

Then there was larger-than-life Laura, whom I'd met at ante-natal classes when she was pregnant with her daughter, Treacle. Despite the ghastly name she'd chosen for her daughter, we'd been if not close confidantes then at least good friends for years until, well, until when? Until Monty was too grown up to play with a girl? That shouldn't have been a reason for my friendship with Laura to wither and die, yet it had. All my friendships had withered and died, bar the so recently pruned one with Charlotte.

The truth was, at some stage I had worked out I didn't really need friends. I had Harry and I had Monty and I met so many people during the day at the shop that I considered that my social life. In addition to Marguerite and Edith who dropped in probably twice a week there were others who were just as regular. Rosalie, the cat woman, came in to look at picture frames for photos of her moggies and always stayed for at least one cup of tea. Julia worked at the estate agency around the corner and had initially sought shelter in our shop from her creepy boss. We got talking and she bought the prettiest pearl ring, then became a regular. There was Rupert, the schoolteacher, who collected Poole pottery and had once whirled me around the jewellery cabinet when Jocelyn Brown came on the radio singing of all things, I wryly remembered, 'Somebody Else's Guy'. These were people whose lives I knew the details of, yet I didn't have a single phone number. And had I, would I have rung them, then, in my hour of need?

No.

Sinead, maybe. Sinead was the Irish girl who came to clean every Friday and had the best-ever stories about bad boyfriends. She'd been cheated on, left in countryside inns, abandoned at sleazy nightclubs, shagged in the loos at Selfridges then dumped outside the hosiery department. She'd had every relationship disaster known to womankind. Or had she? I couldn't remember any boyfriend ever leaving her for another man.

And anyway, I didn't have her phone number, it was at the shop with Charlotte, and I didn't exactly feel like crawling over in my jim-jams with my hair all knotted and scary and asking for it.

So for the next two days I just stayed in bed or on the sofa and talked to Sparky. I had previously been ever-so-slightly sceptical of people who relied on their pets for emotional fulfilment but it turned out I was one.

And is it any wonder? Harry was no doubt getting his emotional fulfilment from this vile cruel nasty Charles person; Monty was on the other side of the world; my sister was with a bunch of face readers; and my parents had yet to provide the sort of emotional fulfilment I sought, so Sparky was actually all I had left.

Harry had never let the dog on the bed but now he was rarely off it. On my third night alone I woke to find his head on Harry's pillow, his paw beside it, like a dog impersonating a human. It may sound stupid, but this little piece of comedy made me smile. And because I had otherwise only had that one early morning moment — an infinitesimal speck of time so small as to hardly even count — when everything was simply marvellous before it all fell horribly to pieces, I needed my smiles.

After five days of my having been left by Harry, however, Sparky was not doing a good enough job and I was in a deeply disturbed place. I was husbandless, jobless and friendless, and could not see from my pit of despair how I would ever climb out of this hole. Not an ugly, stupid, boring, waste of space with the sex appeal of a pot-belly pig like myself.

'Did you ever love me?' I bawled down the phone to Harry when he rang late on that fifth afternoon and I finally answered him. 'Has it all been a lie? A trick? Utter bloody bullshit? I can't believe it. We were happy. I thought we were happy. Did you only love me because I looked like a boy, back then, at the bus stop, waiting for the 268?' This was one theory I had come up with in the middle of the night. 'Did I look like a boy? Were you pretending I was a boy? Oh, I want to die, Harry. I just want to die. I want to kill you with my bare hands. I want to rip you limb from limb! And then I want to die.'

Harry was in his Lancaster Gate bedsit sounding, in all fairness, every bit as desolate as I was.

'I loved you with all my heart, Florence,' he told me, 'from the moment I first saw you. You did not look like a boy. You had that ridiculous padded bra on and blue eye shadow and your hair was down to your waist, which was where your skirt was up to.' He was right. I had forgotten about the outfit. 'I have never seen anyone look more like a girl. And you are as beautiful and sexy now as you were then and I still love you. I pretty much want to bloody die myself at making you feel as though there's something wrong with you because there isn't. This is not about you, it's —'

'How can this not be about me?' I wept. 'Five days ago I was happily married to you and today I'm all by myself. That's me, Harry. The me who this isn't about. You've got someone, this bloody Charles, but I've got no one now and no warning that this was going to happen. It might not have started out being about me but it certainly is now.'

'I know, Floss, you're absolutely right. If there was anything else I could do, I would do it and you must believe I love you with all my heart but —'

'Why does there have to be a but?' I interrupted so

vigorously that Sparky jumped off the sofa and flopped sulkily on the ground. 'Why couldn't you just keep on . . . ?'

'Pretending?' Harry filled the gap in the most awful flat tone and I knew then it really was over. Not just a little bit over either. It was as over as anything ever could be.

'Yes,' I whispered back nonetheless and the silence between us said it all. If only he knew he was pretending, that was one thing. If we both knew, it was another. There was no going back.

'Florence, I'm so sorry.' He was crying again. My big strong Harry, crying like Monty had when he was four years old and fell off his tricycle. 'I'm just so fucking sorry.'

Hearing him swear was even more alarming than hearing him cry and I felt another surge of banana-bashing fury at this. Who was this crying, swearing gay man? How dare he keep such things from me? How dare he?

'So you bloody well should be sorry,' I cried. 'It's all right for you, you have a whole new gang to belong to: the leather and whip crowd with all your bars and internet sites and God knows what else but what is there for me, Harry? For me and Monty?' Oh, Monty! My poor darling Monty.

'Monty is fine, Floss.'

I felt the pitter patter of more fury beating in my chest. 'What do you mean Monty is fine?' I had spent countless hours drumming up different scenarios for telling Monty about Harry. We had to be gentle, so he didn't go into shock the way I had, but we had to let him know it was all Harry's fault not mine, so he didn't blame me, but . . .

'I talked to him,' Harry told me. 'That's what I've been ringing to tell you. I called him in Thailand. Yesterday. I thought it was the fair thing to do.'

'Without even discussing it with me first?' He was truly a

stranger to me now, my husband. I even felt a wave of being glad to be rid of a person who would do something like that. 'You rang our son and told him you were gay and leaving us without even running it past me?'

There was an uncomfortable silence. Of course, I thought, he's not actually leaving Monty, just me.

'I wanted to face the music, Florence. I wanted it over and done with.'

'Well as long as you get what you want obviously everything is all fucking right, Harry,' I said and I threw the phone out the window, which was stupid because I was in the sitting room on the first floor and I heard it smash into smithereens in the courtyard below.

When my anger subsided, which took two more hours of screaming into a pillow and one glass of cooking sherry, I admitted quietly to myself that I was glad that Monty knew and glad that it was Harry who told him. When I'd tried to picture the two of us standing in a room with our son, breaking the news to him, every time the me I was trying to picture either attempted to strangle Harry or broke down and begged him to change his mind or covered Monty's ears so he could not hear the terrible truth. He'd had such a wonderful life, our son, even less blemished by tragedy than my own. No one close to him had died, he had never been in trouble, we'd always been able to afford whatever he wanted. For him to suddenly be thrust into a world where his parents were splitting up and one was gay and the other was bloody furious just seemed too awful to contemplate. His heart would be broken, I was sure, as was mine.

But then I considered that at least he was on his way home, the truth had been told and our hearts would be broken together. I felt a little glimmer of hope then, a smug little glow that Monty and I would be bound by something that Harry could only ever look in on. Having a son wasn't like having a husband, it was for life. Monty could not change his tune and decide I wasn't his mother. Even if he had a sex change, which I prayed to God was not the third rotten thing, I would still be his mother. Forever.

A couple of nights later, Harry came over, which was brave, in the circumstances, but he was in a mood to thrash things out and so we thrashed.

By then I had finally done a bit of research on the internet and found an astonishing number of sites dedicated to wives whose husbands were gay. Depressingly, very few of the stories ended in the husband changing his mind again and coming home.

There were countless religious sites, though, that vehemently exhorted gay husbands to deny their natural inclination and while they were equally depressing, I tested some of what I had learned on Harry.

People become un-gay all the time, I told him. Perhaps he could go to the US and be re-programmed or join a cult or something? Or, if not, perhaps we could stay married and living together but just doing our own thing, sort of, on the sex front.

If he were a non-practising gay man, Harry said gently, that might have almost worked. But there was Charles from the Whittington to consider.

Or there was Charles from the Whittington to bump into in a dark alley and stab a thousand times with the carving knife Harry's hairy Aunt Molly had given him for his thirtieth birthday, I suggested.

Harry did not respond well to my anger, a psychologist would probably say, and he left on very poor terms after that visit. But he came back a few nights later with a bottle of expensive pinot noir and by then, I don't know how, the whole situation had somehow seeped into my consciousness.

I suppose the fact of Harry's gayness was no longer such a shock. It had been a total bolt out of the blue when it first hit me but in not much more than a week there it was, bumpily woven into the fabric of our relationship. Like an amputated limb or annoying permanent house guest, it was something else to get through, to emerge from the other side of. A big something. A huge something. But still, just a something.

I'm not saying I wasn't still desperately unhappy, of course I was. Totally desperate and likely to stay that way I thought, plus enormously angry to boot. And I wavered a thousand times a day between not believing it was happening to being overwhelmed that it was, to hoping against hope that some miracle would occur to make the whole horrible mess go away. But I was no longer surprised. That was the strange thing.

By that second visit, with the pinot noir, we actually managed a moment of strange companionship. It was by mistake, really. My fury would not openly allow such a thing otherwise. But it was the same wine we had drunk on a picnic a few years earlier up near Oxford somewhere, on the river. I only remembered exactly what it was because the entire outing had been highly memorable. Monty was off with a pal and Harry and I were making the most of having a weekend day to ourselves. We'd had ham sandwiches with the wine then both fallen asleep in a big grassy field in the afternoon sun and had woken only when a big hairy cattle beast of some description licked Harry's cheek. Harry roared, like a bull actually, which gave me a terrible fright but it made the cattle beast look very angry and stamp its feet. We emerged unscathed but all the other people in the field who hadn't been licked nearly died laughing.

'Do you remember the big hairy cattle beast?' I asked Harry, forgetting for a moment he was leaving me (which was when the accidental companionship crept in).

'How could I forget it?' Harry answered. 'I couldn't eat meat for a month afterwards. Why it chose me . . .'

Were all these wonderful memories that we shared soiled now, the way things had turned out, I wondered? Was it bollocks, the lot of it, the whole twenty-five years? Because it so hadn't felt like bollocks at the time, when I assumed we would live happily ever after. Now that Harry was gay, I just didn't know.

That picnic had reminded me of something else too. The Black Watch tartan rug on which we lay before and indeed during the cheek-licking was a wedding gift from Harry's lovely Scottish cousin Emily.

(Why hadn't I kept in touch with Emily? What was wrong with me?)

A few years after our wedding Emily's husband John had been in a terrible skiing accident while on a boys' trip to Austria and the last time we'd seen her she'd talked about it over homemade Florentines and a cup of fresh Ceylon tea.

One day her life had been happily tootling along in one direction with every i dotted and t crossed and the future all neatly mapped out in front of them, she had quietly recounted. Then with a single phone call the whole thing had been hideously derailed. John would probably live, she was told in that phone call, but might never walk again. That was her tsunami.

Yet, she informed me, she had found the phone call and the minutes, or hours, after it by far the worst part.

I found this hard to believe at the time. Surely, that was just the beginning of it? But no, she claimed it was the ambush, the surprise, the shock that devastated her. And even by the next day she had got used to the new direction their life was headed in and by the end of the week she was talking rehabilitation and catheters like a pro.

It's like the rubbish man collecting the rubbish all over again. The world keeps spinning. And it certainly didn't bother to stop when Harry came out of the closet. Also, after the first few derailing minutes and hours when all I could think of was myself and Monty, I saw that Harry was just as inextricably tied to me as I was to him and conceded, secretly of course, that it would be easier for him not to be in love with this Charles person. But as they say, the heart wants what the heart wants. And takes other body parts with it.

Later that same night of the accidental companionship, I thought for a split second Harry was even going to change his mind and come home to me. I could see it in his eyes, in the quiver of his jaw, in the desperate way he looked at me, and I knew then how much he loved me. But far from being thrilled and relieved, I felt only pain, the deepest most wretched pain. For there truly was no going back now.

Especially for him. I could see it. While the trauma had given me the look of the wreck of the *Hesperus*, Harry looked good. He was a little grey around the face, as anyone leaving their loving wife would be, I imagine. But something in his eyes, in the square set of his shoulders, whispered of a new happiness.

I loathed him for that.

But I couldn't stop loving him either.

So he went back to his bedsit where working out his position was obviously coming along quite nicely and I went about the business of lying on the couch in my pyjamas, screeching into cushions and talking to the dog.

MONTY

♥ ♥ ♥

You could have knocked me over with a feather when the funny little lady-boy who ran our hotel on the beach at Koh Tao told me there was a phone call for me.

I didn't even realise they had a phone.

Anyway, I was in the beach-side bar enjoying an ice cold Changi beer and playing gin rummy with a drunken Dutchman at the time so at least the lady-boy didn't have to go far to find me.

As soon as he said there was a call I knew it must be Mum or Dad and I knew it must be something pretty serious because I was on my way home and most things would have been able to wait. I didn't panic though. For a start it was my second Changi beer of the morning. Also I thought if it was something really serious, you know, the most serious, the police would be coming to tell me, not the lady-boy in the midriff top and high-heeled flip flops with COOL SHIT carved into the soles. Still, it was pretty intense.

I don't know what Dad thought I would say but pretty much 'Wow' was all I could come up with. I don't mind about him being gay, God, far from it. As my friend Mischa says, what you do in bed is no one's business unless they happen to be in bed with you. It was the shock, I suppose, more than anything else because my parents have always seemed like one of those creepy totally in love couples that make everyone else's warring, bickering, ancient parents look like sad bastards.

Or maybe it was just Mum that seemed totally in love. Maybe Dad has always been a bit, I don't know, distant? Of course I might just be thinking that to stop feeling like a complete idiot for not noticing anything gay about him. Although to be honest I don't think there is anything gay about him. I don't mean I don't believe that he's gay, I mean I don't think there was anything I missed. He was a great father, he is a great father, and I had a brilliant childhood so it doesn't really matter much to me what he gets up to now. He's an adult. He can do what he likes.

No, it was Mum I was worried about. Him being gay might not have had much impact on me but it was certainly going to have an impact on her. I didn't know about the ins and outs of the split, we didn't really get into that on the phone. Would she stay in the house? Shit, I hoped so. She really loved that house. Actually, that would have made me feel sad, if the house had had to go. But in a way it would also have made things easier for me.

I had a surprise of my own, after all.

God. Poor Mum.

CHAPTER SEVEN

A few days later it occurred to me that I was crying less and shouting at the TV more. So, on waking up the next morning, two weeks after being left by Harry, I enjoyed my brief blissful moment before despair again set in, then decided to have a shower and wash my hair. Just doing that improved my world immeasurably.

I was still the blind, stupid idiot who married a gay man but at least I didn't smell like a field mouse.

Anyway, I had worked out that if I was going to survive, I had to talk to someone other than the dog and in the absence of any other field mice with which to converse — and believe me, I was only moments away from considering such a thing — I packed Sparky into the tired Golf and headed for Tannington Hall to break the news to Mum and Dad and Poppy.

I should have told them already, of course I should have,

and it wasn't that I hadn't meant to. I'd eyed up the phone in the bedroom (no longer having one in the sitting room) often enough but I just could not bring myself to do it. And when they rang me, well, to my astonishment I seemed extraordinarily capable of failing to mention that I'd lost my job and my husband and was pretty much just sitting around waiting for the next calamity to befall me.

Poppy was wildly excited about some chap she'd met at her face-reading course. Dad was considering growing some strange herb from the highlands of China that had been proven to reduce the side effects of female menopause. Mum had injured her groin getting out of the lotus position but was getting Dad to rub arnica cream into it every hour which meant they were spending a lot of time having sex, him on top for a change.

In the eye-popping conversational ping-pong surrounding these subjects, whether or not I was still working or still married never came up.

In my defence, I don't imagine anyone exactly jumps at the chance to tell their family their husband is gay. Or bonking his secretary. Or going backpacking on his own in the depths of India. Or whatever he is doing that is going to make him very soon not your husband any more. It felt like a failure, that was all, even though I'd had nothing to do with its architecture. Still, *my* marriage was over. *My* childhood sweetheart was in a Lancaster Gate bedsit doing who knows what with Charles from the Whittington.

Millions of women before me had broken similar news to their loved ones and lived to tell the tale, I knew that. I just didn't know how many came from a family so barking mad they were quite likely to commemorate such catastrophic news with an interpretive dance or an incense-burning festival.

Finally, I just closed my eyes, blurted to my mother that I was coming to visit and just hoped to God that the arnica cream had done its job by then.

Harry thought I should have gotten it over and done with sooner. In fact, at one stage he had suggested he take me there and help me do it. He had already broken the news to his broom-handle-up-the-bottom brother in Edinburgh who told him not to bother ringing again, but had decided against saying anything to his parents other than we were splitting up. I should have resented this probably but I didn't. My parents were loony but loving, his parents were neither. Apart from birthday phone calls we didn't have much to do with them. They showed so little interest in us that although I had forced it a bit when they lived in London and Monty was smaller, I pretty much let them go when they moved to the Scottish Highlands. Mind you, as I had recently come to understand, I'd been doing a bit more letting go of my nearest and dearest than was perhaps wise.

Despite that, I actually agreed with Harry about not giving his parents the intimate details of our marital failure although what I said to him was: 'Tell them what you like. See if I care.'

'Well, you might not care about mine but I care about yours, Floss. Please, tell them. I'll come and do it with you if it makes it any easier.'

It was so hard to be left by Harry, he irritatingly seemed to feel the need to help me do it. You can't just knock a twenty-five-year relationship on the head like that, as it turns out, no matter what the circumstances. I had every right to hate him to bits and I did, at times, mostly when he wasn't there and I was just thinking about what a truly rotten thing he had done to me. Then, when we spoke, the conversations were usually vile to begin with but sometimes that strange chatty companionship crept in. When I realised that was happening, I tended to hang up or revert to the vileness. This was confusing for him but I didn't actually give a shit about that. It was just something I noticed.

Anyway, telling my family was something I needed to do on my own but as I pulled into the driveway of Tannington Hall, I felt sick to the pit of my stomach and not just because I knew Mum was cooking her famous nut roast, a truly vile concoction that looked like dog vomit. Even Sparky wouldn't eat it.

'Are you ready?' I asked the dog as I pulled to a stop. He looked at me sadly. But then he always did.

Poppy emerged from the front door at that point, excitedly waving a wooden spoon at me.

'Just so as you know,' she greeted me, kissing me on each cheek, 'Archie's back in his caftan phase. I know you can't bear them and it probably would be better if he bought new ones or had the old ones mended — how does he make so many holes in things? — but remember Effie, it's just another way of expressing himself and with his prostate the age it is, well, it can only help to have the air circulating so please, Flower, don't say a word.'

She snatched my Charles and Diana wedding memorial cake tin out of my hands and peered inside. 'What? Cupcakes? Made with flour? And chocolate? Oh, really, Effie. How many times do I have to ask? All this gluten and dairy will blow me up like a balloon. I thought you might bring nut bars from Daylesford's. All very well for you with those great long legs and that flat stomach. Gosh, have you lost weight? You have! How do you do it? Some people get all the luck. Bloody carnivores, it's just not fair. Crumbs, Eff, are you all right?

You're ghastly pale now I come to look at you. I hope you're getting enough iron. Still eating meat though, I suppose. Oh, Effie, whatever is the matter? Are you crying? Oh, hell! I mean better out than in, let it go, let it go, but, oh hell! Breathe, Effie, breathe. Mummy! Daddy!' Poppy always could holler well.

An hour later we were sitting inside by the fire, I had developed a pleasant glow from two and a half goblets of I don't know what but it had a lot of alcohol in it, and had told them my awful news.

Poor Poppy was beside herself. She'd had her frustrations with the conventional nature of my life but I know she thought Harry and I were made for each other and I think we'd given her hope that her soul mate might be out there somewhere too, just in need of the universe doing a bit of wrangling to throw them in each other's way.

'Oh, darling,' my mother said with uncustomary sympathy, 'what you must be going through. I can only imagine. I am so sorry. A very difficult growth period for you both. Truly.'

Then she just sat there glaring at Dad and nodding in my direction in a 'Go on, say something useful' way although Lord knows why because the man is as sweet as a nut but not generally known for saying anything useful.

'Yes, well,' he eventually managed, hitching his caftan up as he sat so if I dared look I would no doubt see that he had yet to rediscover underpants, 'I always thought he was a bit, you know, queer.'

'Archie!' My mother was aghast. Even she could tell this might not be considered useful. 'You did not! Although,' she added, as a politically correct afterthought, 'there is nothing wrong with being queer. All Buddha's creatures and all of that.'

'Archie, that's rubbish anyway, you thought he was a macho

swine.' Poppy said. 'Remember? When he came and gave you some advice on how to chop the firewood last winter? He said you were doing it all wrong and took the axe off you and you said he had too much testosterone and needed to drink more liquorice tea.'

'You mean queer in a gay way, Dad? Did you really think that?' I asked, my heart thumping desperately in my chest. Naturally, I had been turning myself inside out trying to recall signs from the past few decades that might have alerted me to any signs of queerness in my husband. But I swear, the man was not even *metro*sexual. He'd been going to the same barber for thirty years, didn't moisturise, didn't even wear aftershave. He played rugby, for goodness sake. He had a deep voice. He loved Cameron Diaz. He loved his son, our son. He was such a good father. Not that gay men aren't but — oh, shit, it was actually quite hard, for the record, to be in my situation and remain politically correct.

'I was only trying to help,' Dad said, looking at me over his bifocals, hitching at his caftan again then running his hands through what remained of his unruly white hair. 'So no, I suppose he was more of a macho swine than a poof. We thought that's what you were after, Eff. One of those rugger bugger types. What?' He looked cluelessly at Mum who was gesticulating wildly. 'What have I said now? What? Bugger?'

'It's OK, Mum,' I said. 'Really.'

'Well, was he OK in the sack?' Dad continued, still trying to be useful. 'You know, performance-wise? I mean you never mentioned anything was awry so we all just assumed . . .'

Mum and Dad and Poppy talked endlessly about sex, never tiring of this erection or that orgasm or the missionary position twice removed with whipped cream on top. Seriously, it wouldn't surprise me if our parents had actually demonstrated positions for Poppy to try with each new boyfriend. These were the perils of being thirty-five, single and living at home although Poppy seemed to not find it particularly perilous.

'I never mentioned anything because there was nothing to mention,' I told them stiffly, blushing at even going that far. 'And when I say "nothing" I don't mean nothing at all I mean nothing out of the ordinary. We had a perfectly normal sex life.'

It was true. Normal for normal people anyway. We had sex as often as we felt like it, sometimes initiated by me, sometimes by him. It had never once ever ended in Harry flopping back onto the pillows and me saying, 'Don't worry, darling, it happens to all men at some point.' He was very affectionate, easily — you know, *interested*.

'Well, I hate to be the one to ask you this,' my mother said, rather enthusiastically, recovering from her sympathetic mode. 'But have you had an AIDs test? I mean the statistics are . . .'

'He didn't cheat on me,' I said loudly. 'He says he didn't cheat on me and I believe him. It's just that he wanted to. For a long time he wanted to and now that we're separated I am sure he has. With Charles from the Whittington Hospital.'

'Oh, poor Flower,' Poppy whispered, reaching out and squeezing my hand.

'Didn't Shirley Haverstock's mother get some awful bug and die at the Whittington?' Dad asked Mum.

'Or was it Julia Whiteley's mother?' Mum asked him back. 'And did she die or did she go blind or lose a kidney or something? Either way she was about a hundred. And they all made such a fuss. But yes, I'm pretty sure it was the Whittington.'

'Oh, poor, poor, Flower,' Poppy said again as she launched herself at me, throwing her arms around my neck and hiding her face in my collar. 'You're separated? Oh, I can't bear it.'

'Of course we're separated, Poppy,' I answered although it had taken me a while to work that out too. 'That's what happens when your husband is gay. And we thought it was a good idea that he had moved out by the time Monty gets home. So it's not too confusing for him.' Our son's name stuck in my throat. How I longed to be on the other side of him coming home.

'Oh, poor, poor Monty,' Poppy breathed into my collar-bone. 'He'll be heartbroken. Oh, that poor darling boy.'

At the thought of their poor darling grandson being heartbroken, Mum and Dad looked pretty sick as well. They were undeniably wacky and inclined, for its alleged antibiotic properties, to drink their own urine (or so they said although no one ever saw them actually do it), but they loved my son to within an inch of his life.

'He'll be fine,' Dad said nervously, adding with an encouraging nod in my direction, 'I mean he's a bit poofy himself.'

'Archie!' My mother, who is not surprisingly rabidly against any form of violence, looked ready to clout him.

'You think Monty is poofy?' I should have been offended and on one level I was but I must admit our son had a sensitive side that did sometimes verge on the effeminate. I'd wondered about his sexuality myself, in the past, but that was before I knew about Harry. Could gayness be hereditary?

'Actually, you're a bit poofy too, Archie,' Poppy said sitting up and dabbing at her eyes. 'You're the poofiest of anybody. You're very in touch with your feminine side, we all know that, plus your voice is sort of high and you are wearing a dress.'

'Trust me, there is nothing gay about your father,' Mum said with a roll of her eyes. 'If you could have seen him earlier on today with his —'

'No!' I cried. 'Please, Mum, not now.' My mother started to raise her eyebrows in her traditional how-repressed-are-you look but then relaxed a little when she considered perhaps I might not want to hear stories of heroic heterosexuality just at that point.

'I don't care if Monty is gay,' I said, realising as I said the words that it was true. It was one thing to have a gay husband, irritating for practical reasons as much as anything else, but to have a gay son, well, that was different. Entirely different. As long as Monty was happy I didn't care what he was or with whom he was it. I just hoped with all my heart that if he was gay he would accept it from the word go and be proud of it instead of getting married and living with a woman for twenty years before blurting it out over the table the same afternoon she was fired from her job.

'I don't care either,' Dad said quickly. 'In fact we would welcome it, wouldn't we Beth? Should we light a Tibetan hoping stick or two, do you think?'

'Ooh yes,' Mum said, quite excitedly. 'Please do. Another layer of sexual complexity in the family? I think so. I'd adore a gay grandson. How wonderful. He can adopt, you know, they all do these days, so we needn't be without great-grandchildren just because he's travelling a different path.'

Poppy sniffed. 'Well, I could still give you grandchildren, Beth,' she said sadly. Poppy had bad luck on the romance front, the subject of much psyche-delving for her and my parents.

'Of course, darling,' my mother was quick to say. 'We pray to the moon for those little redheaded angels to arrive.'

'And anyway,' Poppy continued, 'Monty seemed to be taking the heterosexual route when I caught him shagging that little blonde with the enormous bosoms from the riding school last time he stayed here.'

'That doesn't mean anything,' Mum said candidly. 'Harry's been shagging Effie all this time and look at him.'

They all turned to me. In a normal family this would have been an embarrassing moment but I had learned years ago the only person who felt embarrassment in my family was me and it's a pretty empty sensation when nobody else is sharing it.

'Monty shagged a little blonde with enormous bosoms from the riding school?' I asked Poppy instead. How could she not have passed on this vital piece of information about my darling only son, my precious virginal baby, sooner?

'She was very pretty,' Poppy shrugged, 'and Jethro at the Black Swan has shagged her too and says —'

I held up my hand to stop her. Again, details such as these I did not need.

'Have you spoken to him, to Monty?' Dad asked and the concern on his usually blissfully carefree face touched me. 'Does he know?'

'No, I haven't and yes he does,' I answered, trying to maintain a semblance of control. 'Harry spoke to him somewhere in Thailand. It wasn't a good line but Harry swears he was quite calm about it. I can't imagine what he thinks of it all but anyway he gets back this week. I've had an email . . .' My semblance abandoned me. I could not speak.

'Hang in there, Mum,' was all the email had said. 'I'll be home soon. Everything will be OK. Love you lots. M.'

BETH

♥ ♥ ♥

From the very start Florence showed a certain contrariness.

Fancy being fertilised in the ladies' loo at Luton when she could have chosen the most romantic city in the world!

Anyway, there I was, all ready for one of England's first water births. The Russians had been birthing babies underwater for years and it sounded like such a lovely way to bring a new life into the world. We had the swimming pool all ready and waiting in the sitting room at Primrose Hill. The midwife and I had even featured in the Ham & High. *Such excitement!*

But a month out from Florence's due date she turned to the breech position and no amount of shoulder stands or cat stretches would turn her back again. In the end I had to go to hospital by ambulance and have every drug known to mankind, none of them organic, and to top it all off, a Caesarean. I never even got to dip a toe in the pool. The embarrassment, I can't tell you. The midwife never spoke to me again. I had to go to University College Hospital to get one for Poppy.

She was such a serious baby, Florence, not at all relaxed like Archie and me. She seemed to prefer a routine, which of course wasn't really on the cards for us at the time. But you can't make someone free and easy if they're not wired that way and Florence has certainly never been free and easy. Very gifted in many ways, but none of them easygoing.

I would never say we didn't approve of Harry because there's no joy in being judgemental but I was surprised that she settled down so soon. Archie and I married young too but we both had marvellous fun playing the field first. I don't think Florence even played the garden path.

She and my own mother were bonded in a past life, I think, maybe on the same side of a battlefield. The opposite side from me, I would imagine.

I remember trying to get Florence to help me make a dream-catcher when she was a tot. I had bamboo, I had feathers, I had beads, I had a glue gun and all she had to do was help but she did not want a dream-catcher, she told me. She did not want to catch her dreams, she said. She didn't mind letting them go. How could we ever possibly have given birth to someone so removed from their inner self, I asked Archie, who was no help at all, as I recall.

He did point out, however, that I still had an aversion to handkerchiefs bearing cross-stitched initials because when I was a child my mother used to insist I cross stitch our handkerchiefs. She had such rigid ideas about things like that. It drove me batty. Initialled handkerchiefs? Really, who cares?

But I suppose what he was getting at was that Florence and I do share a sort of stubbornness. Although knowing him he was getting at no such thing and it's just a coincidence I drew something sensible from it.

What did surprise me I suppose was that this beautiful, strong-minded, capable daughter of mine ended up hawking musty old antiques in suburbia. I thought she would do more, go further, but getting married and having Monty seems to have been it.

Not that there's anything wrong with that and she certainly seemed happy enough and has done a splendid job with our wonderful grandson. Still, it seems a limited sort of life.

Of course, you could say the same about me except that my life is full to the brim with my outside interests. I teach yoga for seniors three times a week at Woodbridge. I run the organic gardening co-op, I host the local poetry society, I play old-fashioned tennis in the summer, I swim in the public baths nearly every sunny day in the summer, and I am taking weaving lessons. I've given up pottery just recently, I stuck it out for longer than I should have, to be honest. It was so hard. And who needs that many ash trays? No one smokes any more. Not even roll-ups.

I was heartbroken on Florence's behalf over Harry's departure but that was mainly because if you took him out of her life, what else, apart from Monty, was in it?

CHAPTER EIGHT

After baring my soul to my family, I should have felt better and in one way I did. I was glad that the sorry chore was no longer hanging over me. But it was a bit like being glad the guillotine had dropped. So, I no longer had to worry about how much it would hurt, but then again I didn't have a head.

Once the news was out there, even though 'there' was only Tannington Hall, the certainty of being alone truly set in. On the drive back to London I had to pull over twice because I thought I was going to be sick. And it wasn't the nut roast, even though we'd had it both nights. Actually I suppose it could have been the nut roast but at the time I definitely put it down to nerves.

However, no sooner did I get back to my big empty house than something happened to brighten my bleak new world. It wasn't a big something, but it alluded to a big something.

I checked the computer and there was another email from

Monty. It said he was on his way home, would be arriving in three days' time, would get the Heathrow Express to Paddington, and could one of us pick him up there at around two-thirty in the afternoon?

Ever since Harry had moved out I had used Monty's return as the light to which the moth-like quiver of my tiny reserves of hope fluttered. Awake in the middle of the night, trembling with anxiety, I would remember my son: the chubby flesh of his arm as a baby, the permanently scabby knees of his first year at school, the wispy sprouting whiskers on his lip as a teenager, the way that even at eighteen he would lean into me for a cuddle if he needed one or, I suspect, if he thought I did.

If I could just reach the point where my arms would once more surround my boy, I would tell myself, if I could just see him and have him back to myself again, then maybe the pain where my marriage used to be would go away, or at least not hurt as much.

It turned out Harry had received the same email — he was ever the diplomat, our son — and when I rang him he kindly agreed that I should pick Monty up and have him to myself for a few hours. You could take this to be a selfless gesture, given he was just as desperate to see him as I was, or you could take it to be a recognition that Harry had 'Charles' helping to massage any pain he might be feeling at the loss of his marriage.

I had taken to calling the man who stole my husband 'Charles' in a special tone that suggested his real name was something else and 'Charles' was the obscene nickname I had chosen for him.

'I know what you are doing.' Harry had called me up on it straight away. 'You did the same thing when "Alan" Fairbanks

103

voted against me making junior partner and you did it when Hilary Nicholson's husband got that job in "PR".'

'Oh, and "Charles" only ever says lovely things in the nicest voice about everyone else, I am sure,' I'd said with a bitterness that sounded acrid even to me. 'A real Father Teresa.'

'Don't,' was all Harry said, which made me even angrier.

'What? Don't tease you about your "boyfriend"? Oh, OK!'

Just because I had almost completely accepted the marriage was over and attempted to understand the difficulty for Harry didn't mean I couldn't be a complete bitch. I had spent most of my life and all of our marriage being mature and sensible, not to mention pleasant, but I was now the wronged party. And I might not have had much practice at being a bitch, having never previously been wronged, but it turned out that when pushed, I could dish out the verbal abuse as well as the next harridan.

These outbursts of anger were never planned and indeed seemed to rise up out of me like projectile vomit. At the time, it felt liberating, powerful, to be cruel — but what soon followed, sometimes within a split second, was overwhelming shame and grief. This was Harry I was spitting obscenities at! My childhood sweetheart! How could I be saying these things to the man I had loved for so long and who had always seemed to love me?

I swung dangerously from one end of the emotional spectrum to the next, although at neither end did I feel any better.

Until that email from Monty pinpointing his return to me. Suddenly I had something other than a life of emptiness and penury to look forward to. There'd been another worry gnawing at me in the middle of the night after all. According to my calculations, I was still one rotten thing down. I couldn't believe that the universe would take my son from me as well as my job and my husband but then again, as I had recently learned, the universe was a shit of a place. Hearing from Monty made losing him less likely, I felt, although he was still in a disease-riddled country catching a taxi through lethal traffic — being driven no doubt by a semi-conscious drug addict — to board a plane filled with brainwashed suicide bombers.

Regardless of that, knowing he was getting closer relieved me of the default despair that had settled into my bones like damp in the past weeks. After the email, Sparky seemed to develop a low-level jauntiness I wasn't sure I'd seen before. Warmed by the thought of my son back home I cleaned his room, I washed all his linen, I cleaned his room a bit more. I spent more time than I should have going through his drawers and sniffing his T shirts but at least it kept me from daytime TV.

I even thought at one stage that I would make a carrot cake — Monty's favourite — but my will to bake had eluded me since Harry had left. The cupcakes I'd taken to Tannington had actually been from the Hummingbird in Portobello Road. I'd meant to make them myself but just couldn't quite get my mojo back on that front. Rose always said that a good cake could sniff a drama a mile away and would not rise or would cook too quickly just to add to it, so you were better off going to Patisserie Valerie.

Besides, I loathed carrot cake. It had a touch of the Primrose Hills about it, if you asked me. Not that I'd ever told Monty that but I did try and steer him towards chocolate or fruit.

Anyway, despite the lack of the usual delicious smells, the post-email house had unquestionably lost the gloomy feeling it had adopted in recent weeks. Lemon Pledge, perhaps. Or hope.

And then on the morning of Monty's arrival home, something else brightened my sad little world. Someone, actually.

On answering a knock at the front door I found a startlingly handsome young man smiling at me. This, as far as I could recall, had never happened before. Normally I opened the door to earnest Mormons or freckly Girl Guides or, on three separate occasions, drunken louts looking for 'Rasheed'.

Not today.

'You must be Florence,' the startlingly handsome young man said pleasantly. 'I'm sorry to just drop by like this but I'm Will, the builder, a friend of Stanley Morris. He might have mentioned me?'

He hadn't but I nodded anyway. He was at least six feet tall with dark hair shot prematurely with just the right amount of silver, unlined olive skin and eyes like the Aegean — not that I'd ever seen it, but I'd seen pictures. He didn't look like a builder nor sound like one for that matter. He was very clean, for a start, and not Eastern European, which most of the builders in London seemed to be. He seemed more like a well-brought-up actor who would play the part of a builder. Not Harrison Ford exactly, because of my feelings about him after the Claridge's debacle and because he was now a hundred years old, but not un-Harrison-Ford-like either.

'Stan said you were thinking of converting your house into a tearoom,' Will the builder continued, 'and that you might need a bit of advice. As I was in the area — no, I know that sounds corny but I actually was, just over in Shirland Street — I thought I would pop in and have a look. Is that all right? Is now a good time?'

He was wearing faded jeans, a chambray shirt in the same colour of sun-soaked blue, with a white T-shirt underneath, and buff-coloured Timberland boots. Most men dressed like this would look like Village People impersonators. He did not.

I was acting rather gormlessly, I knew I was. I was imagining Harry in the same clothes and realising that he could never in a million years pull that look off. Although of course he probably loved the Village People these days. Meanwhile, Will stood patiently on the doorstep.

'Sooooo,' he eventually nodded at me encouragingly, 'may I come in?'

'Of course, excuse me, how kind of you to think of me,' I burbled, ushering him in and knowing as sure as eggs are eggs I was about to start in on a long stream of nervous bollocks.

In the three weeks that I had been 'single', I had not — before Will knocked on my door — even so much as considered the word. Single was a current position that announced somehow one's intention not to remain that way. I was not in that position. I had been 'left', which while also a current position, announced that one had no intention of doing anything, that one was still dazed and confused by the hideous trauma of having been left in the first place.

My position, it turned out, upon having this deeply hetero-sexual person in my hallway, seemed ready to make a change.

'This is the hall,' I began rather pointlessly, wishing I had worn my good jeans, 'and it has always been the hall whereas these two rooms here, that's my office over there but this is my son's TV room, used to be my grandfather's office when he had his surgery here. He was a GP, and so was his father, and they saw the patients in here and there's this little kitchen out here and a bathroom and this door goes out into the back garden where there is a separate entrance onto Warwick Place. So I was thinking, not that I've really actually seriously thought about it — it's just something someone suggested to me a while ago — but I was thinking that if the customers came in through the front door then Monty and I, that's my son, he's due back from his gap year this afternoon, could use this back door as our private access and this could be the kitchen and we could open up the hall into — oooh!'

I chose that moment in my scintillating monologue to step backwards and trip over Will's satchel full of tools, which I hadn't noticed him put on the floor. For a moment I clutched uselessly at the empty air in front of me but it was of no assistance whatsoever and I fell backwards, landing heavily on my bottom on top of the bag.

'Oh shit,' I breathed, winded, before feeling his hand on my shoulder. 'Shit, shit, shit.'

'Are you all right?' he asked, mortified, as he crouched beside me. 'Is your back okay? Your arm? I'm so sorry, Florence, that was my fault completely. I should never have dumped it there. What a fool. I meant to leave it in the hall but I was in a rush to hear your plans. Please, let me help.' He held out his hand to me and dazedly, I took it. He pulled me to my feet. 'May I?' he asked politely, and he turned me slightly to the side and started to dust me down. The floor was grubby. I hadn't vacuumed that room quite as vigorously as the rest of the house. I should have tried harder. I should have done more. I should have . . .

I don't know what it was, if it was the enormity of all I hadn't done, or the thought of a man's hand (he wasn't very old but I was sure he still counted as a man) so close to my body, or the ache in my buttocks, or my son about to arrive home, or my husband leaving me, or my third rotten thing still hanging out there somewhere, but as he gently swept dust and lint off my back with the lightest of touches, I started to cry. Not big loud sobs exactly. More a series of strangled snivels.

There was nothing I could do about it. Even in the circumstances I wasn't prone to public displays of emotion and my mortification at being so unrestrained only made the snivels harder to strangle.

'There!' said Will, stepping back. 'That's better.' At which point he must have realised I was having a reaction disproportionate to falling on my arse. Like Stanley Morris before him, he seemed wired to cope with such emotional outbursts, however, and instead of standing around looking awkward or stammering and running for the door, he calmly suggested that perhaps a cup of tea might be in order.

I nodded, still snivelling, and led him upstairs where he guided me to a chair and put the kettle on.

As I fought to get a grip on myself, he fossicked around the kitchen and found the loose leaf tea (not the bags), the cups and saucers (not the mugs), the milk jug, the sugar bowl, the spoons. He was really very handy.

'I don't have so much as a HobNob,' I blurted out. This seemed a tragedy all on its own. 'My cake tins are usually full but it's all been so hopeless.'

Will set the teapot on the table and held his finger up as if to say 'just one moment', then disappeared down the stairs again. He arrived back with his satchel, from which he extracted a small plastic container, squashed on one side from one of my buttocks, no doubt.

It occurred to me then that he could be a heinous murderer about to jab me with a lethal poison and I should be frightened or at least suspicious but when he opened the plastic container and set it on the table, it did not contain a hypodermic syringe and a bottle of snake venom but rather four plump, round, dark, chocolate truffles. Well, three were plump and round and one was flat like a squashed thing.

'Cherry and pinot noir,' Will said. 'Go on, have one. I made them myself.'

My tears had slowed while I contemplated the whole axe-murdering thing, but stopped completely at the offer of truffles.

'You made them yourself?'

'My secret pleasure,' he said with a smile. 'Although no longer a secret.'

A delightfully spoken builder who looked like a non-smoking Marlboro Man and made his own chocolates? I wondered if I was still asleep and dreaming. But my bottom was extremely sore. I thought I could feel the outline of a spanner in an emerging bruise. And the taste of the cherry and pinot noir truffle was real; deliciously, delightfully real.

'My God, how do you do it?' I asked Will, who was watching me roll my eyes in ecstasy.

'I get the cherries sent over from a friend of mine in Spain,' he answered, with the beginnings of a proud smile, 'and I marinate them in pinot noir from Central Otago in New Zealand. Then I make a ganache using the wine I've soaked the cherries in, roll the cherries in the ganache and then cover it all in seventy per cent cocoa solids. French. It's quite a cosmopolitan effort.'

'They are really, really good,' I said. They were. And I wasn't just saying that because I hadn't eaten all day. They were just other-worldly good chocolates. He offered me another one, not the squashed one either, and I took it, lingering on this one a little longer, savouring the tart cherry flavour, the almost bitter chocolate.

Two boozy chocolate cherries down the hatch and I felt a whole lot better about life. Did straight men make their own chocolates, I wondered dreamily? Will did not seem gay but then neither did Harry. I was perhaps not the best person to pick a man's sexuality. This was going to make dating a bit tricky, I imagined, not that I could even contemplate dating anyone. What was dating anyway? It hadn't even been invented when Harry and I started going out.

'Are you all right?' Will asked.

'Fine, thank you, yes,' I answered him abruptly, snapping to attention. 'You must think I'm very odd. I'm so sorry but I'm just having a bit of a time of it at the minute.'

'Stan mentioned,' Will told me simply. 'I'm sorry.'

I managed a weak smile.

'And my tool bag is sorry too,' added Will, giving it a kick. 'It wishes it could have provided a softer landing.'

The tool bag was made of what had once been black leather, which was now soft and scuffed. It looked like it had been around for a long time.

'It should know better,' I sniffed. 'A bag that age.'

'I can take it outside and give it a hiding if you like,' he suggested.

I laughed and sort of floated off into the luxury of a world where you sat around the kitchen table and made easy conversation with a handsome visitor who brought his own hand-made chocolates.

Had I ever lived in that world before? I asked myself. I must have. Yet it seemed so unfamiliar. Was it because I was attracted to Will in a down-below way? I shocked myself with this thought. I most certainly was not. Who was I to find anyone attractive in any way at all? Let alone a man much younger than me whom I had only just met and with whom I no doubt had very little in common.

'So, what do you think of the tearoom idea?' I asked with a cough, returning myself to more practical territory. 'Is it the silliest notion anyone has ever had?'

'Not at all. I think if anyone was going to convert their house into a tearoom then yours is possibly the best place for it,' he said. 'The TV room lends itself pretty easily to being turned into the kitchen and then you can use your office for the indoor seating — if we open it up a bit as you suggest — and the courtyard out the front for when it's sunny. Who wouldn't want to sit down and enjoy their cup of first flush Darjeeling looking out at that view?'

He made his own chocolates and knew about first flush Darjeeling?

'I lived there,' he said, as though reading my thoughts. 'In India. In Darjeeling. I picked tea for a season when I was younger.'

'I'm going to Paddington to meet my son,' I said for absolutely no reason except that I was muddled, to say the least. 'He's been in Australia.' Which is nowhere near Darjeeling. 'He's nineteen.' I'm thirty-nine.

'Where in Australia?' Will asked.

'All around, by the sound of it. You've been there too?'

'To Perth for a while. And Sydney. Couple of months in Melbourne. Then on to New Zealand for a bit.'

'You've been everywhere.'

'Born in Kenya, schooled in England, on the trot for a few years there but happily back in London now,' Will smiled. 'And you?'

'I've hardly been anywhere at all,' I answered. 'I went to France, once, on a school trip but I don't much like boats and my husband, Harry — well, you know, he's not my husband any more or he is but he doesn't want to be or —' I stopped and pulled myself together. 'Harry wouldn't fly and so neither did I. I've always said I was afraid of it but now I come to think of it, he was afraid of it and I just went along.'

'You've got a lot of making up to do then, Florence,' Will said. 'The world is your oyster.'

We both smiled, our eyes met and, as God is my witness, I felt something. I don't know what it was but it wasn't made up or airy-fairy. It was as real as feeling the sun on my face or the spanner on my bottom. It was also ridiculous. He was little more than a child. Thirty, tops. Thirty-one if I was lucky. And it wasn't exactly my month. And thirty-one was still too young. It was even too young for Poppy, although he would definitely be a good match for her. What gorgeous babies they would have. What fun they would have making them. Hell! What was I thinking?

'I was going to say something about the tearoom being your pearl,' Will said. 'But on top of "just dropping in because I was in the area", I thought it might be a bit much. You know, corny-wise.'

'Well, diamonds are a girl's best friend but pearls are usually all we can afford,' I said, 'so you might be on to something.' He laughed, an easy, cheeky laugh, and I felt ridiculously grateful at having such a kind, comfortable, easy person sitting there talking to me when I was so pitifully lame.

'Have we got time before you go to Paddington', he suggested, 'to take another look downstairs?'

We went down again and he talked about structural bones, business zones, council permits, bench tops, electrical wiring and chocolate éclairs at the Ritz. It would only take a month, he said, to do the renovation if Stan was free to work with him and they could rope in an electrician who could come and go as he was needed and not charge too much. Usually zoning would be an issue, he said, because of us being in a residential area but as the house had been used as a business premises before, and because of the pub and the antique store opposite the back gate and the ample parking, he did not think it would be a problem and assured me he could take care of it.

I was halfway through telling him that I would get back to him about going ahead when I had 'checked with . . .' when I realised that there was no longer anyone to check anything with. And there was not really much to check.

He had already said he could do it for the money. I didn't know what the future held on that front but I currently had what was required. Plus I was short on other career options. Did people decide to open a tearoom in their house just like that, though? With less consideration than you'd give the purchase of a decent pair of shoes?

'What's worrying you?' Will asked, seeing I was wavering.

'That I don't know what I'm doing, that it will be a complete and utter disaster, that no one will come, that if they do the food will be terrible, that Monty and I will end up bankrupt and homeless.'

'Or it could be a massive success and you could end up a millionaire,' Will suggested. 'Or just comfortably off doing what you like doing. Although I'm making a few assumptions there. You like to cook?'

I nodded vigorously. 'Bake. Despite the current state of my tins, I like to bake. It's what got me fired from my last job.'

'You were fired for being a bad baker?'

'No, I was fired for being a good baker. From an antique shop. My own one, actually. It's sort of a long story.'

'But it was always your dream to open a tearoom?'

'No, I never thought of it until a few weeks ago. A fortune teller gave me the idea.' I realised how limp that sounded. How silly a notion it really was. 'Well, not a fortune teller.

She read my tea leaves. She saw a house and a teapot and a rose and somehow that added up to mean I would set up a tearoom. Here.'

'You need some roses then,' Will said, leaning to look out the front window. He was good looking from the back, as well, the way some men are, although they're usually Italian.

'Not roses, Rose,' I explained, blushing gently at my own lewdness. 'This house was left to me by my grandmother, Rose. That was the clincher really, at the time, although now I'm just not . . .'

'My grandmother used to take me to tea at the Muthaiga Club in Kenya,' Will said, filling in the gap. 'There's nothing quite like a high tea well done, is there? I think it's the attention to detail, the effort that goes into it, when all it really is is a stopover between lunch and supper. I mean it's a treat, isn't it?'

Was he an angel, I wondered, sent from heaven to re-ignite my reason for living?

'Yes,' I answered. 'It is a treat.' I joined him at the window and we both looked out over the Grand Junction where a canal boat was passing slowly up the waterway towards Ladbroke Grove. 'Rose used to take me to afternoon tea too,' I said dreamily, tracing a pattern in the dust on the windowsill. 'We went to all the best places: the Savoy, the Ritz, the Dorchester, everywhere. But our favourite was Claridge's. Have you had tea there?'

Will shook his head.

'It's lovely,' I said. 'Really lovely.'

'This could be really lovely too, you know, Florence,' Will suggested.

'I could call it Rose's,' I added, thinking of Sanderson sofas, of distant happiness. 'With an apostrophe. She would love that.'

'I don't think she would be the only one,' Will agreed, eyeing up the architraves.

Something shifted imperceptibly inside me then. Perhaps it was the fact that Monty was nearly home and my shrivelled heart was pumping with hope. Or perhaps it was Will's enthusiasm and the spirit of cherry and dark chocolate still dancing in the air. Whatever it was, the tearoom had just been an idle possibility up until then, a joke, almost. But imagining walls being removed to accommodate it and giving it a name, a beautiful name, changed it into a promise.

'When can you start?' I asked.

WILL

♥ ♥ ♥

I thought she was lovely from the moment I clapped eyes on her.

She talked nineteen to the dozen when I first got there but falling over the tool kit put a stop to that. I mean she was fantastic when she talked but fantastic when she was quiet too. Fragile, in a way, and who wouldn't be in that situation, but substantial, too, if that's the right word. Underneath it all. Yes, substantial.

The tearoom was a brilliant idea, if you asked me, and I knew Stan and I could knock it together, no trouble. It's true about my grandmother, too, and the Muthaiga although actually we used to have tea at home every afternoon before I went to school in England: sandwiches on the verandah followed by biscuits and a slice of cake.

I can come across as corny, I know that, but it's absolutely not bollocks. I made a vow years ago to be truthful and I try to stick by it, which means I can seem a bit in-your-face sometimes or fake, I've been told. More than once actually. Funny, isn't it, that not telling lies can make you sound more like a liar than actual liars do.

Would I have been as interested in working on her renovations if it was some fat hairy old bloke's idea? Some fat hairy old bloke's house?

No.

I felt something when I was talking to Florence that first day that I hadn't felt in a long time and I think she did too. I knew it wouldn't be easy, the future, if there was going to be one, if it was not too presumptuous to consider the possibility. I knew she'd need a lot of encouragement and that it would seem too soon and too fast and that I was too young and a bit strange and had too much history that she was yet to find out about.

But I also knew that feelings like that don't come along every day and when they do, you have to grab them with both hands and never let go.

That's what I wanted to do with Florence.

CHAPTER NINE

I thought I'd have a nervous breakdown on my way to Paddington Station. I was so close to having my son back yet the world appeared determined to keep me from him. Lampposts seemed to jump in front of me; oncoming buses swerved in my direction; cars pulled out from every angle with uncommon speed and no concern for my wellbeing.

When I finally found a park behind the taxi stand at the station and escaped the tired Golf, I was trembling like a leaf. I suddenly knew what tenterhooks were: they were pointy and sharp and it hurt to wait on them.

Paddington itself seemed more full of people than I had ever seen before. A polite British voice made nonetheless indecipherable announcements; foreign languages hummed around me; a dodgy wheel squeaked on someone's suitcase; an engine throbbed in the background and whistles blew on a distant platform, further frazzling my jangled nerves.

I wished that Harry was with me, that he hadn't jumped the fence, that Charles had stayed a fat slob (if indeed he ever was one but I hoped he was) who never went to the gym or stole people's husbands, that we were going to get Monty together.

Poor Monty, what was he coming back to? A father holed up in some hideous bedsit berating himself for his selfishness and deceit, and a heartbroken mother about to demolish his TV room and serve tea and biscuits to strangers in it. Everything about us, about our lives, had changed. I paced the forecourt nervously, feeling sick with equal parts of excitement and worry. This was not what I had wanted for my son's homecoming. How would he handle it? Would he be angry at Harry? At me? Would he turn to drugs? To therapy? He was just a boy.

And then I saw him in the crowd of nobodies streaming towards me and suddenly everything was all right again.

I don't think my son had ever walked towards me without my heart filling to the brim with happiness. His first steps on those huge chubby thighs, straight into my arms, sent me into an orbit of delight that kept me smitten with their memory to this day. His little feet running towards me after his first afternoon at kindergarten had the same effect. Ditto his big feet after his first day at high school. Monty heading towards my arms was home every bit as much as the four walls my grandmother had left me.

But how he had changed, this son of mine coming to me fresh from Australia! His hair was long and curly now and he was tanned a fantastically healthy, swarthy shade and was unshaven — plus he actually had enough whiskers for it to look that way, even from a distance. He wore faded linen drawstring trousers, which looked decidedly alternative I couldn't help but notice, and to top it off, he was wearing a pale pink and orange striped muslin shirt with several of the top buttons undone and some sort of a necklace on a leather thong around his neck. He'd lost weight and gained muscle. His cheekbones had taken over his face.

The teenage schoolboy I had sent away had come back as a hippy-chic rock star.

All this I registered in seconds as the hundreds of other plane and train commuters blotted into one indistinguishable blur behind him. This was the moment I had been waiting for since waving my darling off at Heathrow nearly a year before.

I couldn't help it, I ran towards him and threw myself into his arms, making him drop his pack and causing another leather shoulder bag to slide down his arm to the ground. He'd grown about a foot, it seemed, and if I hadn't known he was my little boy I would have taken him for a man. A fully fledged man. He hugged me back with his big grown-up body and I felt the happiest and safest and surest I had done for a long time. My gorgeous boy. It was him and me now. And together we could get through any amount of rotten things. Together, everything would be OK.

My anger at Harry, my humiliation, my grief, all drained away as I stood there in the flow of other sons and daughters the Heathrow Express was disgorging. With Monty's arms around me, I knew that if I felt insecure as a wife, and I had every right to, I felt like the Rock of Gibraltar as a mother. Here was proof, my wonderful, handsome, clever, tall, tanned proof.

'Mum,' he pulled himself away and graced me with his face-wide smile. If I hadn't been so busy drinking up the joy of being with him, I might have noticed a hesitancy around his eyes, eyes he got from me, brown and spaced wide apart. 'There's someone I'd like you to meet.'

I hadn't even noticed the little blonde woman behind him.

She was in her late twenties, I thought, and petite, dressed in a little spaghetti-strap top and a colourful skirt.

I smiled at her. She wore leather sandals on slightly grimy feet and had toe rings and a tattoo made up of a band of tiny Chinese characters around her tiny little arm. Her hair was surf-girl bleached and curly and she too was carrying a pack.

How like Monty to pick up a damsel in distress on the Heathrow Express, I thought. What's the bet he'd offered the woman a ride? He'd always loved his waifs and strays, my boy: guinea pigs, cats, dogs, motherless schoolboys, lonely pensioners — his heart had long been in the right place and as usual, mine swelled with pride at the thought.

'Mum, this is Crystal,' Monty said, smiling at the woman.

'Hello,' I greeted her back, tugging playfully at my son's shirt tail, dragging my gaze reluctantly from him back to her. 'I'm Florence, this one's rather pathetic mother. I'm just so thrilled to have him back home, you'll have to excuse me. Do you need taking somewhere? We're going to Maida Vale, but anywhere in the inner west is fine. I just can't believe it, Monty! I just can't believe I'm standing here talking to you.' I knew I sounded ridiculously bubbly and pleased with myself but I couldn't help it.

'Hi there, Florence,' Crystal said in a low accent that I guessed might be antipodean. 'It's great to finally meet you.'

To my surprise Monty then stepped away from me and moved in behind her, laying an arm across her almost bare shoulder, at which she smiled almost apologetically at me, then shyly up at him.

My bubbliness vanished. My chattiness dried up. My gaze shifted from him to her and I was riveted: that delicate collarbone, the pretty mouth with just a dash of gloss, the tanned skin with a smattering of freckles, the clear green eyes.

I found myself nodding my head in a peculiar fashion as that old familiar feeling of not quite getting it started fluttering in my chest. Nice to *finally* meet me? The Heathrow Express was only a fifteen-minute ride. That didn't warrant a 'finally'. Even if she had been sitting next to Monty on the plane from Bangkok and he had started talking about me before they took off, a 'finally' was still surplus to requirements. How long had these two known each other? Why the 'finally'?

I shifted my confused stare to my son.

'What's going on?' I asked feebly, as the fluttering turned to a banging.

'Don't freak out, Mum,' Monty said, a warning tone in his voice.

Me? Freak out? Why would I?

'Crystal and I are together,' he said with a casual shrug, the sort of slightly guilty shrug you might use if you'd just owned up to buying your second chocolate ice cream of the day. 'Actually, we got married. Mum, this is my wife.'

'You what?' I asked. I could have sworn he had just said that he was married to this woman, this frizzy little over-cooked blonde with the ridiculous name of Crystal, that she was his wife. But Monty was just a boy. He didn't have a wife.

He was talking to me, I could see that, but I couldn't concentrate on what he was saying. I was looking at her, at Crystal, and she was looking straight back.

'What?' I asked again, wishing with every fibre of my being that Harry was with me, that I could share my panic and fear and disappointment and hysteria and did I say panic? I needed him to keep me from feeling that the world was spinning away from me. To grab me and pull me back to the earth's surface.

'. . . met at the health farm not long after I got there and we both knew straight away . . .' Monty was moving towards me, his lips still moving, but I no longer wanted to be close to him, this frightening stranger. I backed away.

'. . . got married by a waterfall in the Currumbin Valley before we . . .'

If this wasn't a dream, I thought, feeling my face ache with the effort of keeping it from collapsing, if this was true, if Monty had come back to me with some hideous dried-up Australian wife attached, then *this* was the third rotten thing in my current roll and it made having no job and a gay husband feel like items Julie Andrews would add to her list of favourite things.

Monty was just a boy, my boy. He would never do something like get married without telling me, without wanting me to help him choose the right person. We were a team, we did things together, we always had.

'Mum!' He reached out and grasped my arm and when I looked down at his hand it seemed so foreign to me that I started to shake it off. His hand was so big and brown. His nails were clipped neat and short. 'Mum!' his grip tightened. 'I'm sorry I didn't tell you. I'm really sorry. But —'

Crystal was still standing back with the bags, still looking at me, not defiantly, but not apologetically either.

'But how old is she?' I asked Monty.

'What has that got to do with it?' he fired back and I saw an unfamiliar glint in his eyes.

'I am your mother,' my voice was getting louder, people were starting to stare, 'and you have just informed me that the "woman" I am looking at over there, the complete stranger about whom I know not a single thing, is married to you, my nineteen-year-old son. I think I have the right to ask how old she is.'

'You married Dad when you were nineteen,' Monty said

forcefully, looking much less like a fully-fledged man and much more like an angry teenager in a way he never really had before.

'I know how old we were,' I tried to smile, 'and I'm not saying I have a problem with you being nineteen.' Which was not true because I most certainly did. 'And let's not get onto the subject of your father right now.' I had so many things to be angry about, I didn't know where to start or stop. 'I just want to know how old this "wife" of yours is.'

'I'm thirty-four,' Crystal said.

She had snuck up on me, was standing at my shoulder now, somehow carrying all their bags, which she placed carefully back on the station floor. 'I'm really sorry this has come as such a shock but I really love your son, Florence, and I hope you will come to respect that.'

'Respect?' I felt a terrible urge to slap her. Indeed my palms were itching. 'Where was the respect for me when you took my son and married him without telling me? He's nineteen years old, Crystal. He is just a boy. What does a thirty-four-year-old woman want with a boy?'

'Oh, Mum, for fuck's sake, you're embarrassing yourself. Just listen to what you're saying. She didn't take me! Jesus, and what does age matter? You're being ridiculous.' Monty was laughing at me and this hurt so deeply my inner fishwife lashed out at him.

'I'm being ridiculous? Just a year ago you relied on me for bus money. Your teddy bear slept in your bed. You cried because Beckham stayed with Real Madrid. Now you have a wife? You don't think that's ridiculous?'

'Fine, be like that then,' Monty said, snatching up his pack and his shoulder bag. I had never seen him like this. I had never dreamed of seeing him like this. 'We don't need this shit,' he said to Crystal. 'Come on, babe. We don't need to go back to her place.'

To 'her' place? When did it stop being *his* place?

'Monty, wait a mo,' Crystal said calmly to my son's angry back and he stopped. Then she turned to me. 'I know you're angry, Florence, and I appreciate you believe you have the right to be and that you are having a difficult time at the moment but if you think about Monty and me, it's not the end of the world, is it? That your son is married and, well, happy?'

What did this little strumpet know about the world and its end?

'I'm not so bad, when you get to know me, despite my age,' she continued with an ill-timed attempt at humour. 'I hope you'll come to see that. Don't you have any faith in the choices the son you brought up would make? Don't you think he would choose a wonderful person to share his life with?'

This kind of talk made me feel weak at the knees, and not in a good way. I'd had a lifetime of this kind of talk. The worst thing about it was that it somehow made perfect sense — just not the right sort of perfect sense. Of course I had faith in Monty's choices. Supreme faith. I just wanted to be there when he made those choices to make sure there weren't any hiccups. Crystal was a hiccup. And just like a hiccup, she needed to be suppressed. But as I stood there wishing I knew kung fu or some other more lethal form of martial art to aid me in this suppression, I caught Monty's eye and he looked so hurt, so wounded, my need to inflict severe physical harm on his wife (*wife?*) evaporated.

I never could bear to see that look in his eyes, let alone be the one to cause it.

Oh, I loved that boy. With what was left of my heart, I just loved him. He was the best thing I had ever done. I couldn't bear that he'd hurt me like this but neither could I bear to hurt him. I was the adult (although Crystal came a pretty close second) in the situation. It was up to me to lead the way. I took as deep a breath as my shock would allow and held out a hand to him as though he was four years old and I needed to get him out of the playground and inside for his afternoon sleep. 'Don't go like this, Monty,' I pleaded. 'Please, come home. Please. I'm sorry.'

I didn't know what to do or think or feel but I knew I could not survive having him walk away from me just then.

He looked at my hand and then at Crystal, who nodded encouragingly. Then he asked where I had parked the car with a brusqueness that broke my heart before striding off in front of us.

'Thank you, Florence, I know this must be hard for you and it means a lot to us that you're trying to be understanding,' Crystal said as we followed him out of the station.

'You don't have the tiniest clue about what anything means to me,' I told her, keeping my voice light and non-threatening in case my son could hear me.

'Well, thank you, I appreciate your honesty,' she answered, without missing a beat, and skipped ahead to catch up with him.

I watched her tiny little skirt shimmy and shine as she moved in front of me and hoped against hope that this tough little nut would never get to meet my parents and sister because I knew for a fact that they would just love her.

CRYSTAL

♥ ♥ ♥

It wasn't my idea not to tell Florence and Harry but then they weren't my parents, it wasn't my deal. And Monty seemed pretty sure he knew the best way to handle it.

He definitely didn't want them getting wind of it before we got married but I think he toyed with telling them soon afterwards. Then he got the call from his dad while we were in Thailand. No way could he drop anything else on his mother, he said, especially from a distance. It would freak her out too much.

I loved it that he was so concerned about her, that he thought so much about her reaction. I knew he was a little afraid of how his folks would take it, but I also knew he loved me with all his heart and was not afraid of what we had done.

She pretty much flipped out at the train station though.

At first she just stared at me blankly with her mouth opening and closing and then she kept saying, 'What? What?' in a louder and louder voice even though Monty was trying to tell her what.

When she finally got it, she was so angry I thought she was going to slap me. Monty was really pissed off too but you know I sort of understood how she might be feeling. When he'd talked about his mum while we were in Australia I had imagined someone older. I knew her age but I had still pictured someone much more matronly than Florence. It's her name, I suppose, and the fact that she is my husband's mum. When I saw her at the train station, though, my first impression was that she didn't look that much unlike me. Taller, obviously, and darker, but otherwise? And if I was thinking that, then so must she have been.

Don't get me wrong, I have no problem with being an older woman, with Monty's age. He's wise beyond his years and besides, I fell in love with him before I knew he was only nineteen and I couldn't fall back out again, no matter how hard I tried. Sure, I probably wouldn't choose to get involved with a guy so much younger than me but if there's one thing I have learned in my years on this earth, it's that timing is everything. We met, we made an instant overwhelming connection and all obstacles had to be overcome. It's as simple as that. I just couldn't feel about someone the way I do about Monty and not pursue that simply on the grounds of our age difference. What if I never felt like that about anyone ever again? What if that was my big shot at true happiness and I gave up on it because of, basically, mathematics?

No, Monty and I were meant to be and so we were.

From a mother's point of view, though, I could accept that I might not have been the sort of girl, the sort of woman, she had envisaged her boy ending up with and therefore just the sight of me, the idea of me, would be disappointing to her. Then, adding in the surprise factor, the unexpectedness of having a daughter-in-law, on top of the unexpectedness of Monty's father having a boyfriend, she really deserved to be shocked and angry.

When I saw her standing there at the station, wanting to spit at me, but so desperate to have her son come home, I tried to put myself in her shoes.

How would I feel if my son turned up married to a woman fifteen years older than him?

I can't answer that. I wish with all my heart and soul I could, but I can't.

CHAPTER TEN

She came from Melbourne and was a massage therapist but dabbled in reflexology. She told me this in the car on the way home as I drove in astonished silence, concentrating on keeping my eyes on the road. They wanted to close, or spin like marbles in their sockets.

Monty was married? To an Australian massage therapist who dabbled in reflexology? Who was old enough to be his . . . well, I don't know what, but she was old. Too old. And she was his *wife*.

I felt sick. Helpless. Furious. Sad. Frightened. Sick again.

Jobless, husbandless, and now, son-less. Oh yes, try arguing my theory of three rotten things with me now, Harry, you bloody gay bastard.

I rang him the moment I got into the house. But it was not my day, my week, my month, possibly my year, for it was not Harry who answered the phone at the Lancaster Gate bedsit.

'Who is this?' I asked of the polite male voice at the other end of the phone, some unknown emotion clipping my words, making them small and hard and mean.

'It's Charles,' the voice said on the other end. 'Is this Florence?'

Well, if Harry's intention was to test my easily plucked filaments, this was definitely doing it. My heart was now officially not just broken, it was shattered. It was shattered and jumped on and burned and then the ashes were spread across the Arctic Circle and frozen and when that was melted they were eaten by some strange creature with a long nose and shat out again and picked at by birds.

I ached. Not just emotionally but in every part of my body. Even my hair hurt. The tiny holes in the corner of my eyes where the tears strained to leave my tortured body hurt.

'Please ask Harry to ring me urgently,' I told 'Charles', trying to sound cold and unforgiving but I was too upset for this to be truly authentic. So much for Harry being holed up in his bedsit crippled with remorse.

'There's no need,' Charles said. 'He's right here. I'll pass you over.'

I heard the muffled sound of grown-up men talking and then Harry was on the line, sounding falsely cheerful and uncomplicated.

'Floss, darling, is he here?'

'Don't you "Floss, darling" me, you snake,' I hissed. 'What's he doing there, answering your phone? You knew I would be calling, Harry. Why would you do that? Are you trying to hurt me? Any more than you already have?'

Harry seemed genuinely surprised.

'Of course not, no, oh Floss, I'm so sorry. I thought you would want to spend a couple of hours with Monty first and actually I thought it would be he who rang me but I just didn't think, really at all. The last thing I want to do is upset you more than I already have. Please believe me. Charles is just here to give me a hand with, ah, to help . . . I've been to Ikea.'

I had tried very, very hard over the past few weeks to not imagine what Charles was helping my husband with. Every now and then I caught a flash of something that made me gulp: two naked male torsos on a passing bus advertisement, two men holding hands walking along the canal, Frankie Goes to Hollywood's 'Relax' blaring out of a passing car radio. It wasn't that I was even interested in what grown men did with each other, I wasn't, I didn't care at all, that had nothing to do with it. What upset me was the reminder that out there existed another world, a world Charles had taken Harry into, where there was no place for me, no matter how hard I tried, no matter what I did or didn't do.

'Tell "Charles" to shove your bookcase and come home at once. I need you here,' I said.

'For God's sake, Floss,' Harry said tiredly.

'Monty has come home with a wife,' I then told him, doing my best to keep calm. 'An Australian woman practically old enough to be his mother. She dabbles in reflexology, Harry. He's married. Monty is married.'

There was silence at the other end.

'That bloody idiot,' Harry finally breathed. 'What the devil has he done? He's just a bloody kid.'

It should have been a bonding moment. It had potential to be our best since the split. Here we were joined again by virtue of being parents locked into the same nightmare. But I was still too raw to feel completely joined with Harry just at that point. Something to do with Charles giving him 'a hand' with his Ikea, no doubt. In fact, in a fit of complete contrariness considering I felt pretty much the same way myself, I found Harry's reaction thoroughly galling.

I was angry that Monty had married Crystal without mentioning it in passing, I told Harry. Not that he was young when he did it. Harry and I had indeed been the same age when we married and before Harry changed his tune we were the poster children for marrying young.

The battles we had to fight with those who thought they knew better!

'Marry in haste, repent at leisure,' my whiskery Great Aunt Violet had warned me three times in the course of one short visit before our wedding. Had it not been for the divine ginger flapjack she had the presence of mind to bring with her, I might have throttled her.

Harry's parents had been totally against it too. They never quite made it clear just who they'd set their sights on for their younger son but did make it clear it wasn't me, his childhood sweetheart, a secretarial college drop-out with a doo-lally family who never stopped kissing and hugging and all smelled overwhelmingly of lavender oil.

My own parents were hardly more encouraging although their objection was that I was getting married at all — such an over-rated institution according to them — not that I was doing it at nineteen.

We'd showed them though. For twenty years our detractors had been forced to eat humble pie. And even now the ones who were still alive couldn't blame the age at which we were married for its awful end. They could blame Harry. And 'Charles'.

'It's not him being a kid that is the problem,' I whispered angrily down the phone to him because I could hear Monty and Crystal, or 'Crystal' as I was already calling her, clattering around in the kitchen. 'It's her being old. Older. Harry, he's just a boy and she's a fully grown woman! It's bordering on obscene. She only has another two minutes of child bearing left in her and Monty is not ready to be a father. Oh God, I can't even believe I'm having to think these things. Monty, a father? Jesus Christ, Harry, you're right. He's still just a child. He's got a pimple on his forehead, for heaven's sake. There must be something we can do.'

'Too bloody right there is,' Harry agreed, full of bluster. 'I'm going to come around and give that woman a piece of my mind and we will take it from there. Don't worry, Floss, we'll get Monty out of this mess.'

Don't worry, Floss. You see, it's things like that no one warns you about missing when you're left by your husband: there's no one to tell you not to worry. It's a small thing, I suppose, which is why there aren't books written about it, but it's a big thing too. Because without there being someone you trust to tell you not to worry, what the hell is there to stop you from doing so?

Monty was making a terrible mistake and I was worried— beyond worried — I was beside myself that he was throwing his young life away and not visiting any of the promise that he had shown since, well, since he was born. Monty was just meant to do great things, everyone knew that. It stuck out like dog's balls. But married at nineteen? He had a wife to look after now. It would tie him down. It would halve him.

My worrying binge was exacerbated by the realisation that perhaps this was what I had done to Harry. Had I arrested his development, tied him down, stopped him from being the best he could be? I didn't think so, I thought I'd always encouraged him to do exactly as he pleased. But perhaps a more mature person might not have done so. Perhaps a more mature person might have guided him differently, challenged him more. All I knew for sure was that what I had done had ended up with the wrong result, which left open a multitude of different courses I could have taken but didn't. I'd always simply supported Harry because I believed in him. I didn't care if he was a lawyer or not, and encouraged his decision to chuck it all in to become a writer even though, truthfully, it seemed an odd choice. He was never much of a fan of reading, after all. Still, I didn't care. I just wanted him to be happy.

And that was what I wanted for Monty too. I wanted him to be happy. But although I had thought, when briefly considering he might be gay, that I wouldn't mind who he was happy with, I realised now that was not the truth. I wanted him to be happy on his own or with a nice girl about his own age in a few years' time. Not right now with an aged Australian wife who dabbled in reflexology.

Any brief respite I got from having Harry tell me not to worry, even though I had everything in the world to worry about, disappeared when he showed up about an hour later and his bluster seemed to have blown.

For all his talk of giving Crystal a piece of his mind he seemed to have changed it. For a start, he couldn't contain his joy at seeing Monty and I could hardly blame him for that. Then when it came to talking to Crystal I could see he was somewhat fazed by her good looks and cool demeanour. Plus, rather annoyingly, she really didn't look thirty-four.

'You must understand our concerns about having this dropped on us with such unexpectedness,' he told the pair of them as we stood somewhat awkwardly in the sitting room, Harry and I sipping wine, Monty a beer, Crystal a glass of water at room temperature.

'Dad, I was going to tell you but you have to admit —'

Monty started but Crystal put her tiny hand on his arm and quieted him instantly. The look he gave her! Such adoration.

'Of course we understand, Harry,' she said coolly. 'I'm sure any parent would feel the same way in the same situation and of course he is your son, your child, but Monty is also an adult. He has adult feelings and based on them he makes adult decisions, one of which was to ask me to marry him.'

'And you had to say yes?' I couldn't help asking, thinking as I did that she was talking about Monty as though he wasn't even there, which seemed pretty bloody rude.

'Didn't you?' Monty shot back at me, his venom stunning me, making me think he didn't mind having Crystal talk for him.

'Yes,' Crystal jumped in. 'When Harry asked, didn't you?'

'We're perhaps not the best people to be canvassing right now,' I answered, in a sour tone I hadn't been aiming for but which got the better of me anyway. 'Our marriage having just finished.'

'Oh, Mum . . .' Monty shook his head and looked at his feet while Crystal consoled him with another irritating pat.

'Come on, Floss, is now really the time for that?' Harry was using his grown-up lawyering voice on me and I didn't like it. It made me feel . . . well, I couldn't put my finger on it but I was experiencing an awful sort of shrinking sensation.

'It is a difficult time for you to speculate on the sense of marrying young, I can appreciate that,' Crystal said earnestly. 'But you and Harry have had twenty amazing years and if Monty and I have half as long and half as solid a relationship then I think we will be doing brilliantly.'

I looked at Monty to see if he was devastated by this spectacularly gloomy marital forecast.

'You'd give it ten years?' I faced her, aghast.

'Well, if you are angry that we're married shouldn't you be pleased it's not going to last?'

Monty was looking at me in such a way that I all but disappeared. There was not a trace of adoration in that look. There was not a trace of anything I recognised. Where was the son who had done nothing but make me happy all these years? The boy who cared so deeply how I felt? The angel that everyone adored, no one more than I?

'What have you done to him?' I burst out at Crystal. 'This is not the Monty I know. We were a really happy family before and now . . .'

And now what? Now my son was back yet I felt more lonely than ever. Lonely. That was the feeling that was shrinking me, making me disappear. The recognition of this stunned me into silence. *Lonely?*

My husband, my son and his wife were all staring at me with variations of the same look on their faces.

They think I am the enemy, it dawned on me.

But I had never been the enemy before and on top of my new-found loneliness and the awful bitterness that kept erupting from the darkest, deepest parts of me, I was suddenly overwhelmed by being such a foreigner in my own beloved country. I froze, right there in the middle of the Persian rug I'd been given by my mothball Granny and had never really liked, never less than right at that minute.

How was it that my darling husband and my gorgeous son could both be looking at me this way when just a month ago I had believed the former to be wildly in love with me and the latter utterly devoted?

Either I was the unluckiest person in the world to have these two things so suddenly not be true, or I was the stupidest person in the world for not realising it sooner.

And to feel lonely, truly lonely at the same time, for the first time?

I could not for the life of me imagine what I had ever done to deserve such hurt. I turned on my heel, grabbed the wine bottle and a glass, and taking the stairs two at a time I fled to my bedroom. It wasn't until I was settled under my duvet with one glass already down the hatch and *The Bill* blaring on the telly as the tears slid down my cheeks that I realised Sparky had stayed in the sitting room.

Another traitor. Another enemy. Oh, the pain.

GREAT AUNT VIOLET

♥ ♥ ♥

We all married in haste and repented at leisure in my day but that didn't mean Florence should. I was only trying to be helpful. She was such a lovely young girl. Just a bit lacking in confidence, I always felt. Those sort of girls often marry young. I should know, I was one myself. My George was never gay, of course, but he wasn't terribly interesting either. And talk about bossy. Wouldn't let me plant marigolds in my own garden or try spaghetti. Foreign muck, he called it.

Still, it was a terrible shock when he died. He was such a stickler for his daily constitutionals. Who would have thought? Anyway, I've got marigolds as far as the eye can see now and I eat spaghetti all day long if I feel like it although it does give me wind, as it happens.

She didn't listen to me, Florence, just the way I didn't listen to my great aunt. Mind you, my ginger flapjack went down a treat. It always does.

CHAPTER ELEVEN

Monty and Crystal made themselves scarce for the next few days and I suppose I could hardly blame them. Although they needn't have worried about running into me because I barely ventured out of my room. I was tired, so tired. All I wanted to do was sleep. It was a blissful escape.

I woke up one morning however with a hammering in my head that seemed to shake not only my body but my bed, the floor, the whole bloody house.

I moaned but the hammering continued. I got up and went to the bathroom but the hammering continued. I closed the door and it dulled a little. That seemed odd. I opened the door and there it was again.

Then I remembered Will, the chocolate-making builder with the startling blue eyes and the magnetic calm. What had possessed me to tell him to go ahead with turning my house into a tearoom? To start today?

Despite my misery, I got up and threw myself in the shower then dressed in the True Religion jeans Monty had chosen for me before he went away. They were loose, the jeans, which surprised me as they most certainly had not been the last time I'd worn them. I'd had to lie on the floor and pull the zipper up with a coat hanger hook. Plucking at the waistband I moved to the full-length mirror to check myself out. I did look thinner. I also had black rings under my eyes and my cheekbones looked sharper than usual. I peered closer. I was pale too. In fact, I looked revolting. I delved into my make-up drawer and doing the best I could without having put lids on anything in the past five years or being able to find the necessary brushes, I made myself as presentable as possible.

Downstairs Will had started deconstructing the wall between Monty's TV room and the hallway. It gave me a shock, to be honest, took my mind off my distress over the whole daughter-in-law business. I hadn't thought about the process of changing the house into a tearoom as being noisy or brutal but it was. My house! My lovely house! The only thing it turned out I could rely on and here I was cutting into it, making it bleed plaster and scrim and ancient shards of wallpaper. Will had pushed all the furniture to the far end of the room and covered it in drop cloths before starting to rip off the lining to expose the wall's framing. This was hardly dramatic, yet it changed everything. The light was different. The look was different. I had been coming to this house for my whole life and it had looked exactly the same: the carpet, the light fittings, the phone table without the phone. What had I done? Wasn't there enough unwanted change in my life right now? What the hell was I thinking orchestrating more?

Will appeared through the doorway from the office and saw the panic in my eyes.

'This is the worst bit,' he said. 'Don't worry. It'll be over by the end of the week.'

Indeed, by the end of the week he had transformed, albeit roughly, the bottom level of the house. Gone were the walls that separated the rooms from the hall and in their place was one admittedly delightful open space, filled with the natural light streaming in through the tall sash windows that looked out onto the canal.

'It's going to be a corker spot for a cuppa,' enthused Stanley when he came by to work out his schedule with Will. 'Better than the Spanish Steps any old day, I bet.'

It was a pleasure having the two of them in the house, to be honest. It cut through the tension that swelled between Monty and me like a fast-moving river full of rolling logs. Neither of us had the dexterity to try crossing at this point, so the twin distractions of a gobby plumber and a mysterious builder could not be more welcome.

'Cope with it all right, did he?' Stanley asked me after meeting Monty for the first time. 'The news about you and your old man?'

'He had some news of his own, as it turns out,' I told him, as I delivered a pot of Prince of Wales tea on a tray along with a packet of chocolate digestives. 'You'll meet her any minute.'

Crystal duly appeared and proved to be utterly charming, wearing another cute-as-a-button surfer girl outfit and managing to talk plumbing at a fairly knowledgeable level with Stanley and tai chi with Will before skipping happily out the door with my surly son.

'New girlfriend?' Will asked me, and I felt a pang of something. Something ugly. Crystal was closer to his age. She should be with him. But . . .

'New *wife*,' I said in a clipped voice.

'Woo-hoo,' howled Stanley. 'That must have come as a shock, eh? The little beggars never fail to surprise, do they?'

I bit hard on my lip to keep any more unwanted tears from paying another visit.

'I suppose you've had enough surprises lately,' Will said, gently. 'But I bet you're glad to have him home.'

And although I spent most of my waking hours trying very hard to imagine how I could keep myself from wringing his stupid bloody neck I was, I truly was. How could I not be? It's just that I'd barely had a chance to talk to him. She was always there, Crystal. Never left him alone for a moment. We'd not had any of the heart-to-hearts I'd been dreaming of. I didn't even really know what he thought about Harry, about us, about 'Charles'.

News of the impending tearooms had been greeted with little more than a raise of his eyebrow. It was Crystal who said she thought the house had such a lovely feel that it should be open to more visitors. And what did she know?

I stood at the kitchen window one morning and watched as she and Monty hung out their laundry in the back yard. I'd never seen him hang out washing before. I'd always done it for him. They worked side by side, him helping her reach up to the clothesline Harry had strung between two trees at the back of the garden. They were laughing, nudging each other, stopping every now and then to kiss and mess about.

'I got married without telling my mother too,' Will said behind me.

'You're married?' I asked, quickly trying to camouflage my distress.

'Was,' said Will, unloading the contents of the tea tray on to the kitchen counter. 'Divorced five years now.'

'Five years ago? You don't look old enough to be married,

let alone divorced.'

'I'm thirty-one,' he said, and he looked at me with an unreadable expression, which nonetheless made me blush. Under such scrutiny, I turned my attention back to the laundering lovebirds.

'He could have had any woman in the world and he chose her,' I said. 'Why? I just don't get it. And why now when he has his whole life ahead of him?'

'Maybe he wants his whole life to be spent with her and he just wants to get on with it,' Will said as he rinsed the tea cups and put them in the dishwasher. 'That's what I felt like when I met Natasha.'

'Well, we're neither of us very good advertisements for marriage, though, are we?' I challenged him, my voice more brittle than I meant it to be. 'Yours was obviously short and not very sweet and mine turned out to be long and bollocks.'

He leaned back against the kitchen counter and shrugged. 'Would you have it any other way though?'

I thought of the way Harry had looked at me on our wedding day, despite the width of the shoulder pads (what was I thinking?) in my white satin dress. Regardless of what had recently come to pass, he had loved me, truly loved me, that day, and I knew it, which was a precious gift. What's more, he had loved me for many days after that and I knew that too. Then there was Monty, our darling boy, who burst into our world and exploded all my fears that he would break our magic spell of happiness, that there wouldn't be enough to go around. There had been. So, he was currently breaking my heart but for nineteen years before now he had done nothing but fill it with joy.

'No,' I admitted. 'I wouldn't have it any other way. And you?'

'No,' he said. 'There are a lot of things I would do differently, but getting married isn't one of them.'

'What happened then, with you and your wife? And please don't tell me she left you for a woman.'

Will smiled. 'I'll tell you some other time. When you know me better.'

There it was again, that glimmer of something deep and wonderful between us, the promise of close encounters to come, but I stuffed it down beneath the complicated mixture of hurt and bitterness that didn't involve him yet was churning inside me.

A mixture that was stirred, as it happened, when my family came for supper on the first Sunday after Monty's return. It was bound to be fraught with tension as Monty had asked if Harry could come. I didn't want him there, the sight of him still made me too angry, and sad, and angry and sad again, especially as he continued to glow with health and vitality while I shrivelled in comparison. But Monty, in a rare bout of speaking to me, had said it would mean a lot to him if we could all hold it together for a night so I told my inner fishwife to stick a sock in it, smiled as magnanimously as I could manage, and said, 'Of course, darling, if that's what you would like.'

Just seeing Harry there on the day, however, catapulted me into a foul temper, as did watching Dad eye Crystal up with what was unquestionably a pervy look.

'Monty, you sly old thing, eh?' he said, ruffling his grandson's hair. 'Quite the looker. And a masseuse as well, lucky boy!'

Crystal and Poppy bonded instantly over their twin skills in the homemade dream-catcher department, of all things. Mum had long been mad for them and Poppy had made one for me the year before, a twitty circular thing made of twigs and feathers, which hung on the rear-vision mirror of the tired VW for about twelve seconds before Sparky pounced on it, attempted to have sex with it, then ate it. I'd not asked for a replacement and upon hearing of its demise, she'd not offered one.

Now, she and Crystal were joined at the hip at one end of the table twittering on about the Ojibwe native American tribe while my mother was gazing at them so thrilled and delighted and full of the joys of the universe I wanted to poke her in the eye with a crochet hook, although of course I didn't have one.

Afterwards, I retreated to the sitting room and let Harry and Dad and Monty do the dishes as was the habit after our Sunday suppers. Crystal excused herself, saying she was off to visit friends in Earls Court, giving Mum and Poppy the opportunity to practically cream themselves offering their congratulations, welcoming her to the family and insisting she come and stay at Tannington Hall as soon as was humanly possible.

'You could always take her tonight,' I suggested sweetly once she was out of earshot.

'What is it about her that threatens you so much, Florence?' my mother wanted to know. She had her psychologist hat firmly wedged on her out-of-control hair, never a good metaphorical look. Mum had not trained as a psychologist but you would never guess this by talking to her. She had read a lot of books on the subject and could have made quite a career out of offering unsolicited advice to those she felt were in need of her particular brand of 'therapy'.

'She doesn't threaten me at all, Mum,' I answered. 'But allow me a little room to express my "feelings" about a woman Poppy's age arriving on my doorstep announcing herself as Monty's wife.'

I had long learned to throw the whole expressing-your-feelings business back in my mother's face but on this occasion it fell flat.

'Hostile,' Mum mouthed to Poppy.

Harry's cellphone, which was sitting on the coffee table, started to ring at that point but when I reached for it I saw that the name 'Charles' was flashing up on the caller ID.

I had been extremely pleasant to my husband all evening despite fighting a dreadful urge to fling myself across the dinner table and rip his throat out. He was so much his old self it just didn't seem right that he in fact lived around the corner and had a boyfriend. He wasn't even uncomfortable with my family which he jolly well should have been because he had betrayed me so awfully. And they should have been very cross and quite mean to him in a show of solidarity for me, their actual daughter and sister. Instead there was a slightly congratulatory mood in the room. Jovial almost. This enraged me so much that when I saw 'Charles' flashing on the phone I opened the window and threw it out into the courtyard.

Hostile, my foot.

My mother pursed her lips in a very cat's bottom fashion and decamped for the kitchen.

'Oh, Florence, please, please, don't be angry,' Poppy pleaded, her freckles sticking out adorably below her imploring blue eyes. 'I can't bear to see you like this. I know you're hurt but anger won't help you heal, you know it won't.'

'Am I not allowed a moment or two of wanting to kill the former love of my life for abandoning me?' I asked her.

'Yes, of course you are, but you've already had those moments,' she said. 'You must think about moving forward. And anyway, it's not Harry I'm worried about. He can look after himself. It's Crystal.'

'What do you mean?'

'I mean she seems like a thoroughly decent person and the universe has brought her and Monty together so you shouldn't be the one to drive them apart.'

'How exactly am I driving them apart?' I asked my sister. 'By having them living here in my house, by feeding and watering them?'

'You are not being very nice to her,' Poppy said. 'In fact, you're being quite horrid. And she's Monty's choice. They're in love!'

'Just because he chose her doesn't make it right,' I snapped. 'For God's sake, grow up, Poppy. And what do you know about love anyway?'

I couldn't have hurt her more if I had spent weeks working on it. She was right, that was the problem. I was being horrid. But it wasn't my fault. My hurt had curdled into anger and was giving my inner fishwife the upper hand which was helping no one. Especially me. Poppy bit her trembling lip.

'Don't let what has happened to you turn you into a terrible person, Effie,' she said, and she too scuttled off to the kitchen.

I sat there in the sitting room where I had spent so many happy occasions over so many years and felt misery seep into every corner of my body. Then a funny muffled ringing tone trickled up the outside of the house and warbled in the window just as Harry came in asking for his phone.

It was not my night.

'She's making a terrible mess of the place,' I heard my father say as the family departed not long after.

'Oh, someone can always put it back together the way it was,' my mother said cheerily.

I slumped back on the sofa and pulled Sparky awkwardly into my lap. He wasn't that keen on me now Crystal had moved in but I wasn't having a bar of that. I needed him.

The truth was, I'd made a terrible mess of everything. And no one could put it back together. Ever. Plus, as Poppy had pointed out, I was turning into a terrible person and it didn't make me feel better, it made me feel worse, so what was the point? I liked myself much more when I just wanted my son to be happy, no matter what, although of course I had never imagined a 'what' the likes of Crystal.

Try as I might after that night to be a better person, to be more open and accepting of Monty and Crystal, most of the trying was done theoretically. In practice, I just wanted my son back and felt extremely resentful of her for stealing him from me.

I would manage to be my pleasant old self on the rare occasions when it was just him and me together but the moment she appeared in the kitchen, in the back yard, on the stairwell, my charm would evaporate.

Something despicable in me, previously untapped, made me turn my nose up at the vegan meals she cooked even though they smelled quite heavenly. I left pork chops sitting boldly in the fridge where she could be repelled by them. I barely thanked her when she did my laundry although no one had washed my smalls for me for years. I let conversation fizzle out when she attempted it. Still, I couldn't help but learn a few things about her, about them.

They had met at the health spa where they were both working. He'd been doing gardening and maintenance and had torn a shoulder ligament, she was the resident massage therapist who'd tended to it. It was love at first sight, for both of them. Yes, Cupid had drawn back his bow and now here she was living in my house, bringing organic peanut butter into my kitchen, and no doubt having large amounts of sweaty erotic sex with my previously pure and virginal (busty riding-school girl notwithstanding) son.

Worse, my previously pure and virginal son revealed that he was no longer planning to do a business degree as he had always said he would, but wanted to become a film director.

He chose an evening when Crystal was out with her Earls Court friends to drop this on me and his father, who had not been to visit since the phone out the window incident but was there for another restrained attempt at a family supper for which I had to give him credit. I wouldn't have come near me with a forty-foot barge pole. But still, he came, kissed me nervously on the cheek (which for the first time I allowed) and said: 'Will you promise to leave my telecommunication devices alone?'

His good humour disappeared when Monty mentioned his change of heart on the career front. 'Are you bloody mad?' Harry exploded. 'Do you know how many unsuccessful film directors there are out there? Most of the successful ones can't even get jobs, let alone the newcomers.'

'Well, thanks for the vote of confidence, Dad,' Monty said, 'but I met a producer in Australia who said the industry is always looking for new blood and anyway what was all that bollocks about following your heart when you gave up law?'

'That was entirely different,' Harry snapped. 'I already had a lucrative career to fall back on. And with all due respect, what would a producer in Australia know? By all means, become a film director, Monty, but show some sense and do it when you are my age.'

'How do you even get to be one?' I wanted to know. The only other film director I could think of was Madonna's husband and he came from a wealthy background, I thought. Plus he had a rich wife and Crystal didn't look as though she had much more than a Tibetan hoping stick to her name.

'There's a two-year MA course at the London Film School,' Monty told me. 'It's pretty highly regarded actually and the fees are a bit steep but I could work in the evenings and at the weekend and Crystal will help support me. She's behind me completely.'

Well, she would be, wouldn't she? Little madam, talking Monty out of the dream we'd had for him and letting him follow his stupid heart.

'There's no money in it, Monty,' Harry said, exasperated. 'There won't be, ever.'

'Who says I care about money?' Monty challenged him. 'There's more to life than money, Dad, as you should know. How's the writing going, by the way? Making any money out of that yet?'

Harry turned puce with rage or embarrassment, I wasn't sure which. In all our years together there had been very little turning puce. This sort of stand-off was totally alien to us, we'd never had one before, and all I wanted to do was soothe the waters even though I too thought being a film director was pie in the sky.

'We just want you to have some security for the future,' I told him. In case you get a real wife when you are older, I added, silently. 'Is that so bad?'

Monty's cellphone rang and his eyes lit up when he saw who it was.

'Back in a mo for more of this scintillating patronising,' he said, and went to his room to take the call.

'Could Monty wanting to be a film director be the beginning of another roll of three?' I asked Harry, sick to my stomach, once he'd left the room.

'Please, Florence,' Harry answered grumpily, 'you know I

don't believe in that nonsense.' He seemed particularly agitated. Nervous, almost, once I came to think about it. 'He could have such a future in the City, that's the shame of it. He's so clever, he has the right personality and I always thought he had the drive. But now? I just don't know. There's no money in film-making, God, any halfwit knows that. It's what rich kids do when they can't think of anything else. Monty's too clever for that.'

He checked his watch, not for the first time, and it occurred to me that 'Charles' was waiting for him somewhere, which tickled my anger bone.

'Oh well, as long as he's happy, I suppose,' I smiled, doing a complete turnaround while taking a noisy slurp of wine. 'And he did always love going to the movies.'

Harry, of course, was on to me straight away. 'Yes, Crystal must be a movie lover too, I suppose. Indie types, I imagine. With sub-titles. And she certainly seems to make him happy.'

I plonked my wine glass down on the coffee table with an angry thunk but I couldn't think of anything to say.

'What? Going to throw that out the window too?'

I considered making Harry the target, but decided against it. I pictured my mother mouthing 'hostile' across the room. Besides, if he left, I would be on my own and I really didn't feel like it.

'Was it us?' I asked instead. 'Did we go wrong somewhere along the line? He's always been so sensible, so, normal. And now . . . I hardly recognise him.'

'I've been over it a hundred times myself, Floss, and I'm damned if I can work it out,' he answered. 'I try putting myself in his shoes but you and I were married at the same age so there's not much of a leg to stand on.'

'Yes, but . . .' I started but I didn't have the energy to continue.

There were so many buts. But we had known each other for years. But we were both the same age. But Harry went to university as planned.

Perhaps we could try using the collapse of our own marriage to — well, that was the thing. To what? Stable door unlocked. Horse bolted.

'I'm going to go and hook up with Crystal,' Monty said, popping his head around the door. 'See you later, Mum. Catch you tomorrow, Dad.'

'Hang on a minute,' Harry said. 'I don't think we quite finished what we started. Your mother is right about getting some security, Monty. Would you please not just consider getting a business degree first and then pursuing the film thing, if you still want to, afterwards?'

'Dad, enough with the security,' Monty said. 'I mean what security do you have now, anyway?'

I thought Harry might be hurt by this but he shot me a strange, twitchy look.

'Actually, the subject of security has been weighing heavily on my mind lately,' he said. 'I've been meaning to mention it but it's been . . . well, the thing is I'm going back to the law. As of Monday I'm working for Johnson Klint Boyle in the City.'

I could not believe my ears. 'You are what?' I demanded. 'Please tell me you are joking. That's ludicrous, Harry. You hate the law. What happened to your novel? The one you've always dreamed of being published? The one you have been working on all these years? What happened to exploring the truth instead of lies? What happened to all that?'

'Yeah, Dad,' Monty chipped in. 'What happened to that?'

Harry faltered. 'I just decided that in the circumstances the law was the best place for me,' he said, somewhat limply.

'The circumstances?' Monty and I repeated at the same time.

Again, Harry faltered. 'I'd like you to keep the house, Florence,' he said. 'I think that's only fair. And you should be able to do with it what you want. The tearooms, I mean. It's Rose's place and you've always loved it more than I have. But I need somewhere to live and I need an income and to practise what I've been trained for seemed the best way to achieve that.'

He flicked a look at Monty, which I took to mean he didn't particularly want our son in on this conversation but it seemed a little late for such considerations.

'You said that the law crippled you, that it was killing you, that it made you dangerously unhappy,' I reminded Harry.

'Yes, I said that,' Harry admitted. 'And at the time it was true. It's just that now . . .'

'It's just that now what?'

'Let it go, Floss,' Harry warned me gently.

'Let it go?' I felt yet more anger building from somewhere deep inside me. 'It's just that now what, Harry?'

Harry bit his top lip and looked around the room.

'For God's sake, Harry, stop pissing about. You have a boyfriend and Monty has a wife. Do you really think my life could get any worse? That anything could shock or surprise me more than it already has?'

'It's not the worst thing in the world, me having a wife,' Monty said. 'Or Dad being gay. It doesn't mean we don't, you know, love you or whatever.'

Was it me putting my son in a position where he had to point something like that out? Of course I didn't think he didn't love me any more just because he now loved someone else. More. Like Harry did. Or did I think that? Was I that pathetic? No, I bloody well wasn't.

'I just want to know what happened to the whole being

dangerously unhappy thing, Harry,' I said, anger pushing me further than I ideally wanted to go. 'Am I allowed to do that?'

'There's nothing to be gained by hashing it out any more than we already have, Florence,' he said. 'It's just the way it is.'

'The way what is? Am I not entitled to find out why the change of mind? For years you tell me something is crippling you, killing you, making you dangerously unhappy and . . .'

I've said it before, I can be slow at times. But I get there in the end.

Of course. It hadn't been his job making Harry unhappy all that time, I realised as I watched him avoid my gaze.

It had been me. It had been us.

A little cold hard nugget inside me expanded in that moment, pushing out any of the spare bits of loveliness I had been trying to keep tucked away in case I needed them. I hated Harry with all of what was left of my heart. Hated him. So, me loving him had crippled him and made him miserable. Well, boo bloody hoo.

'So, everything is somehow my fault, is that it?' I asked brightly. 'I've been responsible for being your wife and mother of your son and chief cook and bloody bottle washer all these years and I've done such a terrible job and made you so unhappy? I should have tried harder, you are right to take no responsibility for yourself, to completely blame me . . .'

'I don't blame you. This is not about —'

'Get out of my house,' I told Harry. 'And don't ever, ever come back.'

'Mum, I don't think —' Monty started to placate me again but I turned on him too.

'Please, go and meet your "wife",' I said. 'Don't worry about me, darling. Don't either of you worry about me. I'll be absolutely fine. Just go.'

I didn't want Monty to go, I wanted him to stay and give me a hug, tell me everything was OK. But everything wasn't OK. And I didn't see how it ever could be.

They both left, at which point I had two choices: I could go upstairs and hang myself from the coat hook on the back of the bathroom door even though it had been wiggly for about four years and sometimes fell off when you hung a bathrobe from it, or I could do what I did best: bake. It had been a while but the urge was suddenly overwhelming.

I started off with a dozen chocolate cupcakes. When the smell of them baking in the kitchen chased away a small fraction of the angst reverberating around the house, I baked a dozen more: vanilla. When that improved the atmosphere yet again, I made a dozen chocolate and vanilla marbled. And when I ran out of chocolate, I made lemon cupcakes that were so delicious Sparky and I had two each and could have polished off the whole lot.

The act of measuring the ingredients precisely into my favourite bowl seemed somehow therapeutic. And I know you are not supposed to beat a cupcake mixture too vigorously, but at times I could not help it.

Harry was a real bastard, I could see that now. For all his careful consideration he was still ultimately blaming me for something about which I had no knowledge and over which I had no control and that was not fair. The trouble was that every time I saw him I felt worse. It would be better, I decided, if he was dead. But unlike me, who was getting thinner and paler as the days went on, he was still rather irritatingly looking the picture of health. All that going to the gym and getting 'a hand' with 'Charles' was turning him into some sort of a stud. Yes, I decided, dead would be good.

But as I whipped up a fourth mixture adding some frozen

berries I'd found in the freezer, I remembered what Will had said about not wanting it any other way. Without Harry, there would be no Monty and without Monty it really would be the wiggly coat hook. So, I found Crystal hard to accept, but as I've said, she was quite a difficult person to actively loathe. She had so far proved to be so sensitive and obliging it was hard to find fault — I had to really work at it. True, I was enraged to see her organic peanut butter hidden behind the toxic kind on the pantry shelf, but deep down I knew that organic peanut butter was not really in itself a heinous crime.

Still, she had taken my son and made him her husband at a time when I really needed him just to be my son. I wavered as I put the experimental berry cupcakes into the oven and thought I would be better off if she was dead too.

But by the time I took them out again I felt differently. So, I'd lost my job, crippled my gay husband, and my son was going to leave me. These were three of the rottenest things that could ever happen. But that was it. Over and done with. There was nothing else that could go wrong.

And on the plus side, I had a roof over my head, this particular roof, and beneath it I was going to make a living, to make a future, for myself. And Sparky. It may have been a sugar buzz from licking the spoon so diligently over so many hours, but despite everything I actually felt a glimmer of hope.

Forty-eight cupcakes can do that to a person.

POPPY

♥ ♥ ♥

I thought Crystal was lovely, and so did Beth and Archie.

You could tell from a mile away how much she was in love with Monty and he with her. It was so romantic, I thought. Meeting all the way over there in Australia and getting married despite the obstacles.

I think I would marry a nineteen-year-old too if one met me and fell in love with me but there don't seem to be a lot of nineteen-year-olds in East Anglia. There's Russell who helps Dad mow the lawns but he doesn't have any of Monty's sort of grown-up-ness. He still seems like a spotty teenager to me. Not that I've got anything against spots, they're only toxin build-ups, but still, I am thirty-five. I should aspire to spot-free, even though I wouldn't let spots stand in the way of true love if they were attached to the right person. Russell, I think, is not the right person. He has a scotch egg for lunch every day, for a start. That's sausage meat. The worst kind.

Anyway, I was worried about Florence after meeting Crystal because I could see how hurt she was by it all. And who wouldn't be? Archie's being silly when he says Harry was always poofy. He and Beth thought they were a match made in heaven (just like they are, only square). And so did I. It's dreadful what's happened, although of course Harry must be true to himself. I know Effie believes that but still. She's been a bit robbed on the happily-ever-after front and we all know how that feels.

It would be terrible if she turned her hurt into something mean, though. She's done that before, a few times, just over little things, without realising it, I think. She doesn't know how tough she is, Effie, how strong. But I do. It's one of the things I so admire about her. I wish I was that tough and strong.

CHAPTER TWELVE

'We've struck a bit of a problem,' Will told me a few days later. Stanley was standing behind him, looking worried, which should have struck fear into my heart but didn't.

Despite the generally serious atmosphere that lurked ominously in the hallway, I just could not focus on the problem, whatever it was. It was not foremost in my mind. It was far from it. Much closer, so close as to be taking up nearly all the available space, in fact, was Will himself. Yes, Will was on my mind. Completely and utterly. The thing is, I had dreamt about him. In a rather explicit fashion.

And as he stood there looking at me the dream, which I had until that moment forgotten, came back in a blinding rush and sort of tackled me, starting down near the floor and ending in my cheeks by way of a chronic blush.

In the dream he had come into my room and sat on the side of my bed and just smiled at me in the most patient, understanding, adoring fashion. Then he had pulled back the covers, slipped off my nightie (transformed for dreaming purposes from the usual T-shirt with the hole in one armpit to a saucy see-through Agent Provocateur-type thing) and run his hands down my body, like a blind man, feeling every bone and hollow and bump until I was totally exposed head to toe, naked and moaning with longing.

Then he had stood up, his clothes sort of dissolving into a puddle on the floor, and he had climbed into the bed next to me. He lay there, just stroking me — my breasts, my collarbone, my ribs, my hips — and then his fingers had slipped down below. He'd pulled me on top of him then and with his hands on my thighs he had guided us both to an extremely erotic and satisfactory ending.

Plus, the dream hadn't ended there. Unlike in real life where sex is often followed by the immediately gentle snoring of one or other or both parties, Will and I had lain on our sides facing each other on the bed, holding hands. He had told me that he loved me, that he would always be there for me, that with him beside me I had nothing to fear and never would ever again.

In the dream, I had wanted to cry because I was so happy.

Now I wanted to cry again because it hadn't really happened. As well as not having recently had sex, I had also not recently (cupcakes not included) had happiness. And now here was Will trying to explain to me what was going wrong with my tearooms-to-be and I was too busy wondering if it had been the cheesiest dream in the entire universe or the loveliest one to concentrate. I knew I should have been nodding or shaking my head or going 'tut tut' but instead I could only gaze blankly at the space just to Will's left because I could not bring myself to look at him.

'I can't fix the pipes with things the way they are down

there, Florence,' Stanley chipped in morbidly, which brought me out of my torpor. 'Dry rot's the enemy of the plumber as well as the builder, you know.'

'Dry rot?' So that's what we were talking about.

'Yes, it's wicked stuff,' Will said. 'We went to detach some of the old plumbing in the basement and one of the joists just about disintegrated in my hands. They're in a pretty bad way and we'll need to replace them and some of the floorboards before Stan can go any further.'

'So, what does it all mean?' I couldn't just at that minute think what a joist might be.

'It means time,' Stanley said.

Well, actually, I had plenty of that.

'And money,' added Will.

'Oh shit.'

Now he had my attention. Forget pulling me on top of his naked body. Hell, now I was thinking about that again. I reverted to thoughts about joists which brought me back down to earth. And on earth time was not a problem but money was. Will and I had budgeted the renovations at exactly £30,000 because that was exactly what I had.

'How much more do you think we will need?'

Stanley looked even more worried.

'I'd like to say ten thousand but it could be more,' ventured Will.

'Oh shit, shit, shit.'

Any residue of my delicious dream vanished into thin air, taking any fleeting happiness or hopefulness I had felt with it. Where the hell was I going to get another wodge of cash? I hadn't even had the brains to get the first one. That had been a mistake. And I was living as cheaply as I could but I was still perilously close to dipping into the £30,000 just to feed myself and Sparky and keep the pantry full to choking with flour and butter and sugar and raisins and chocolate and . . . My knees buckled beneath me and I swooned. Not in an adoring way but in a losing consciousness way. Will sprang to my aid and steadied me. I felt unbelievably weak and woozy and needed to lean on him as he helped me to the kitchen, sat me at the table, and as he had done the first day we met, set about making a cup of tea.

He was talking and I was nodding but I couldn't really make out what he was saying. There was a film of something floaty in between me and the rest of the world. It muffled everything. It should have been scary but was actually rather nice. I lingered in the middle of it and would have been quite happy to stay floating there but as soon as I tried to extricate myself from whatever it was, I slid off the chair and hit the floor.

'Florence!' I heard a muffled version of Will calling. 'Florence!' He was a blur, a blue denim blur, so I knew it was the real him, not the dreamy one because the dreamy one would be flesh coloured.

'I believe you,' I told him, because I really wanted someone to love me and always be there for me no matter what, the way he had in my dream. Or was I still dreaming? I couldn't quite figure it out. 'I believe you,' I said again. 'I do.'

'Florence, can you sit up? I need to sit you up.' The blurriness started to sharpen and all of a sudden the crisp version of Will was trying to scrape me off the kitchen floor. His voice was as clear as a bell. His look radiated a concern, a caring that penetrated my bones and I felt suddenly overwhelmed with longing: not the sexual longing of my dream but a yearning of another kind. What it was for — him or the past or just your average everyday common or garden happiness — I'm not sure but it chased away any airy-fairy floatiness, that was for sure. It was sharp and hard and real.

I felt my body settle into my consciousness again, my bones start to stiffen, my brain tick over.

'Florence?' Will scooped me up by my armpits, sat me back on the chair, then bent me forward over my knees. He had his hand on the back of my neck. I could feel the calluses on his fingers. The rough sandpaper of his skin against mine. 'Can you hear me? Are you all right?'

I was not all right. I was pretty sure nobody who had been through what I recently had would be all right. But still, in the strange clear aftermath of a dead faint, I registered that I really was not all right. Deep down inside I was not all right. Physically, I was not all right.

I had lost weight, maybe as much as a stone; I was pale as a ghost beneath my make-up and any passing blushes; and my troubled circumstances were playing havoc with my digestion, which had become more sluggish in recent years but come to almost a standstill in recent months.

I had previously put this down to my three rotten things but now I thought about it, now Will had my neck in his warm, worn hand, it occurred to me that maybe there was more to it.

'I think I need to see a doctor,' I said in a funny feeble sort of a voice that barely belonged to me. Hearing it made me feel better though, and I sat up straight.

Will smiled, relaxed, felt my forehead. One of those calluses scratched gently above my left eyebrow. I imagined it leaving a scar. A permanent one. Proof he'd been there.

'You don't seem to have a temperature,' he said. 'But the doctor's probably a good idea. You're very pale, Florence. And at the risk of sounding like your mother, you need your strength.'

'You've clearly never met my mother,' I told him, my vocal cords sounding more familiar. 'She thinks strength is over-rated. I'm supposed to celebrate my frailties.'

Will laughed.

'Anyway, we can sort something out about the rot, about the money,' he said. 'Please don't worry about that. And I'm glad you believe me. I don't know what it is exactly that you believe, but I'm still glad.'

I managed a weak smile, possibly even a half-hearted blush. And when I felt my heart rate return to its regular pace, I crawled up the stairs, exhausted, and fell into a deep sleep, free of luscious dreams, free of riotous sexual congress, free of anything but blissful oblivion.

Later on, I rang and made an appointment with Nick March, our ancient family doctor. As it turned out, it was Nick's son, also Nick, who I eventually saw a few days later.

Old Nick had retired seven years before, Young Nick told me, to my great astonishment. It had obviously been a long time since I'd needed medical attention although I couldn't believe it was quite that long. Seven years earlier, I had been the healthy, happily married mother of a twelve-year-old boy.

Now, here I was, according to his scales seventeen pounds lighter than I had been then, newly and involuntarily single, and the perfect example of the sort of mother-in-law innocent newlyweds have nightmares about.

Young Nick sat very sweetly through a quarter of an hour of me crying about my rotten things before gently suggesting I jump up on to the bed so he could have a good old poke around my abdomen and ask a few questions about my 'movements'.

I was a bit like Granny Rose in this department, I didn't like talking about that sort of thing and I still don't, but the truth of it was I had been chronically bunged up for weeks and had come to the doctor partly to seek relief so it only seemed fair we swap a bit of chit chat on the subject.

Rather than simply prescribing me some extra strength laxatives or giving me a lecture on the benefits of fibre, however, Young Nick surprised me by suggesting an internal examination.

I did not know what sort of an internal examination he meant before I agreed to it and found it deeply undignified, to say the least. In fact, when I realised he was actually going to use my rear end like a glove puppet I just about died and started blushing and stammering and suggesting I come back another time. Perhaps when I was feeling better, in which case I might not have to bother at all. Young Nick smiled comfortingly and said he did this all the time and it wasn't as bad as one might imagine and anyway would be over in a jiffy.

When he extricated his hand from my nether regions, however, his smile had definitely gone. So had mine, but then I hadn't had one to begin with.

'I might just refer you on for another test, Florence,' he said, with a certain false brightness.

'Why?' I asked, panic rising. 'Is there something wrong?'

'I very much doubt it,' he said calmly, 'especially considering what you have been through of late. One's bowels can often bear the brunt of emotional upheaval. However, you are coming up for forty and with your family history there's no harm in having a bit of a look-see. It's nothing to worry about, Florence. I'll get the nurse to ring and make an appointment for you to have a colonoscopy. She can call you with the details.'

Upon extensive questioning of the nurse I found out that a colonoscopy was a camera that went up into the colon —

just another word doctors liked using instead of bowel, as it turned out, not a whole different organ as I originally assumed — and had a look around to make sure everything was tickety-boo. Lots of forty-pluses had colonoscopies, she told me, even though I wasn't forty-plus, and they didn't hurt a bit. It was less invasive than an internal examination, she added, because the clinic gave you lovely drugs so it didn't hurt and you didn't remember a thing.

Looking back, it would be easy to say that I sensed something was wrong, that I could feel it, that I knew something dangerous lurked within me, but the truth is, I didn't have a clue. I missed the first colonoscopy appointment because I forgot about it and it's only because the nurse was so cross when she rang up to reschedule that I turned up for the second one. There was so much wrong on the outside of my world that I could have been twelve months pregnant and had twenty sluggish colons and still would not have noticed anything untoward.

The camera up the colon had no such other-worldly distractions. It slithered its way into my body while I chatted happily, totally on top of the world thanks to God knows how much Valium; then it had a look around, spotted the tumour and was out of there — with photos — in less than twenty minutes.

Thanks to the Valium I remained pretty upbeat about this discovery as I was wheeled into the recovery room and brought dreary grey tea and slightly stale digestives.

The colonoscopist — if that's what they are called, I thought it hilarious at the time — couldn't be sure it was malignant (that's the bad one, right? I had to ask) until they had sent it off to the pathology lab for testing. But I could tell by the way the colonoscopist looked at me, the way his receptionist patted me on the back, the way the no-longer cranky nurse escorted me to the door and told me she'd be in touch as soon as possible, that no one expected the news to be good.

And it wasn't.

By the time Young Nick rang and told me, I did know it, I had sensed it.

On top of everything, I had the 'measles'.

YOUNG NICK

♥ ♥ ♥

Some days I just want to chuck it all in and buy a yacht and go sailing around the world.

The week Florence was diagnosed with colon cancer, I had already lost three patients: one to old age, thank Heaven, but one in her forties to breast cancer and one in her fifties to a heart attack at the Porchester Baths.

It's devastating all round obviously, this sort of thing, well, you know, death, but I think perhaps it's particularly awful for the seemingly healthy ones who are diagnosised and have to live with it. Dropping dead at the Porchester Baths is a terrible shock for everyone else but for the one dropping dead, well, it's almost entirely pain and anguish free. A patient hears the word 'cancer' though and their life is never the same again and the awful thing is, once it's been diagnosed, there's nothing I can do. I'm just a GP, I'm the know-a-little-about-a-lot chap. By the time the patient has had the right test and talked to the right specialist, they already know more about whatever it is they've got than I do. How can I help? Apart from the odd sleeping pill here and anti-depressant there, I'm all but useless.

Of course, if you're going to get cancer, the bowel, or colon as we call it, is quite a good place: a lot of it can be removed without too much inconvenience to the rest of the body and often that gets rid of the cancer for good, as long as it hasn't gone through the bowel wall.

I didn't know how advanced Florence's cancer was, as the histology didn't really tell me. What I did know was that she would need to have the tumour and surrounding part of her bowel removed and have the lymph nodes tested to see if the cancer had travelled. If it hadn't, she had every chance of living a long healthy life.

Even if it had travelled, her condition still wasn't necessarily terminal, although the survival rates certainly drop dramatically if the cancer isn't detected early enough. Chemotherapy would still treat it in her case, is what I thought, and modern drugs can do a wonderful job of, if not of getting rid of it, keeping the dreadful bloody disease at bay.

People think we have all the answers, about medicine anyway, but what we know is only a drop in the bucket. It's terrifying how little we know. Utterly terrifying. In fact, if I thought about it too much I simply would not get up out of bed in the morning. I don't know how Dad did it for sixty-odd years without getting totally depressed. Mind you, he did hoe into the Scotch most nights, rest his soul.

I've not headed down that road — yet — but I came bloody close when I got cc'd Florence's colonoscopy report. It came in the morning mail so it can't have been past eleven o'clock. The poor thing had had so much to deal with in the past few months and then this. She was a lovely woman in seemingly good nick. My Dad was always immensely fond of her.

As a doctor of course you don't wish illness on anyone but there are at least two cantankerous old hypochondriacs who in an ideal world should have got colon cancer before Florence Dowling.

CHAPTER THIRTEEN

I've seen *Beaches*, I've watched that other thing with Debra Winger and Shirley MacLaine, I cried for months when my own grandmother died of the measles, but here's the thing about actually having them yourself.

It doesn't hurt and it's not sad.

It's just plain terrifying.

When I put down the phone after hearing from Young Nick that my tumour was the bad sort, that I needed to see a surgeon as soon as possible, that his nurse could make an appointment for me, that time was of the essence, that I should get a friend or relative to come and sit with me as I'd just had a terrible shock, my eyes stayed stretched wide open, unblinking and dry.

My heart thumped in my ears, my breath came in shallow little puffs, I sat frozen in a hunched position on the end of the bed.

I was sick. I was deeply sick. I was deeply *mortally* sick. I had the measles.

My thoughts started to tumble about in my head nonsensically, not gripping on to anything, hopping from hospital beds to graveyards to images of diseased body parts to Rose's funeral, time sliding by as if it suddenly hadn't just become the most precious commodity, something I'd frittered away without so much as a by-your-leave my entire life and now had nothing left of.

Sparky slunk across the floor as though he too had heard Young Nick's dreadful news and slid behind my legs, twisting his head to rest it on my foot, staring up at me with his huge mournful eyes, his stump of a tail wagging slowly, hitting the bottom of the bed like a muffled glockenspiel.

My body felt strangely removed from my thoughts. It was an unpleasant sensation, unconnected and hollow. I forced my dry eyes down on to my hands, spread out as they were on either of my thighs. I didn't recognise them. Were my fingers really that shape? Long, and knobbly around the knuckles, with veins that stuck out and a big freckle by my now empty ring finger? Surely I would have noticed that freckle before if those hands were truly mine. Surely I would have nicer nails than that.

With great effort, I twiddled the fingers of my left hand just above a splodge of chocolate on my jeans and with some relief felt the corresponding drumming sensation on my thigh. My hands suddenly looked ridiculously familiar again, exactly the same as they had half an hour ago before I picked up the phone. Long fingers, knobbly knuckles, slightly ragged nails, my ring finger freckle.

I wiggled that finger. I could clip that nail, if I wanted to, I thought. I could clip all of them. I'd have to find the nail clippers first but when I did, I could clip them. They were mine, those nails. They were on my body and they were part of me. I was in charge of them. I was in charge of moisturising my skin too, even though I had chosen not to, or forgotten. I was in charge of deodorising my armpits and combing my hair and nourishing my body with food and drink and removing the hair from it and strapping up my bosoms to stop them getting in the way. I was in charge of going to a gym and getting muscles if I wanted them. I was in charge of going to a tanning clinic and getting a spray tan. Or not. I could have Botox. And collagen injections. I could exfoliate every time I had a shower. Those dead skin cells were mine to exfoliate, after all. I was the boss of me and totally in charge of everything to do with myself.

And yet I was in charge of nothing.

This was the shocking truth. Somewhere in the recesses of my mind where I never actually bothered to explore such things I had somehow assumed that when you got a terrible illness you had more or less asked for it. Smokers asked for it, miners asked for it, people who worked in asbestos factories asked for it, poor people asked for it, old people asked for it, hypochondriacs asked for it, people sitting around in their damp bedsits eating cat food asked for it.

As much of an unformed theory as it was, I had never had reason to doubt it. Well, I had never even had reason to properly form it in the first place.

Until now.

Because here I was a healthy person who had not smoked, mined, worked with asbestos, been properly poor, or eaten cat food — and I was far from old.

Yet somewhere deep inside me lurked a hideous disease that could rise up and kill me, actually kill me. Cancer. My stomach lurched at the thought of the hateful word that encompassed that hideous, common disease. The cheek of it! As far as I could fathom I had not done a single thing to encourage it, invite it in, feed it or welcome it. It had just barged in and made itself at home and now I had to deal with it somehow.

Well, how bloody rude. And how bloody awful. And how . . . how everything. How nothing. How what difference did it make? If your body could turn against you like that without so much as a whisper of warning — other than a perfectly understandable bout of teeth-clenching constipation — then really, what was there to be done?

I have never in my life, not even during the recent bit, which had spiralled so quickly out of my control, felt so utterly helpless.

Suddenly, all my other problems dropped away like pearls from a broken necklace and bounced insignificantly off into the distance, to gather dustballs in foreign corners.

I mean I could always get another job; after all, I was already on to that, construction issues notwithstanding. I could even get another husband, which secretly I thought was pretty unlikely but that didn't mean it was impossible. Fat, ugly people with bad teeth on reality TV got husbands all the time so there was no reason why I couldn't if I wanted to. I could even get another son, for that matter, if Monty really turned against me, which I prayed to God he would not, but it was not beyond the realms of possibility to add a sibling if I so desired. I would need a small fortune to spend on IVF or to go to Africa for a little black baby like Angelina but I could still do that. I was still able.

But I only had one body. This was it. This strange assortment of personality and hair and flesh and blood and bone was me. And without it . . .

I'd always been under the impression that I had my place in the world and that it was somehow guaranteed. This assumption had been rocked by recent events but still I felt . . . well, 'important' isn't the right word. If there's a word like that but with less arrogant overtones, that's what I felt. That someone like me, someone sort of worthwhile, shouldn't be fired by her partner or left by her husband or betrayed by her son. Worthwhile? What a joke!

Now I felt so bloody trivial that a flea could breathe on me and I'd disintegrate. I was suddenly overwhelmed by my total insignificance in the great scheme of things, a scheme which as it turned out was being manipulated by the same people that operated the Thunderbirds puppets, for all I knew, and for all they seemed to care.

I would die, I think I knew that then. I knew that I was not enough of a battler and that I didn't have the thing that measles survivors who lived to write books about coffee enemas and macrobiotic diets had. I didn't even have a husband. Not that everyone needs one, but I needed mine, and the fucking bastard was out there being gay while I was at home being attacked from the inside out by rogue cells carrying loaded guns.

Worse, Monty would be left motherless. My heart contracted at the thought, although I had to admit that with Crystal on the scene, now was probably a good time for me to die. He would be devastated, despite our current problems, but that tight Australian certainty of hers would hold him up, help him through, get him past the horror, the pain.

Mum and Dad would be shattered but they had Poppy and transcendental meditation. Actually, they'd be OK, my parents. They were quite robust in their eccentricity. There'd be a lot of chanting and incense and genuine grief but eventually, they would be OK.

Even bloody Sparky would be OK. He'd miss me more than anybody else would but he'd still be OK. Monty would walk him and he loved Will and Stan, the new male blood in the rumpty old house. Maybe Will would even adopt him.

Will! I sat up straight and one lone, wet sob escaped me. My hands flew to my face, covering my mouth, teeth biting down on my bottom lip beneath them. Now I'd never get to have sex with Will!

I take it back, maybe it did hurt, the measles, and maybe it was sad. I was sad. I'd never get to have sex with anyone again. I'd die an almost virgin, having only slept with one man my whole entire life; and with him being gay, he probably wasn't even very good at it, although I'd had no complaints but what did I know? What had I been missing out on? I should have shagged Eddie Carmichael at the toga party. I should have shagged the entire first XV. And the cricket team. And the water polo players who had bad hair but lovely shoulders.

Then they could all come to my funeral, in their various sports uniforms, and the cricket team could form a guard of honour through which my coffin, a Union Jack one sort of like Austin Powers' Mini only obviously a box, would be carried by the England rugby team with Jonny Wilkinson at the helm. Or even sitting on top like an old-fashioned king.

I was surprised, to be honest, at how clearly I saw my own funeral. I'd never given it a moment's thought before, that I could recall, but now it was unspooling in my head as clearly as if I was sitting in the Electric Cinema in Portobello Road watching it on the big screen.

Mum was there, dressed in bright orange, weeping dramatically and rattling her jewellery. Dad was clinging to her, stunned, in a purple cheesecloth shirt with one of those awful Chinese collars men of a certain vintage so love. Why I imagined so clearly what they were wearing, I can't say. Maybe it was the colour. So vibrant. They looked like flowers. Poppy was, strangely, in black and crying quietly, her freckles floating in front of her sad little face, her eyes dull and empty, as she held a little basket of rose petals. She'd had one at our wedding, she'd thrown the petals in front of us as we walked into the reception. I'd loved it although Harry complained afterwards that the petals stuck to the bottom of his shoe and went gooey, causing him to slip later on the dance floor.

His dancing was a bit gay maybe, I idled. Something to do with his hands?

Anyway, in the film version of my funeral, my former friend and partner Charlotte was there, clutching at Martin while her three gorgeous daughters all howled with anguish, Abigail crying that she wished it was Charlotte who had died, not me, even though I'd not been in touch with her since I left the shop, which quite possibly made me the most terrible godmother.

Still, I figured Charlotte was more terrible for what she had done to me. So I edited Whiffy O'Farrell into the church to sit next to her and annoy her with his odour while he cried quietly and said a lovely blessing, the one about not standing at the grave and weeping. I loved that.

Oh, Marguerite was there, with her twins! And Sinead, lovely Sinead who used to clean the shop. I made an extra mental note to find out where she lived so I could get in touch with her before I died or she might feel awkward coming to the funeral.

Would Harry's miserable parents bother, I wondered? Would his tight-sphinctered brother come down from Scotland with his thin-lipped wife and their pale, churlish children? And where would Harry himself be?

I imagined him hiding behind a pillar at the back of the church with a sheepish Charles. I had decided Charles was ginger, not a rich beautiful ginger like Poppy, but a harsh carroty ginger with piggy blue eyes. He was sort of Uriah Heep-ish, hunched over and fawning. Harry would be devastated at my passing and so he bloody should be. The last few weeks of my life and he had ruined them. I gave Charles very ugly facial hair. And a limp. And a tiny little dog that he kept in the pocket of his bright green chequered suit. He was hideous.

And then I realised that in real life I was no longer statue still, hunched on the bed, but was trembling from head to toe. My hands quivered on my jiggling thighs and it only occurred to me just in the nick of time that I needed to dash to the bathroom to avoid losing the contents of my stomach on poor Sparky's head. I supposed the measles had spread from my colon already, that those pirate cells were bouncing their way around the pinball machine of my internal organs. I supposed I might die at any minute right there as I lay on the bathroom tiles, chipped and not especially clean, without having even had the chance to reacquaint myself with the people I would soon rely on to mourn me.

Sparky was outside the closed bathroom door and scratched at it, as was his wont. I heard his disgruntled body slump against it and slide to the floor with an agitated sigh. Young Nick was right: I needed a friend or relative to come and sit with me because I'd had a terrible shock and could not now stop imagining my funeral. It was getting grander and grander with every passing moment. There was a choir of little boys singing George Michael songs now. And George Michael was there himself, although he was very emotional, so upset to be losing me when he'd only just got to know me. In my imagination I made sure that Harry had left by the time George Michael showed up or otherwise he might have whisked him off and ruined my funeral as well as my whole life leading up to it.

My hip ached where the bathmat had bunched beneath it. It would not be altogether unpleasant to die, I allowed myself to think. Life was hard. At the moment, too hard. The tearooms, although a lovely dream for the future, were beyond me. The house was revolting. Maybe it didn't want to be opened to strangers again. It was costing me more money than I had and I didn't want to confront that particularly. I'd lost my husband and son to people I didn't know and I was tired and lonely, which was also hard to confront. Maybe slipping away to a better place would be easier than staying in this one.

I felt my poor frantic heart beating unhappily against my rib cage. You know, if I could have died right then, I would have. But the chipped, grubby tiles were no place for a half-dead completely mad woman to die, or lie, for that matter. I was cold and my hip was getting sorer. Slowly I got up and washed my face in the basin, which at least warmed my hands. And then I looked at myself in the mirror.

There it was: the sadness. In fact, I was the picture of sadness. My eyes filled with tears as I stared into them, my mouth crumpled, my cheeks wobbled, everything pointed horribly downwards. I placed my hands on my abdomen, so flat and firm. But what chaos lay behind that paltry muscle?

How could this be happening to me? On top of everything? How could it?

I had not even known my colon was so important until being told it was in grave danger. It was just part of the boring bit of being alive, as far as I had always been concerned; the mechanics of it all. You breathe so the oxygen can do something or other with your blood; you eat so you have energy; and you drink so you're not dried up like a coconut. If you're in a car accident and hurt your spleen it can be chopped out and you'll never even notice. I knew nothing about colons. Would never have guessed how essential they were. I mean when breasts got diseased it was tragic but you could still lop them off and go about your business with the right bra. What would happen if I lost my colon? Why hadn't Nick told me? Why hadn't I asked? Why was this happening to me?

I thought about ringing my parents but again couldn't picture myself saying the right words. And anyway, they would probably think I had brought it on myself by eating white bread. And maybe they were right. But I didn't need to hear that right now. Had I been wrong to mock vegetarianism all these years? I ate red meat but to be honest, I didn't even like it that much. I preferred chicken. Was it the hormones and antibiotics in the chicken that had killed me? Was it Khan's prawn korma? Pumped with toxins from some hideously polluted ocean on the other side of the world and laden with full fat cow's milk cream?

I considered calling Tannington Hall and asking to speak only to Poppy but I knew she would just cry. And that would be as hard to stomach as a lecture on the perils of salami.

Harry? Well, I wasn't sure if he was still a relative. Or a friend for that matter. In a perfect world, the perfect world that up until recently I had inhabited but from which I had been wrenched thanks to him, he would be there already. There would be no need to call him. He would be holding my hand or standing behind me as I stared into the mirror, assuring me that I was just being silly, that it was all so sudden, that I wasn't dying, of course I wasn't, that everything would be all right, he would see to it.

But there was nobody behind me, nothing but a butterfly kimono Mum had given me for my birthday years before, which had hung on the back of the door on the unreliable hook ever since because the sleeves collected marmalade and got stuck on doorknobs.

There was Monty but I couldn't really go worrying him because he was just a boy. And how awkward would it be anyway, given we were barely speaking to each other? I didn't quite know how to go from, 'I'm not that fussed on your secret wife,' to 'I'm dying of the world's most boring disease.'

Never in my life had I been so alienated from so many people, I thought, in astonishment, as I continued to stare at my sad self. And what kind of a life was I having anyway?

Then I heard the sound of something being dropped on a foot two storeys below and turned to look at the kimono-covered door. It was Stanley's foot, I deduced, by the sound of the curses that followed. Then there was the low murmur from Will, no doubt offering consolation.

I turned around and caught my reflection again. To my surprise, this interruption from the outside world had pointed my face slightly upwards once more. It was the bloody garbage man all over again! The planet was still spinning! Yes, my eyes were still great wells of sadness but my face was no longer the picture of it.

I looked just like I had before the phone call.

How the hell could I have cheered up so quickly? It wasn't right. Nothing was right. I couldn't even go about having a fatal illness the normal way. I'd lost my job, been left by my husband, had a secretly married son and a half-renovated house, and now I was no doubt going to make a complete and utter mess of being poorly and, soon enough, dead.

This terrible truth made me ache all the more. And even

the ache wasn't normal as it wasn't, the way one might expect, for a cure for cancer or the secret to eternal life. It was for dark chocolate and banana cake with fresh raspberries and sour cream icing.

Rose had made this cake for me once, after Janie McPherson invited everyone in the class but me to her twelfth birthday party. Truly, biting into that decadent slice piled high with gooey chocolate made me forget, if only briefly, the pain of such a bitter blow. It wasn't the secret to eternal life, but it was bloody delicious.

So, I might not have the coffee enema thing but I had something: the will to bake.

Or the will to at least think about baking.

At least it was will.

ROSE

ROSE'S BANANA AND CHOCOLATE CAKE
WITH FRESH RASPBERRIES

1¾ cups all-purpose flour
100g granulated white sugar
50g light-brown sugar
1 teaspoon baking powder
1 teaspoon baking soda
¼ teaspoon salt
150g dark chocolate
3 large very ripe bananas, mashed well
3 large eggs, lightly beaten
120g unsalted butter, melted and cooled
1 cup raspberries

Preheat oven to 180°C and place the oven rack in the middle of the oven. Butter or spray a cake tin.

In a large bowl combine the flour, sugars, baking powder, baking soda, salt, and chocolate. Set aside.

In a medium-sized bowl combine the mashed bananas, eggs and melted butter. With a rubber spatula or wooden spoon, lightly fold the wet ingredients (banana mixture) into the dry ingredients until just combined and the batter is thick and chunky.

Add raspberries and spoon the batter into the prepared tin. Bake about one hour or until a toothpick inserted in the centre comes out clean. Place on a wire rack to cool for five minutes and then remove from tin.

Let cool and ice.

Icing
250g dark chocolate
1 cup sour cream
⅔ teaspoon vanilla

Melt chocolate in a double boiler or a large metal bowl set over a saucepan of simmering water, stirring occasionally. Remove bowl from heat, then whisk in sour cream and vanilla. Cool to room temperature, stirring occasionally (icing will become thick enough to spread). You must work quickly and spread it before it becomes too thick. (If icing does become stiff, reheat over simmering water, then cool and try again.)

Top with a layer of fresh raspberries.

CHAPTER FOURTEEN

As it happened, the will to bake, or think about baking, or live for that matter, came and went over the next couple of hours.

I stayed in my room to begin with, but the telephone tortured me with my inability to pick it up and use it to ask someone, anyone, for help. This gave me the shakes, which in turn meant more violent outbursts in the bathroom.

Meanwhile, my funeral had turned into a state event like Princess Diana's during which no one would be able to get to the hairdresser's or the supermarket, causing the population in general to end up hating me.

I needed a break from myself, I knew I did. Lurching between visualising my mourners and my diseased colon was starting to overwhelm me. Rose's banana and chocolate cake with fresh raspberries would definitely sort this out, I reasoned, and I was trying to summon up the energy to go out and shop for the ingredients for it when I heard Will's voice sail up the stairs and snake its way through the cracks in the door to find me.

'Florence, fancy a cup of tea?'

Stanley must have gone home. I imagined Will standing at the bottom of the stairs by the kitchen, thinking of me, calling up to me.

'Yes, please,' I answered in a voice I knew he could not possibly hear.

'Florence?' He called again. And again. Then I heard his boots on the stairs, his voice getting closer until he was obviously just outside the bedroom door.

'Florence, are you in there?'

'Yes,' I answered, dully, again. I was in a sort of a trance. Quite pleasant actually. In my own feeble way I was luring Will towards me. I don't know why. Or I pretended I didn't.

He rapped gently on the door.

'I'm here,' I said, although who knew for how long. And anyway, I had been ordered to seek out a friend, had I not?

Then the door opened and his head appeared around the side of it. 'Florence, are you all right?' he asked, looking around as if expecting to find someone else there.

I just looked at him. He had a white shirt on, as crisp as you like, and not at all dirty. How could that happen? He was a builder, for God's sake. I couldn't wear white from my bedroom to the bathroom without getting thirty-two different-coloured stains on it.

'May I come in?' When I didn't reply, he stepped cautiously into my bedroom.

As I looked at him I felt every healthy cell in my body stand up and go, 'Oh, yes, please!'

It was a bit like being electrocuted or shot with a Taser gun, only none of the outside of me moved. Just the inside.

But it wasn't a made-up thing, it was real. It was more real than the measles. I'd only been told about them — mysterious people in white coats had identified them under a microscope somewhere, had written reports, had maybe even felt a quiver of emotion themselves at delivering their malignant opinions — but I couldn't feel the measles. I couldn't feel them at all. Will, on the other hand, I felt. In the marrow of my bones, in the flow of my blood, in the goose bumps of my skin, I felt him.

'Florence?' he said softly again, moving towards the bed.

I did nothing, just kept looking at him, feeling him and wondering just how my insides and my outsides could be at such odds. I don't think I had experienced that sort of distance from myself before. How strange, that in the space of a single day, my body would deliver two such peculiar revelations.

One: that I harboured a disease that was probably killing me.

Two: that Will and I were quite possibly made for each other.

Scientists may not have had a piece of that in a Petri dish to poke at but it was every bit as much a lethal diagnosis as the colon one. It was what my cellular structure was telling me. My silly cells had been looking the other way when the measles walked in the door but when Will arrived they had stood up and paid attention.

Did I believe in love at first sight? Yes, of course I did. It's what I thought had happened with Harry. But in retrospect, what did a fourteen-year-old's cellular structure know? That chocolate fuelled pimples and a boy with a cute fringe smiling at you meant you finally had a boyfriend. And a good boyfriend, too, there was no denying that. Well, I'd never worried about him cheating on me with my girlfriends, although as it turned out there was a reason for that. And we loved each other, there was no denying that either. From the beginning, we loved each other. But maybe it was a brotherly/sisterly sort of love? I couldn't remember Harry setting me on fire with lust or whatever it was that set people in love on fire. It was more like he fanned whatever fire I already had.

Will and I, though, were two good old-fashioned sticks just made to rub together. I don't mean that we were made for each other in a lovey-dovey romantic novel sort of a way; the way where it all falls perfectly into place just because one's a square hole and the other's a square peg and oh, whoopsie, here we both are, how marvellous.

No, it was chemical. I reacted to him. It was as simple as that. And it wasn't because I'd just found out about the measles and was losing my marbles. From the moment I had first opened the door to him there'd been a whiff of it: a stiffening of the arm hairs, a darkening of the pupils, a scent of something wonderful just around the corner. And then there'd been the moment at the kitchen table when he'd made the cup of tea when it became a tangible thing. Or as tangible as something invisible can get, especially something invisible that may or may not exist.

Yes, we were made for each other. I knew that now. Maybe that was a measles or a marbles thing but I still knew it. But what a truly, deeply awful time to figure it out because for a variety of different reasons — I was so much older than him and so recently separated from the love of my life, and mother of a son with whom I was engaged in a complicated sort of war I didn't know how to fight or surrender from *and* I was ill — nothing could ever come of it.

Will crouched in front of me and put one hand on my knee, the chocolatey one. He had such concern for me, this surprise addition to my household. His eyes were full of it, his face was full of it, his body too. And there was something else. Something more than concern. In my current state I seemed to be able to see right through him, like Superman, and what I saw was that Will was full of all this wonderful love, wonderful endless unused love. I could tell that because I recognised the symptoms. I was full of wonderful endless unused love too.

This was how we were made for each other. It was too tragic for words.

'Florence, you're worrying me,' he said. 'You look so upset. Whatever's the matter?'

The tears I had been holding back, keeping teetering within the brim of my eyes, spilled over and flowed down my cheeks. Why is it that sympathy brings them on? Shouldn't sympathy dry them up? What was that about?

'Oh, Florence,' Will said. 'Whatever it is, please tell me. Please let me help.'

If only he could. He squeezed my hand and I realised I could trace his calluses already, so familiar was the territory of his lovely, young, healthy body, its geography somehow already imprinted on my mind.

I looked into those blue eyes of his and right down at the bottom of my heart where I trusted only a few scant droplets of truth — like Monty was the best thing that ever happened to me, I actually had really good legs, my fresh date scones were better than anyone else's — I knew that in this tiny pocket of time Will felt the same way about me as I felt about him.

But even if I'd had the guts to act on this instinct, I'd just been told in no uncertain terms by my body that it was not to be trusted and that it was the boss, so I could take my delicious chemistry and stick it up my arse, along with every gloved hand known to medicine.

While I was busy not acting on my instincts, however, Will kissed me. His lips swept away my fear like a smooth velvet curtain. I don't think I had ever properly been kissed before, no offence to Harry, sort of, and actually I only thought of him embarrassingly fleetingly. To be kissed by Harry was lovely, is what I actually thought, but to be kissed by Will was exquisite. I felt it in my toenails.

His hand was on the back of my neck, stroking some little strip of me that I didn't know until then only existed to be stroked just like that. The smell of him was like baking bread and sunshine and salt. His energy, without wanting to sound too Tannington Hall, pulsed from his lips to mine and down my body to the poisonous parts and I could almost feel it light up the dark like a shooting star or an emergency flare.

We perched on the end of the bed, twisted around each other, kissing like teenagers, although not the teenager I had been myself, and I could almost see a neon light blinking the word DESIRE above us. I desired him. I desired him like I had never desired anything before ever in my life. And because of our cellular bonding, I knew he desired me.

And then we were lying down and I could feel his weight on top of me, his hips on my hips, his thighs on my thighs, his chest on my chest, his tongue on my neck and the power of him, the good health of him, was suddenly too much to bear. I was damaged goods, in more ways than one, and he deserved better. Better, younger, stronger, other.

'No!' I cried and turned my head away. 'No.'

We lay there panting, then I pushed him off, sat up, buttoned my shirt, bit my aching lips, and ignored my invisible quivering.

Will stayed on the bed. I couldn't look at him but I could see out the corner of my eye that he was lying on his side, up on one elbow.

I would have thought he would be embarrassed or apologetic, but he wasn't.

'But why not?' he asked, with almost laughably polite curiosity.

I ran my fingers through my hair and straightened my collar.

'Florence, why not?' He reached for my elbow and I was amazed I didn't burst into flames at his touch. 'There's something there, you know there is.'

Why was I being tortured like this? What woman in the world did not pray to God to be sent a man who looked and felt like Will and who said such things? But to be sent *this* man on *this* day? Someone somewhere was having a huge laugh at my expense. Someone somewhere knew that today was not the day to have sex with the man I was meant to be with.

If I had sex right now with the man I was meant to be with and I got pregnant then I would die and leave him with a poor little motherless baby. Although this was a slim chance because I was old and my ovaries were buggered and my body was riddled with some disease that no doubt ate pregnancy hormones for breakfast, it was still not a chance I could take. Even if I didn't get pregnant I would still die and leave him anyway. And the fact of the matter was I couldn't do that. Because if the shoe was on the other foot, if Will died and left me I would not want to survive without him. I knew now what it was like to be left and just imagining leaving Will, even for a really good reason like being dead, tore a piece from my heart and I couldn't do it.

'I'm sorry,' I said, covering my face, shaking my head. 'I'm so sorry.'

He sat up then and took me in his arms, rocking me gently

and resting his perfect chin on the top of my head.

'No, I'm sorry,' he said. 'It's too much for you, Florence. It's just all too much. And too soon. There's time,' he said, in a lullaby voice. 'There's plenty of time.'

Only now I didn't believe him.

WILL

♥ ♥ ♥

She tasted just the way I'd imagined. Like chocolate, but sort of floral. I'm not much good when it comes to flowers so I couldn't exactly pinpoint it but there was definitely a hint of something rose-like, I think, or maybe lavender. It was a very feminine taste, anyway. Not girly, not even womanly, just feminine in all the best ways I could possibly imagine.

I shouldn't have kissed her, I kicked myself afterwards, it really was too soon, but it's just that the moment seemed so right. And a woman doesn't kiss back like that, with her whole entire body, with everything she has, unless the moment is right. I'm sure of it.

But something was holding her back. The thing that had her holed up in her room in the first place, I suppose. It wasn't Harry, or Monty, or Crystal, or the construction problems. It was something else.

I wished she'd tell me, let me help her. I could have, I was sure of it. But there was no point me having all the confidence in the world, because she was the one who needed it. She needed to have it in me because I was a step ahead of her. I already had confidence in her. Florence wasn't a risk for me, she was a certainty.

Do I believe in love at first sight? I have to say, yes, I do. Unravelling it from lust at first sight is the problem but I've learned that the hard way. I've learned everything the hard way.

But at least I have learned.

The timing for me and Florence was not perhaps right, although it also wasn't wrong. She'd only just split up from her husband but at least she had split up from him. Because the truth is, if I'd met her anywhere else, at any other time, I would have felt exactly the same way about her. It's an odd sensation: like having known a stranger already, intimately, forever.

I believed it would work out. I believed she would eventually trust me, trust herself.

Of course, I wasn't exactly a catch. I didn't have much money. I didn't even own a house or my own flat. Just my truck and a few bits of furniture and the odd painting. But I knew I could take care of Florence, I really could. And I knew I could love her like no one else could ever love her, no disrespect to anyone who has. I knew that for a fact.

CHAPTER FIFTEEN

It was such a peculiar thing, being desperate to see Will and to avoid him all at the same time. It barely gave me time to concentrate on having the measles. I kept wondering what would have happened if I hadn't gone to see Young Nick, if I hadn't had the colonoscopy, if I hadn't been given the awful diagnosis. Would we still have met on the edge of my bed? Would we have kissed? Kept on kissing? Ripped off our clothes and had wild, passionate sex? Got married and had babies? Grown old together and turned into one of those ancient couples that never go anywhere without holding hands?

Of course it was possible that had I not got that phone call, Will would not have come into my room because I probably wouldn't have been in it. And I most likely would not have realised that we were meant to be together because I wasn't usually the sort of person who thought like that. Staring death in the face had brought that on. I'd never stared death in the face before. I'd stared over its shoulder, I suppose, when I went into labour with Monty but even then I didn't believe there was any reason for anything to go wrong. I was too young and silly to know how many complications the world was full of.

Now, I knew. And it changed everything.

Before Young Nick I'd felt something for Will but it was a by-the-by sort of a something upon which I don't think I would have acted because I had so little experience in that field. Plus, I'd only been separated from my husband for five minutes and it seemed a trifle indecent to be contemplating a lover quite so quickly. Before Young Nick, I would not have admitted that the something I felt even involved contemplating a lover. Before Young Nick, I don't think I had ever even used the word 'lover'.

Before Young Nick? Yes, it's interesting. With the buzz of a dial tone my previous life as a healthy thirty-nine-year-old was whisked impossibly far, far away dividing my life into two separate chunks. I was in some other world now. The 'after' world. Everything after Young Nick, however long that may or may not be, would be in this strange new territory, I supposed. With that phone call I had stepped over an invisible line; I could look back but I could never step across it again.

For the next few days, as my before and after worlds were extricating themselves from each other, allowing my muddled emotions to settle, giving me time to adjust to my lack of future, I managed to avoid seeing a single soul, bar Sparky. I was astonished at how easy this was. I'd never had to do it before. I'd never wanted to. Usually when I heard Monty's voice in the house I would follow it until I found him but I discovered the opposite was just as easy to do.

Monty. I couldn't bear the thought of looking at him, knowing what I knew. The things I would miss if the cancer claimed me: him getting over this teenage nonsense and growing up properly; getting married, the right way, to a real wife and having gorgeous little grandbabies and a house in the country and a big golden retriever dog called Bill or Bob or Barney and a job in the City and a lovely car that didn't make a knocking noise when you went around corners and beautiful clothes.

I would never hold those grandbabies in my arms, I now believed, I would never rock them to sleep, read them stories, take them to Regent's Park to play on the grass. These were the things I had dreamed of for me and my son, the future I had stitched together for him as surely as if it was a patchwork quilt like the ones Charlotte made for her each of her girls.

In the present, Monty was making it easy for me to avoid him because he made such a bloody racket. He seemed to rattle the door a thousand times louder than anyone else when he came home from wherever he was going these days. I swear his feet were heavier on the stairs than even Stanley Morris's. The sound of him getting a glass out of the kitchen cupboards could probably be heard in Chichester. And most of the time, to boot, there was the sound of his roaring laughter; his overwhelming, uncontrollable, ineffably audible joy at being in the company of Crystal.

He'd always had the best laugh, Monty, and a smile to go with it. A smile that took up his whole face. His entire school life I'd been told that his exemplary record had been helped enormously by that smile. It could right a hundred wrongs, his home room teacher Mrs Whiting told me once, not that there were a hundred wrongs involved, she hastened to add, but there were one or two, though only quite small and in fact hardly worth mentioning now she came to think of it.

Will had a lovely smile too. Not as wide as Monty's, but

then Monty was young. Younger. Will's smile came with the baggage of having been around longer. But not much longer. Thirty-bloody-one? What had I been thinking? What was I thinking now? How much longer did I have to think?

In the days following our little incident in the bedroom, I married him in my mind sixty-five times, died a hundred more and imagined God knows how many lavish funerals.

I also baked not one but two chocolate and banana cakes, burning the first one while I was busy avoiding Monty and Crystal by taking a bath in the middle of the day. I got the second one right but icing it was a mission. I went three times to Tesco to get sour cream for the icing, forgetting it the first time and getting cottage cheese by mistake the second. Trips to Tesco were rather more complicated these days because I went out of my way to not go up Warwick Place past my old shop. As a result, my thoughts were often dark and filled with bitterness and resentment as I went the long way around, which in turn led to quite a bit of bungling on the shopping list front.

I'd been particularly addled on the sour cream expeditions, thanks to not passing the shop and not seeing Charlotte. The subject of Charlotte upset me just as much in the after world as before, if not more. I had, after all, a rather glaring hole in both places where a good friend should be.

As it was, with no one but my shattered self for company, I was starting to lose my grip. My poor mind bounced from cancer tragedy to motherless son despair to unrequited love angst without stopping for a breather until in one brief window of clarity I accepted that I was in danger of my inner turmoil getting the better of me. I was icing my stale cake when I decided, as I licked the spoon and tasted salt from my tears, that I really should drive to Tannington Hall and tell my family what was happening to me. On the cancer tragedy front, that is, not the unrequited love angst front, although I'm sure they would have preferred the latter. Not that there was really anything to report with the latter other than I had it and would have it forever, however long forever was.

'Not scaring you away, are we?' Will asked with a sad smile when he caught me sidling down the stairs with my overnight bag.

I couldn't meet his eyes, but I recognised his smell. It was like vanilla, only sort of lemony. Thoroughly delicious. Totally cruel. My eyes swivelled around erratically, landing every now and then on Stanley, who grew nervous under such odd scrutiny.

'I'm going to see my parents,' I said to the space where the wall between Monty's TV room and the hall used to be. 'I need to speak to them about something. Not much. But something. You know.'

I sounded twelve. It was atrocious.

'What's happening with the pipes?' I then asked trying to claw my way back to appropriateness.

'Pipes? Well, nothing just yet. We're sort of working around that. It's the dry rot we need to sort out first.'

'Oh, yes, of course.' I had actually completely forgotten about the dry rot.

'We've had a mate of Stan's around to give us a second opinion,' Will said. 'I thought you might have seen him? Or heard him?'

I shook my head. I'd been busy.

'Rattly little bugger,' Stanley laughed. 'Could talk the hind legs off a donkey.'

'He had quite a few suggestions, actually, that could save us a bit of money, if not time,' Will continued. 'The good thing is that the rot is contained to the foundations near the kitchenette plumbing and the floorboards above that so we just need to cut out the affected parts and take another metre from the floorboards to make sure it doesn't spread.'

It hit me then, like a ton of the proverbial, that the house more or less had the bloody measles too. It had started in the joists and was spreading its poison throughout this whole safe, solid, precious building, threatening its very existence.

The rattly man with the donkey's hind legs was in fact the glove inserting itself up my house's basement and determining how long it had to live.

What sort of an unhinged universe was this?

'But is it terminal?' I asked abruptly. 'The dry rot? Is it terminal?'

'Terminal?' Will repeated.

'What do you mean by terminal? ' Stanley asked as I trembled pathetically on the stairs.

'I mean terminally terminal as in the end!' I blurted out. 'I can't have terminal rot in Rose's house, I just can't. This house is . . . it's . . . if it's terminal I can hardly have a tearoom. There would be no point, no future. It would be an utter waste of time. And money. Money I don't even have. And who knows if a tearoom is . . . ? I just can't see now how it could work. No, I can't see it at all. I think we need to stop. I need to rethink this. The tearoom is too much for me, I realise that now. It's probably too much for me without terminal rot but with terminal rot it's even more ridiculous. I can't. I simply can't. No, no, I think we need to stop this right away.'

I looked around at the debris, the exposed pipes, the crumbling walls, the flaking wallpaper, the dust. What had I done? I flopped down on the stairs, astonished at my own ludicrous enthusiasm. What had I been thinking?

Will and Stanley swapped a bewildered glance.

'Well, Florence, I don't really think you need to panic. There's really no such thing as terminal rot,' Will said, carefully. 'The whole house isn't rotten. Just bits of it and we can replace the bits. It's really not a great big problem. It's a medium-sized problem. Small to medium, even. And we can fix it completely. Honestly. There's nothing terminal about it.'

'There you are,' Stanley agreed. 'Listen to the expert.'

'If anything, we can probably make the house stronger than it was to begin with,' Will continued, 'but it will just cost money and we know that could be difficult for you so Stan and I are throwing around some ideas — and Sid the rattler is helping us out — to see if we can come up with something.'

'Make it more affordable,' Stanley interjected again.

'Just so as we're clear on there being no such thing as terminal rot, Florence,' Will repeated. 'The tearoom is a fantastic idea. There is a point, of course there is. There is a future. It's not ridiculous.'

I looked at him, albeit fleetingly, and thought my heart would break. The tearoom was too much for me, rot or not, and so was seeing him, smelling him, imagining him, imagining the life we would never have.

'I'm sorry,' I said, getting to my feet. 'It's just not going to happen. The money, I mean, there's no way . . . I just don't . . . You've both been so lovely but I'm sorry.' And like the mature thirty-nine-year-old I was, I fled out the door, leaving the two of them standing there like stunned mullets, while I flung myself into the tired Golf.

I cried all the way to Suffolk, Sparky at one point howling in sympathy next to me as I sped up the M11. It was so unfair! How was I supposed to deal with all the rotten things? How was one person supposed to — oh my God, I thought, just about swerving off the road at Newmarket. This was the beginning of another roll of three! I'd had the job-husband-son threesome and now there was the house-with-its-sodding-dry-rot and there was me-with-mine. Which meant there was one more rotten thing to come. How inconceivable! I howled myself then, which actually shut Sparky up. He looked most put out: I'd out-saddened him.

My howling became hiccups by Bury St Edmonds and by the time I turned into the lane leading up to Tannington Hall I had quite a firm grip on myself.

That loosened, however, when I pulled into the driveway.

There was an ambulance there, the back door of it open, nobody inside. The front door of the house was swinging open, almost closed and open again with the sway of the gentle breeze.

Rotten thing number three? Stage two? So soon?

Sparky slumped down on the front seat and put one paw over his eyes.

I wished with all my heart I was able to do the same.

STANLEY MORRIS

♥ ♥ ♥

Things got very strange over at the Dowling house there for a while, I'll tell you that for nothing.

I've known Will for years, he's a good lad is Will, the very best. And a ruddy good builder too. But the day the boss headed off to see her family in a bit of a lather, it occurred to me that Will had a bad case of the galloping hots for her.

Well, in some ways, you'd be mad not to fancy her — she's a corker — but the poor girl had been in such a state, what with all that had been going on in her personal life, not to mention the effing dry rot. That was a shock to me and Will and all. Who'd have guessed? We was both gutted when we found it but these old places, honestly, you don't know what's lurking about down below until you get in there and have a look.

We'd already decided to help her out, me and Will, call in a few favours, get the materials on the cheap and throw in the labour for next to nothing. Frankly, I already had all the money I needed and it was worth coming to the Dowling house for the company. Will, he didn't have tuppence to rub together but as I say, my guess was he was mad for Florence.

Good luck to him, that's what I reckoned. It probably wasn't the best idea in the world to get involved with a lady with quite so much on her plate but there's no such thing as the perfect woman, so they say, and she'd be closer than most.

Of course, her giving us the sack, even though we were working for free anyway, was a bit of a fly in the oinkment, as my uncle Jimmy (a pig farmer) used to say. But I'll hand it to Will, it did not make a dent in the lad.

He's a dark horse, is Will.

CHAPTER SIXTEEN

An eerie sort of stillness descended on me as I stepped away from the car and moved toward my parents' house, my own turbulent concerns retreating to the corner of my anxiety vault, whipped into submission by whatever dreadful news the ambulance heralded.

Such moments tell a girl a great deal about herself, a great deal about her lot. I had long joked about not really belonging to my family. It was what someone who felt like an outsider did to deflect the twinge of feeling that way. But as I loped along the empty hall, swept through the deserted kitchen and mounted the gloomy stairs, I realised I would be lost without them. Especially now. They were bonkers, they really were, yet I suddenly needed them in a way I had never needed them before. Dress code and lentil preferences aside, I was one of them, we were all part of the same nutty unit. If something was happening to me it was happening to them too; and if something was happening to them, vice versa, although I already had quite a lot of somethings to be getting on with, but still . . . Together perhaps we could get through the worst of whatever the universe had to throw at us. Even if one of us thought vegetarian burgers tasted like wet toilet paper and the other three thought salt was the work of the devil.

'Mum, Dad!' I called up the stairs. 'Mum!'

It would be her, I was sure. The measles would have got to her first. They were in our genes, our filthy bloody genes, and she had never had a camera up her colon and was probably riddled with it and didn't even know and now it would be too late and I had been such an awful daughter. Such an ungrateful girl, woman, person.

Then she appeared at the top of the stairs, looking terrifyingly frail, for her. Her yoga posture had gone to pot; her shoulders were slumped, making her look unrecognisably small, even in her voluminous peasant blouse; and her lovely face was lined with worry, her organic mascara that was prone to smudging anyway blotched beneath her eyes.

'Oh, Effie,' she cried, bursting into fresh tears. 'I can't believe you're here. We haven't called a soul.'

I threw myself into her arms, which is not something I usually did, and she clutched me as though she would never let go.

'What's happened?' I whispered, my voice faltering. 'Is it Daddy?'

He was such a trouper, my Dad. I mean pretty much all he ever did was go along with my mother, no matter how twitty her persuasions, but really what was wrong with that? He was happy if she was happy. And he had nearly always been happy. Without him . . .

But then he came out of the corner bathroom, alive and

upright, and he too was crying.

'Oh, Eff,' he said, brokenly, in a repressed sort of a gasp. 'Oh, Beth.' He came up behind my mother and caught us both in a heartbroken bear hug.

'They think she'll be all right,' he said, into my mother's hair. 'They think they got here just in time. They think it will be OK. Oh, Beth!' And he wept as if his heart would indeed break.

I stood back from them then. They moved in closer to take up the space where I had been, clasping each other desperately as though each was stopping the other from toppling off the edge of a cliff.

Now I could hear the sound of shallow murmurings from within the corner bathroom and as if in a dream, a nightmare, I moved slowly down towards the open door. When I looked in, all my fears for myself, for my health, for my future, slithered away.

Poppy lay in the bathtub, which in this bathroom was dramatically stationed in the middle of the room, with two ambulance men kneeling on either side of her. Someone had emptied the bathwater and covered her with a towel but there was still blood everywhere. One of her wrists was bandaged with a mass of cream crêpe, and one of the ambulance men was attending to the other.

Poppy's head was leaning back against the end of the old-fashioned claw-foot bath. Her eyes were closed but tears slid down her white, white cheeks, those crazy freckles now seeming to float a foot above her miserable face.

'Poppy?' I knelt beside her, one of the men moving aside to let me in. I took her hand, the one that belonged to the already bandaged wrist. Her fingers were icy cold. I squeezed with all my might.

'It's me, Poppy. It's Effie.'

She opened her eyes and turned slowly to look at me, the tears not stopping for a moment.

'I just wanted to die, Flower,' she said in a tiny, tired voice. 'I just wanted to be done with it all.'

I saw one of the ambulance men raise his eyebrows as he fastened the bandage on her other wrist and for a moment I felt an anger so pure I could have slit his wrists for daring to react like that. But then he looked at me with such sympathy that the anger slid down the drain with the rest of Poppy's blood. Poppy's blood!

'It's OK, precious,' I said kissing her fingers the way I remembered I had when she was little and I very first adored her. 'It's OK. Don't worry. Everything will be OK.'

'We can help get her out now if you'd like,' the other ambulance man offered.

'No, I'll do it,' I said. 'Thank you. But I will do it. Mum and I will do it.'

I kept holding her hand while they cleared up and quickly left us. Then Mum came back in, her eyes falsely bright and her mascara smudges gone, and we picked my little sister's curvy white body out of the bath, wiped her down till there was not a trace of her dreadful attempt left, other than those tell-tale bandages, and we dressed her in a pink flannelette nightie with big orange flowers that she had made at school when she was fifteen.

She let us lead her to her room and over to her bed, under which Sparky lay, looking too sympathetic by far if you asked me. Poppy barely registered him, just slipped under the covers and sank into the mattress, sighing with a deep teary flutter that just about did in my over-plucked filaments yet again.

'We'll let you rest, my petal,' Mum said, softly, as she put a little bottle of rescue remedy on the nightstand. 'Unless you want us to stay.'

'I want Effie to stay,' Poppy answered, wanly. 'Will you get in with me, Eff?'

I wanted to go with Mum. I wanted to find out how this had happened, why my parents hadn't seen this coming. I wanted to yell and scream and stamp my feet with violent unadulterated rage at Poppy for being so stupid, so selfish, so bloody cavalier with her precious life, but of course I didn't. I slipped off my shoes and got into bed next to her. She reached for my hand and I took hers in both of mine, turning on my side to look in her big blue cornflower eyes, avoiding the feel of the crêpe beneath my fingers.

'Why did you do it, Poppy?' I asked as softly as I could manage. 'Why would you want to do something so terrible?'

'I'm so lonely, Florence,' she burst out, with an accompaniment of fresh tears. 'I'm just so lonely. I've got no one to love. I'll never find anyone to love. And I'm here with Beth and Archie all the time and they've got each other but I've got no one. And I just can't bear it any more.'

I was so shocked by this I couldn't come up with a quick response. I'd known she wanted a man, a 'life partner', but I had never for a moment imagined she was lonely. Poppy had more friends than anyone else I knew. She collected them without even noticing. The mother of one of Monty's friends whom she spoke to for half an hour at his sixth birthday party still sent her Russian fudge every Christmas. The postman's sister-in-law wrote to her regularly from Rye after meeting her one summer a dozen years ago. Yoga enthusiasts the world over corresponded with her by every means known to mankind, including psychic ones. She still had tea twice a year with her kindergarten teacher. She belonged to every club within chanting distance of Tannington. How could this insanely popular bundle of joy and enthusiasm be so lonely she wanted to die?

'But you have lots of love, Poppy,' I told her, although I was still so stunned I lacked appropriate conviction. 'Everyone loves you. You must know that.'

'I don't want everyone to love me!' she cried. 'I want one special person to love me. Even if it's just for a while. I don't need forever.'

'But, but, what happened to the chap from the face-reading course?' I asked. 'Mum said you were seeing him and it was going fabulously.'

'He has a perfectly lovely wife in Swingleton Green,' Poppy cried. 'And two little babies! Which I only found out about after we'd had sex three-and-a-half times. What sort of a person would do that, Effie? To me? To his wife? To those dear, sweet little babies?'

'Oh, Poppy. He's only one bloke.' If the face reader had been within reach I would have rearranged his features, never mind the lovely wife and dear sweet babies.

'No, he's not,' she wept. 'He's every bloke I've ever known. They're all married or not ready for commitment or just want to be friends or in the wrong head space or the biorhythms are out of sync. There's always something, Effie, and I know what it is. It's me. I'm the problem. And I don't want to end up all on my own, I really don't. I've tried to prepare myself for the possibility, you know, positive reinforcement and chanting and visualisation — I went to a whole weekend workshop on visualisation, for heaven's sake. I could visualise better than anyone else there. I *excelled* at it — but where does it get me? Nowhere! Nobody! And I know this is awful for you because of Harry being gay and everything but at least you've had

Harry. At least you've had *it*. At least you've known *it*. You've had all those wonderful years with him and you have Monty.' She started to really wail then. 'Lovely, gorgeous, beautiful Monty.'

What little extra room I had inside me for emotion, and I was understandably quite jam-packed at that minute, instantly filled with guilt.

I had been so busy supping on my self-pity, and not without reason, that I had not stopped to appreciate what I'd had, even though I no longer had it. Poppy had a point. My life had turned to guano, but I'd had plenty of lovely years when I believed it to be perfect. I might have been blind and as it turns out possibly unfulfilled, but at the time I'd thought I had it all. At the time, I'd been unbelievably happy.

And there was lovely, gorgeous, beautiful Monty.

'Yes, well, lovely, gorgeous, beautiful Monty isn't actually speaking to me right now,' I said, thinking this might make Poppy feel better. 'We're sort of agreeing to disagree on quite a few things. Crystal, of course, being one of them but I am trying, Poppy, because of what you said I really am trying.' This was a lie but I resolved then and there to attempt to make it the truth from then on. 'But he's given up his plans to do a business degree and wants to be a film maker which we think is . . .' Oh God, it sounded so awful now I was saying it out loud. What kind of a mother had I turned into? The sort that foisted her own stubborn opinions onto a child that had hopes and aspirations going in a different-but-who-was-to-say-not-just-as-viable direction? Yuck.

'He's such a great boy, you're so lucky to have him,' Poppy wept.

All I could do was hug her because she was right. He was a great boy and I was lucky to have him.

'The truth is I don't even care so much about a life partner any more,' she sobbed, 'but I want a baby, Effie, I really and truly and completely want a baby.'

Poppy had always been fantastic with children and I knew that like most women she hoped to have some one day but I don't think it had registered that this was her be-all-and-end-all.

'A little girl,' she wept. 'I just want a little baby girl. I can see her, Effie, I really can. I think about her all day long and when I go to sleep I dream about her and she's so beautiful, she's just so utterly beautiful. She's perfect.' I felt goosebumps emerge head to foot. I could actually picture the little ginger-haired dot nestled in my sister's arms myself.

'And then every morning I wake up and she isn't there, it's just me, there is no baby and most days I can keep breathing and I smile and I tell myself "You can do it" and I visualise getting up and feeling positive about the universe then I put my feet on the floor and get up and do my Pilates and have Beth's Bircher muesli for breakfast and go about my business but not every day, Effie. Not every day. Some days it's just too hard and I can't do it and I can't imagine keeping doing it and today was one of those days.'

I knew that sensation. I had recently had some of those days when I was so lonely and scared I'd felt my own life was too hard and that slipping away would be easier than carrying on.

But I could not bear to think that Poppy felt the same way.

Despite the measles situation, I was stronger than my sister. I think I had always known that but I never knew it more than in that moment. Yes, my life was in the toilet, literally, but as hard as these recent times had been, as the world after Young Nick's phone call in particular had been, it had only fleetingly felt unbearably hard. If only by a hair's breadth, it had always been within the bounds of what I could manage, even though I didn't want to manage it, thought it cruel and unfair that I had to do so. Still, I had managed. It had never been as hard for me as it was for Poppy.

She had spent her lifetime being so sweet, so lovable, so kind and caring towards everybody within her radar but now I saw that those very traits that made her so giving to others had left her bugger-all resources to fend for herself.

I lay there with my poor baby sister in my arms, so inconsolable with grief that she had tried to kill herself, and tried not to think about my rotting colon. Never mind out of sync, the biorhythms were totally fucked if you asked me.

Poppy drifted off to sleep eventually and I lay there for the best part of an hour, watching those long golden lashes on her pale cheeks, smelling her buttery breath and feeling something so complicated and painful and odd I couldn't put it into words.

All I knew was that without Poppy the world was a truly shit place. I needed her in it. Forever. However long that was, etcetera etcetera etcetera.

When she was truly conked out and snoring the fluttery puppy-dog snore she'd long been known for, I extricated myself from the bed and crept downstairs to the kitchen where I knew Mum and Dad would be waiting for me.

'How is she?' my mother asked. 'Oh Effie, I'm so pleased you are here. Your father and I are at our wits' end. I thought she'd seemed better, didn't you, Archie? Just lately I thought she seemed better.'

I pulled up a chair and helped myself to a goblet of whatever they were having. It tasted like gin, only worse.

'I just don't know where to start,' I said, surprised that I didn't feel more angry with them. 'What's been going on? What do you mean you thought she seemed better? What's the matter with her?'

'I can't tell her, Archie,' my mother wailed. 'You do it.'

Dad hitched at his corduroy trousers. He was looking quite conservative for him. But so old, the poor thing. His brow was furrowed so much his glasses sat higher on his nose than normal, which made him look quite foreign.

His hand shook as he raised his goblet to his lips and took a sip. Then shook again as he put it down.

'Poppy's been depressed,' he said, with such disbelief I felt a huge surge of affection for him, living in his perfect happiness bubble. 'You know, clinically. We tried St John's wort and reiki and quite a lot of acupuncture but we had to resort to conventional medicine in the end. Pills and things,' he said, still bewildered, 'since the last time.'

'The last time?' I was aghast.

'Ginseng tablets. About a hundred of them,' my Dad said, his voice breaking. 'Last year, just after Monty had gone to Australia. We didn't want to upset you by telling you.' He looked nervously at Mum as if to check he was getting this right. 'She's been so bloody fragile, Effie, and we've been trying to look after her, haven't we, Beth, but it's not been easy. She's such a precious soul.'

'Why didn't she tell me?' I was aghast, totally aghast, but also hurt, I think. 'I'm her big sister.'

Mum blew her nose so loudly I was surprised her ears didn't fly off.

'Well, that's just it,' she said. 'You're her big sister. You're the one who has done it all first and done it well and she doesn't feel she can compare to you, Florence. She never has.'

Compare to me? Was I hearing things?

'But I'm a mess,' I said. 'My marriage has collapsed, as has my relationship with my son, as have most of the interior walls in my house. And on top of that, I . . .'

Shit.

My parents were looking at me, both of them so crinkled and ground down with sorrow that suddenly I knew I could not tell them about the measles. Robust? What on earth had given me that impression? The two of them were as tough as spun sugar. They would snap at the gentlest of tweaks.

I just couldn't bring myself to drop my bomb when they were so obviously already shellshocked by my little sister lying upstairs with her wrists bound up in cream crêpe bandages.

'On top of that, what?' my mother asked.

'Yes, darling, whatever else is the matter?' Dad's goblet shook in his hands.

I just loved them then. I just truly, really, enormously loved them. They did such a good job of looking after Poppy and she needed them so much more than I did. I could get by without them in a way that she couldn't, especially now. I'd got this far, hadn't I? So I decided that I would tell them my awful news, but I would wait until the impact of Poppy's suicide attempt had settled into the creases of the past. When it was not so much a real live tragedy but more of a whispered 'remember when?' under the covers at night or a stolen look between the two of them over the breakfast table.

'The house has rotten foundations,' I answered, rather limply. 'I know it seems silly in comparison with what's happened to Poppy but the thing is that apparently the joists are all turning to dust and need fixing or the whole jolly house could fall down and it's going to cost a bomb and, well, that's it, really . . .'

My parents looked at each other, clearly thrilled, and I

swear they both sat up an extra two inches as they beamed. You'd have thought I just told them I'd converted to Hinduism and was going to live on an ashram in Goa.

'If it's money you want, darling, that's no trouble at all,' my father said, quite delighted.

'Yes, get out the chequebook, Archie!' my mother crowed.

This lottery-winning delight was not the reaction I had expected. I had expected them to collapse with relief that I wasn't turning my house into a common cafe to which ne'er do wells with their white sugar addictions might flock, to their, and no doubt my, ultimate detriment.

'Which drawer?' my father shouted from the study.

'The chequebook drawer, Archie,' my mother shouted back, rolling her eyes.

I had never before asked my parents for so much as a penny and it felt totally despicable to be doing it now. Or, should I say, it should have felt totally despicable and I had always imagined it would feel totally despicable but then again, I hadn't really asked them. Seeing what pleasure it gave them, I could not help but be warmed a little by their sheer delight.

Here, I realised, was a problem they could solve, just like that.

I had absolutely no doubt they had tried as hard as they humanly could to help Poppy, to curb her loneliness, to improve her sex life, to get her that little red-headed baby she so deserved, but really, against the will of the crooked universe, they were powerless.

Reinforcing the basement of Rose's house so I could serve orange pekoe and lemon yo-yos, even though I wasn't going to, now that was a different matter.

'What will it take?' Dad asked, taking the lid off his antique fountain pen with a dramatic flourish. 'Twenty? I can't see how you'd fix dry rot for less than twenty.'

'Well, the builder says ten,' I started to say.

'So, you can take that, double it, and add another ten,' scoffed my mother.

'Thirty it is then,' Dad quickly agreed and again he and my mother shared such a triumphant look I damn near called them up on it. I wasn't such a stubborn old goat that I would never let them help me, was I?

'Thirty is more than enough,' I said weakly, then snatched up my goblet and drained the hideous liquid that was settling, pond-like, within. If only they knew. Here I was letting them help me but not in the way in which I actually needed their help.

I took the cheque, kissed them both good night, then trudged upstairs and climbed back into bed with my poor sad darling sister.

POPPY

♥ ♥ ♥

I could have died all over again but properly this time when Effie walked into the bathroom. What a silly twit she must have thought I was. And she'd be right. All that's going on in her life and I have to make a fuss about something as nonsensical as not having a boyfriend.

It's just that it didn't feel nonsensical. I really needed a boyfriend to get me my baby. And I always tried to throw so much light out into the world, I really did, but I just wasn't attracting the right sort of light back in again.

Gideon, the face reader, I really thought he was it, my future force. He was so kind and thoughtful and gentle and brilliant at sex. He picked wildflower posies for me and took me on picnics with three different sorts of sprout sandwiches and gave wonderful massages with Fair Trade jojoba oil.

We lay in a meadow one afternoon laughing at the clouds, just holding hands and talking about what we wanted out of life and it was so beautiful. It felt so honest and hopeful. I mean never bloody once did he mention his wife and two daughters.

How could a kind, thoughtful, gentle person do that? He knew I was looking for a life partner, he knew how much I wanted a baby, and yet he lay there in the long grass with me and pretended to imagine our future together. Is it just me or is that the cruellest thing you could possibly imagine?

I met his wife at a Feldenkrais workshop in Sudbury, that's how I found out about her. She was this wonderful, tall, blonde, beautiful powerhouse of a woman with a perfectly toned body and the most warrior-like posture. She was telling me about her husband and how he collected Tintin *first editions and I knew straight away it was Gideon and sure enough it was.*

He came to pick her up with the two little girls in the car and when he saw me he didn't even look surprised or worried or anything. His eyes just slid over me as if I wasn't even there and I realised then that it had all been a big fat lie and he was just like Bruno the rugmaker and Jimmy the farrier and Gerald who managed the secondhand bookshop in Bury St Edmonds.

They'd all told me one thing and meant quite another, which I simply can't understand, no matter how hard I try. Is it just me that these seemingly lovely men tell such terrible lies to or do they lie to everyone?

There are good men in the world, I know that. Daddy is a good man. Harry is a good man. Monty is a good man. That's three just in my family. So where are all the others?'

CHAPTER SEVENTEEN

I stayed on a few more days at Tannington Hall because Poppy, Mum and Dad each separately asked me to and in the circumstances, I could hardly say no. Besides I was scared to take my eyes off my sister. I didn't think she would try to do anything silly again, she seemed embarrassed by it, really. But she was still undeniably sad.

When we were together, however, chatting about this, that and the next thing, she seemed to perk up. I could see the mist of loneliness and depression lift a little, and it did my own aching heart good to be of some help.

In this climate, again, keeping my own awful secret wasn't as hard as I might have imagined. I've heard it said before of people who have been in terrible accidents that they don't feel all their injuries at once, only the worst one: the head injury overwhelms the shattered leg, which covers up the broken wrist, which blocks out the multiple lacerations, and in a way

I suppose the same could be said of me.

I felt terror on Poppy's behalf, first and foremost, and that obliterated my other worries. They would be there, waiting for me, when distress over my sister lessened, I knew that, but in the meantime every time I looked at her or my parents my own problems blurred into the background.

Apart from first thing in the morning, of course, when myself and my situation were crisply reunited in the harsh light of day and found each other extremely lacking. I'd wake up, stretch out in the bouncy single bed piled high with the goose-down quilts that I'd had since I was three and for those few blissful moments all would be right with the world. Then I'd remember that Harry was gone, Monty was married, Poppy wanted to kill herself, and I had cancer.

I thought I could feel it then, physically, my disease, lurking in my innards. It felt like a big, oily, slow-moving, dark mass that was oozily forcing its way into the various corners of my body, like some sort of sinister asphalt. Why me, I would think, over and over and over. What had I done to deserve this? As those bleak morning minutes ticked by, this historical disinterment took over my worries, shadowing my fear for the future. I upturned every flowerpot of my past looking for a hidden reason why I might have attracted cancer when I felt as though I had done nothing in my life but pay attention to my manners, be kind to strangers, and generally try to do the right thing.

Was it because I had turned my nose up at Mum and Dad's alternative lifestyle? For all I knew cynicism was the number one cause of cancer. Or was it because I'd been secretly pleased when school bully Susan Steiner was hit by the number 18 bus and broke both legs and her big ugly nose? I didn't know how far back cancer searched when it invaded a life looking for a reason to visit hell upon it. Had it chosen me because I'd been a bit smug at ending up a happily married mother of one at such a young age? It had made life easy for me being Harry's wife and Monty's mother, I sort of knew that, although I only knew it around the edges, not down the middle. I hadn't had to go out in the big wide world and find a husband or a career but that wasn't a deliberate statement, it was just happy coincidence (or not so happy, as it turned out). And anyway, as far as I knew being unambitious and a tiny bit smug wasn't a crime, especially not one punishable by what was being dealt to me.

It was more plausible, I supposed, that I should blame white flour and red meat and an absolute inability to meditate for more than a split second without wondering whether you can still buy those little mushroom things to darn socks with; or whether chocolate cream best fills the gap between the layers of a coffee cake or whether it should be coffee cream or just plain cream.

Whatever it was, I didn't like to be left alone for too long applying such twitty forensics to my past life. This propelled me out of bed on those Tannington days, despite the cosiness of the goose-down quilts, and into the freezing cold bathroom for a shower so I could then get about the business of helping my family get over Poppy's near-demise.

Still, every morning as I dried myself in front of the pathetic one-bar heater in my room, I imagined myself telling Mum and Dad about what was happening to me. I could see Mum's face crumple, Dad's fade to ghostly white, him clutching her, she falling back into her chair. But when it came to picturing the words I would use, I choked. How would they bear it? How would Poppy bear it? If I was terribly ill, if I was terminally ill, and I had fairly much talked myself into the fact that I was, what would be gained by talking about it now?

If I kept it to myself, I reasoned, teeth chattering, when it came the blow would fall short and sharp, as it had with Rose. Charlotte's father, on the other hand, had died a year or so before after a very long drawn-out battle with pancreatic cancer. I swear the family had done so much grieving before he actually popped his clogs that his death and the funeral that followed it all seemed a bit of an anti-climax. Everyone was thoroughly exhausted by then, physically and emotionally. Charlotte's sister had all but had a nervous breakdown trying to deal with her loss. An aunt had thrown a spectacular hissy fit at the graveside — over the matter of some dusty heirloom as it turned out. The stress had caused Charlotte to starve herself down to Posh Spice proportions and her mother had been hospitalised four times in a single week with what emerged to be panic attacks.

The old bugger damn near took his entire family with him and I most certainly did not want to do that to mine. Nor did I want the looks of pity and the hushed whispers behind my back and the gentle pats telling me how brave I was, which were all sure to come if I spilled the beans. It was all so horribly public. Like being pregnant, only in a bad way. When I was carrying Monty I had been embarrassed that my status was so apparent to complete strangers, some of whom felt the urge to actually touch my growing belly. I didn't want to share my pregnancy. And I didn't want to share what was happening to me now.

Until the time was right I would deal with it my way, without bothering anyone else. That was the decision I made shivering in front of the rusty three-legged Belling in the spare room at Tannington Hall, pulling my clothes on before I was properly dry for fear of freezing to death right then and there.

In my interest and the interests of the dwindling numbers who knew and loved me, it was better to not say anything, not do anything, not even know any more than I already did.

Poppy, meanwhile, remained as delicate as a rose petal and my parents remained utterly shaken by this, by her. I granted myself my wretched mornings, but for the health of my family I vowed to remain a pillar of strength otherwise.

After nearly a week of Mum's kidney bean casserole, however, she and Dad seemed to be getting back to their old selves — their gas emissions were overtaking their rotating updates on Poppy's state of mind as a topic of conversation — and I knew I needed to think about going home.

I did not want to talk about gas emissions. I was off the subject of digestive systems. And I did not like the bean casserole in its first incarnation, let alone when it returned as bean casserole 'bake', followed the next day by bean casserole bake 'pie' and, worst of all, the following morning, bean casserole bake pie 'jazzed up breakfast fritters'.

I don't even want to imagine what jazzed them up. A hundred million mould spores, most likely. Or hashish.

Had my digestive system been in perfect working order to begin with, it would have been lucky to survive such an insult. As it was, I could not help but feel extra concern for its welfare.

Also, I needed to do some real baking. I had been doing my best in Mum's country kitchen but it just wasn't the same with rice flour or spelt. Everything I made looked and tasted like bricks and no matter what anyone says, I just do not believe that carob is a proper substitute for chocolate. I do not believe anything is a proper substitute for chocolate.

I did what I could — carob zucchini cake (harrumph), dairy-free oatmeal cookies (not bad), blueberry and parsnip muffins (disgusting). Dad ate everything and asked for seconds. Mum suspected me of sneaking butter on to the premises (if only) and refused to partake; Poppy picked sadly at whatever I placed in front of her before eventually pushing it listlessly away.

I felt confident that my parents were now in better shape to take care of her, though, even if she herself had not appeared to gain quite as much ground as I had hoped.

'It's not over for you, you know, Poppy,' I told her as we sat out on the porch overlooking the vegie patch one crisp afternoon, Poppy tucked under a pale cashmere throw, me in one of Dad's old jumpers. 'Just because the face reader was a lemon, it doesn't mean the right person isn't out there for you somewhere. It doesn't mean that there isn't some way to get your baby girl.'

'I've thought about a sperm donor, of course I have,' Poppy answered, patting Sparky, who'd made a suitably mournful companion during our stay. 'But I'm not sure if I'm a sperm donor sort of person. I want to know where my angel's come from. Is that wrong? I think I have to aim for a life partner, even though I am thirty-five and people are writing books and making movies all the time about how hard it is when you're thirty-five. Or about how everyone thinks it's hard but it's not, if you follow a few simple rules like . . . oh, I don't know, settling for someone who bores you to tears and kills puppies for a living and has buck teeth and no hair. And a sperm donor could be a puppy killer too, couldn't he? I bet they don't ask specifically on the form. No, I think an actual non-puppy-killing flesh-and-blood man is the way to go, although I've got more chance of getting hit by lightning than finding one at my age.' She shuddered suddenly and her jaw dropped open, her eyes widening in horror. 'Oh, I'm so sorry, Effie, I don't mean

. . . I didn't want to . . . oh, what is the matter with me?'

It took me a moment to realise why she was upset but it soon dawned on me that if it was hard to get a life partner when you were thirty-five, it was most likely impossible when you were four years older.

'God, don't worry about me,' I laughed, and I meant it. 'That's the last thing on my mind.' The last in a pretty impressive list, mind you, I thought, a collage of faded blue denim and tanned skin flashing in my brain.

'But if it wasn't the last thing on your mind,' Poppy said wistfully. 'What would you do?'

If my life was totally different, if my world was turned upside down again, or right way up again, to be more precise? If finding a life partner, oh bugger that, a boyfriend, a husband, a whatever, was the first thing on my mind? I knew what I would do. I had an option. I would find Will, wherever he now was since I'd fired him from my house, and I would spend all day and all night having wild, abandoned, extremely un-gay sex with him, and then I'd live happily ever after with him.

If.

'Oh, Effie, please don't look like that,' Poppy said desperately. 'I'm just a total ninny talking nonsense, as usual. Why would you be thinking about that with everything else that's going on in your life?'

'Of course I've thought about it,' I said breezily, my balloon of blue denim popping. 'In fact, I saw an episode of *Oprah* after Harry left and she said San Jose in California was the best place to get a husband. All the men there are apparently super fit and healthy and straight and what's more there are a lot of them.'

'San Jose?' Poppy didn't look convinced. 'I wouldn't last five minutes in the Californian sun. And all the fit, healthy, straight men would like the tanned girls better than me anyway.'

I couldn't truly see Poppy as a Californian either, but nonetheless perhaps Oprah was on to something. If the life partners weren't coming thick and fast wherever Poppy was, perhaps the trick was to go somewhere else.

'Do you think you could bear to get out in the world a bit more, Poppy? Maybe move to Bury St Edmonds or maybe Norwich or . . .' I couldn't see it. She needed too much looking after and she knew it, she was shaking her head.

'I'm a home body and that's the truth,' she said. 'If my life partner isn't going to find me here then he's probably not going to find me at all. I'm not like you, Effie, I don't feel at home in the city. I feel lost. You, you just fit in so well.'

Was that true, I wondered?

'I just love that house,' I said. 'And I've never wanted to live anywhere else so I suppose I must fit in there.'

'And you like the Tesco,' she said, 'even though the organic department is woeful.'

'True,' I agreed.

'And the Formosa Dining Room, even though it's a rort.'

'True again. And Gordon Ramsay's bought the Warrington pub just up the road.'

'Never mind him, soon you'll have your tearoom!' Poppy crowed, colour crawling across her cheeks. 'Something to really look forward to. How wonderful for you.'

It was a delight to see her face wrenched away from its sadness and I only wished I could hand Poppy something to really look forward to.

'Did Dad tell you about the dry rot?' I asked her.

'Yes, but he said half of London is rotten. And the other half is radiated. And anything that's left is politically incorrect.'

'He's loaned me some money to fix it,' I confessed, blushing, because I felt so guilty about the money.

Poppy smiled, albeit wanly, and rested her head against the back of her chair closing her eyes, her gold-red lashes pearlescent on lily-white cheeks.

'He's so chuffed,' was all she said. 'I can't tell you.'

She was so still, so lifeless, sitting there, I couldn't even see her chest rising with her breath and it frightened me.

'You'll be okay, Poppy, won't you?' I asked her, suddenly desperate for something to go right, to be all right. 'Will you promise me you won't try anything, you know, again?'

She turned to look at me, pulling the cashmere throw closer around her shoulders and offering me another sad smile.

'I'll do my best,' she said.

'Because Beth and Archie would just die,' I said, wondering how they would survive if both their daughters were taken from them.

'And I would . . .' But I couldn't finish. For a million reasons I couldn't finish. Poppy reached her hand out for mine.

'Will you promise to make at least one gluten-free goodie at Rose's?' she asked, giving me a squeeze. 'And while you're at it, could you please just for me skip the dairy?'

She was so solemn, I meant to laugh but instead I just made a strangled gurgling noise. There wasn't going to be a Rose's, after all. I was more than likely going to spend the £30,000 on shoes and hair extensions. But I couldn't tell her that. Not then.

'Of course I will, silly,' I croaked instead and I was off my chair and giving her a hug in the blink of an eye. 'Just be good to yourself,' I whispered into her hair. 'Please, Poppy, just be good to yourself.'

ARCHIE

♥ ♥ ♥

The girls laugh at me for being in touch with my feminine side but it was my masculine side I worried about when Poppy was so ill.

I felt like I had failed her, as a father, that I hadn't looked after her well enough. Beth doesn't hold much truck with that line of thinking, she insists we're on equal footing and we are, mostly, but just because I can do macramé doesn't mean I don't expect to be able to protect my family.

I've had the most wonderfully lucky life but by far the best part of it has been being a father to these two remarkable people, Florence and Poppy. They're like chalk and cheese in so many ways, always have been. Florence is extremely self-contained whereas Poppy is open to the universe, too open, possibly.

She can't take the blows the way her sister can. Just look at the way Florence handled Harry changing sides, or however they put it these days. She just boxed on, quite incredible really. She's never been one to ask for help, ever since she was a tiny little thing insisting on walking around the place on her own, no hand-holding thank you very much, despite the falls and knocks and scrapes. 'I do it myself!' she would say. 'I do it myself!'

That's why I nearly fell off my chair when she told us about the hiccup with the tearoom and then, blow me down, accepted a bit of assistance. Money is the one thing we have enough of in this family. It's embarrassing, actually. I've had the most extraordinary luck with the share market and believe me it is luck, there's no skill involved. Even when I make ridiculously risky investments that the white collars wouldn't even sniff at, they seem to pay off. I can't help it. Green stock mostly. Who knew being environmentally friendly would take off so well? We have more money than we need and even though we are funding an irrigation scheme in Darfur and a school in Sri Lanka, it keeps adding up.

If I could have solved Poppy's problem with money I would have been a happy man but money couldn't buy what she needed just then.

As for Florence, well, I was chuffed, obviously, when she took the cheque but then I saw the two of them sitting outside talking by the vegie patch. Florence was wearing an old jersey of mine and it swam on her. She looked so small inside it. So pale. She'd lost quite a bit of weight, I suddenly noticed. In fact, I couldn't help but think both my girls looked like they were suffering.

CHAPTER EIGHTEEN

It wasn't until I got in the car to drive back to London that I realised how much being a tower of strength had taken it out of me. I blubbed all the way back to Little Venice, thrilling the dog, of course.

I quite enjoyed feeling sorry for myself for a while, to be honest, but then I developed those hideous sad hiccups which gave me a hell of a stomach ache and encouraged me to pull myself together. When I got home it was after five and Will's truck wasn't there, but the secondhand mint-green scooter Monty had recently bought was. I hated it because scooters seemed such a dangerous way to get around in London and what if he was killed? Or lost a leg? Or suffered a terrible head injury and was in a coma for the rest of his life?

Inside the house, to my enormous shock, to the right of the front door where the floor of my old office used to be, there was now a large jagged hole, about the size of a dining table, from which emanated a smell like a thousand rotting cabbages.

I stood there, my mouth hanging open, and stared, despite the vile vapour wafting around me. I could see some sort of complicated scaffolding holding up the bits of floor that weren't a hole. It seemed glaringly obvious that the hole had not made itself and that Will and Stanley and possibly the rattly man had been working while I was away, despite my asking them to stop.

How dare they? When they knew I couldn't afford to pay them!

Although, of course, now it turned out that I could afford to pay them three times over so I needed to come up with a whole different excuse to keep them from turning my house into the tearoom that I would soon be too sick to run.

It was all quite tricky really, but I couldn't stand there another second contemplating the trickiness because the smell was making my eyes water and I'd only just finished an extensive bout of eye watering and did not fancy another one.

I stomped tiredly up the stairs, leaving the putrid stench of rotten whatever-it-was behind me, and to my great dismay found Crystal in the kitchen making a cup of lemon and fresh mint tea.

'Would you like one?' she offered me but I shook my head. 'Monty's gone for a job interview in the West End,' she told me, 'so it's just me here.'

Despite my overwhelming bone weariness, I felt a terrible almost electric urge to be bitingly snippy, but remembering my promise to Poppy, struggled to suppress this.

'So, he didn't take the scooter?' I asked.

'I hate that thing,' Crystal said, frowning for the first time since I'd met her, as she stirred a teaspoon of honey into her drink. When did sugar become public enemy number one? 'Fastest way to do yourself a serious injury, if you ask me, which he didn't when he bought it or I would have begged him not to.'

Don't expect me to gang up against my son with you, I thought to myself, even though it fell into the snippy category and I totally agreed with what she was saying.

I made myself an instant coffee and loudly poured lashings of full fat milk into it while Crystal got about the business of marinating tofu in a low sodium organic soya sauce and some strange foreign-looking herb that looked a bit like green armpit hair.

'Nick March, your doctor, has probably rung six times over the past few days,' she said, quite matter of factly. 'He's pretty stressed out that you haven't called him back. He wanted me to pass that on. You might want to consider giving him a call?'

I was so shocked that Young Nick had dobbed me in like this, with Crystal of all people, that I could not think of a single thing to say. He had left a message or two before I'd gone to Tannington Hall but I had not been in the right frame of mind to answer them and still wasn't.

'I haven't mentioned anything to Monty', Crystal continued, threading cubes of tofu onto a bamboo skewer, 'because I don't want to worry him — but I get the feeling Nick wasn't just ringing to remind you the verruca clinic is coming up.'

My mouth opened, but still nothing came out.

'If there's something wrong, you can tell me, Florence,' she said evenly. 'I may even be able to help.'

As if I would tell her! Crystal? As if she could help me! I was suddenly overwhelmingly furious. Furious at Nick for talking to her, furious at there being anything to talk about, furious at the hole in my house, at Poppy, at Harry, furious at this strange woman spraying soy around my kitchen and stealing my lovely gorgeous beautiful son.

'What on earth makes you think you could ever help me?' I snapped. 'What on earth makes you think anything at all to do with anything about me in any way whatsoever? You're just a bloody interloper bloody well interloping in my life! In my house! Doing stupid bloody things with your stupid bloody tofu!'

I knew that this was snippy gone wild, that Poppy would be ashamed of me, that it was not really Crystal I wanted to shout at, yet I seemed unable to stop.

'You know nothing about me,' I raged. 'You have no idea, you can't begin to fathom what it feels like to, to, to . . .'

'To what, Florence?' Crystal asked, remarkably unmoved by my hysterics although she had stopped making the tofu kebabs.

Where could I start? Oh, why was my life like this? 'To lose a son!' I cried, plucking at the closest excuse I could find. 'That's what! To lose a precious son! To someone like you!'

This was not the me I had always tried to be. This was the opposite. So much for minding my manners and doing the right thing. I was lucky she didn't clock me on the head with the meat tenderiser but then she probably didn't know what one was.

A shutter came down over her face though and she leaned back against the kitchen counter and looked at me pretty coldly, for her. Whether I liked her or not, there was no denying she was a warm person. As a rule, she positively radiated warmth.

'Not to someone like me,' she said with glacial calm. 'Yes, that's true, but otherwise I can definitely fathom it.'

'Don't be ridiculous,' I shot back. 'You can't possibly know what I'm talking about. You don't have a son.'

She kept looking at me in such an expressionless way then that it occurred to me that I might perhaps be approaching back-foot territory. Her eyes were landed steadily on mine as if waiting for me to reach some sort of conclusion. My anger started to dissipate and I began to feel that slow, creeping, hot sort of frost that crawls over you when you start to realise you have said or done something really, really awful.

'You can't possibly know,' I said again, all the same, although the conviction was missing and I was no longer sure I was talking about losing a son. I was talking about losing in general. Actually, I didn't really know what I was talking about.

'Well, you say I know nothing about you but you know nothing about me, either, Florence,' she said. 'You've jumped to your own conclusions without bothering to ask me so much as one single question about myself, about my life. But for your information, I did have a son but he died.'

The hot creeping frost spread down from my face to my chest, my heart. I didn't want to hear another word. I wanted to know what happened. I ached for her. I hated her. I hated myself.

'How old was he?' I finally asked, even though it was the wrong question.

'Seven and a half months,' she answered.

A baby? Oh, why was the world, my world, so cruel?

'When?'

'Six years ago,' she told me in a voice devoid of its usual upbeat twang. 'Six years, two months, three weeks and four days ago.'

The heartbreak of counting those days.

'I'm so sorry,' I said. 'Truly, Crystal.'

'Cot death,' she told me then, 'if that's what you call it here. I got up to feed him in the night and . . . well, anyway. We couldn't wake him up. We called the ambulance but we already knew.'

A ghastly silence filled the room and throbbed in my ears. I felt sick to my stomach. She had actually lost a son? A baby? Who was 'we'? She'd been married before? I was a horrible human being and I deserved everything I had coming to me. But why hadn't anybody told me? How was I supposed to know that this foreigner who had pinched Monty away from me was a, a, a . . . A what? A real live woman with her own hideous torments, just like me?

I slid into a chair, my good legs no longer able to hold up the horrible rest of me. 'I'm so sorry,' I said again.

Crystal's eyes flickered, and she too pulled out a chair at the other end of the table and sat in it.

She looked totally different to me now. That serene smoothness I had taken to be some sort of Aussie default position now seemed a veneer as obvious as an alpaca poncho. She perhaps wasn't the cocksure blasé son-snatcher I had initially taken her for.

I was evil. That's why I had cancer.

'I don't know what to say,' I told her. 'I can't imagine how you even . . .'

'Survived?' She finished my sentence.

I nodded. She was silent, then: 'It took six months before I could even truly believe he was gone,' she said. Her voice changed again, as though she still couldn't believe it. She looked out the window, into the patchy blue sky, as if expecting to see a little cherub perched on a cloud out there. 'I checked his empty cot about fifty times a day. Wouldn't let Steve change a thing in the room. And I felt him in my arms sometimes, when

I was daydreaming, you know? Actually felt his skin on mine, for a long time. Then after a while I couldn't even remember exactly what his cry sounded like or how he smelt. That was almost the saddest of all. The not remembering.'

There was nothing I could say to her. Nothing.

'Yep, that was almost the saddest thing,' she said again, smiling, but it wasn't a happy smile, it was the sort that you force on your face to keep it from crumpling. 'So don't tell me I don't know what it's like to lose a son because my son is actually lost, Florence, forever, whereas yours is right here, just with someone like me.'

I deserved her disdain. I deserved much worse. 'And you know what?' she continued although her voice faltered, making me hate myself even more. 'I make Monty happy, I know I do.' A tear slid out of one clear green eye and travelled determinedly down her cheek. 'And he makes me happy, which I never thought anyone else in the world would ever, ever be able to do.'

I wanted to tell her right then that I was dying of cancer to show her that I was not a spoiled bitter housewife or a frightful old bitch, just not my usual self. Blurting it out now though would only seem like I was trumping her in the tragedy stakes and I couldn't do that.

'I'm so sorry, Crystal,' I said again. 'I didn't know. Monty never said.'

'If you don't want to get to know me that's fine,' Crystal told me and I admit I admired her strength then; her ability to survive her baby dying and stand up to a prickly old sourpuss like myself. 'Really, that's OK, up to a point. But I am a human being with feelings just like you are, Florence, and we need to find a way to somehow exist together in some sort of harmony while Monty wants to stay here.'

I felt a glimmer of something vaguely joyful at hearing that Monty wanted to stay, but it was quickly overshadowed by the grief I felt at her dreadful loss and my awful behaviour.

'Poppy tried to kill herself,' I said, feeling only slightly ashamed at pulling this out of my hat. I would have told her anyway, most likely. 'I've been at Tannington Hall with my parents as she begins the, you know, healing process.'

I coughed, although it could have been a choke. I never used words like 'healing process'. I wasn't stooping, I told myself, and I don't think I altogether was. I was trying to speak Crystal's language. And I think she got it. Her face returned to its usual understanding self.

'That's terrible,' she said. 'What did she do?'

This question took me by surprise, I admit. It seemed so practical.

'She slit her wrists in the bath,' I answered. Hearing it out loud like that, in the kitchen of my house, having just learned that this woman I'd been so horrible to had lost a child, I felt shocked to the core all over again.

The world was an appalling place and I was an appalling person.

CRYSTAL

♥ ♥ ♥

I could see that Florence was struggling with something huge. I saw it in her aura actually, that first day at the train station although I don't think she was aware of it herself then. Her colours were fuzzy greys and browns then whereas by the time she came back from Tannington Hall they were crisper but much, much darker.

The grey was the emotional upheaval of having her sister try to take her own life, as well as the marriage break-up and me, I suppose, but the brown, I believe, was related to her health. I suspected that from the beginning but then when her doctor kept ringing, well, it seemed obvious.

But we're all responsible for our own bodies and Florence was definitely passing the buck on hers. Even she would agree with that, I think. She hadn't been eating properly, that was pretty clear. She seemed to live on white sugar and bacon and egg pie. And not enough of either to put much meat on her bones, if you'll pardon the expression. She looked hollowed, is how I would describe it. She's a beautiful woman but it's as though she was wearing the shadow of her beauty, if you know what I mean, not the beauty itself. She didn't fit her skin.

Of course, it wasn't just her physical self that was suffering. Her unhappiness, I think I can call it that and not offend anyone, was as clear to me as her hip bones, her cheekbones, her long slim arms and legs. Her unhappiness was so obvious I could almost reach out and touch it. That's what I was trying to do when I told her about Jamie. I wasn't emotional game-playing or trying to make her feel guilty or anything like that. That's not me, I would never do that. I was just opening up to her in the hope that she could then feel able to open up to me. To be honest, I was also a bit sick of her shit by then and I wanted to put a stop to it. I knew I wasn't really the enemy but I didn't realise then just who, or what, the enemy was.

I don't tell everyone about Jamie. I keep him locked inside me most of the time. I express my feelings about him, of course I do, or I have in the past, and it used to feel like I thought about him every minute of the day but with time that's actually changed so my thoughts about him are more fleeting now, not all-consuming the way they used to be. It's like he's a thread in my tapestry, not the whole wall hanging, if you know what I mean. I don't cry when I think of him any more, but if I happen to be crying I make sure there are some tears for him. And if I happen to be smiling, I make sure he gets a bit of that as well. He's my angel. And I wouldn't bring him out like that and introduce him to someone unless I thought it would be of some help.

You don't need a diploma in intuitive therapy to see that Florence was in trouble back then and I was probably the last person she thought could help her but I could.

I knew from what Monty had told me that she had led a more or less blessed life up till then, apart from the passing of her grandmother before Monty was even born. While this charmed existence had made her the wonderful mother he has told me she always was, it had not prepared her to deal with the shit hitting the fan.

The fact is, and I'm not sure if Florence got this to begin with, in my experience nobody gets to lead a totally charmed existence. Nobody escapes the pitfalls of being a human being. It's what separates us from the zebras. Or that's my theory anyway, formed when my first husband Steve and I went on safari in Tanzania after Jamie died, when we still thought that our relationship could withstand what we'd been through, when we thought going on an expensive trip as far away as possible could get us away from 'it all', which was a crazy notion but it was a crazy time.

I think I already knew it was over. We'd had a good relationship, a good marriage by most standards, but I don't think I was really myself until my son died and stripped away everything that didn't matter. The house, the car, the suburbs, the coffee mornings. I couldn't remember why I'd ever wanted those things, what I had ever liked about them.

'It's grief, you'll get over it,' everyone said, including Steve. I had my doubts but I trusted everyone else more than myself then and so we went on this African trip, which was amazing, which made everything crystal clear.

We were standing in the back of a truck watching a lioness in the long grass of the Serengeti staking out her newborn prey when I realised my old life was over. The lioness started to track this female zebra and her baby, peeling them away from the herd. Steve was going nuts with excitement, the driver had to tell him to stop hooting, and he was taking a million photos as he watched it all happen, while I was just standing there crying.

Did you know that when a lion takes down a baby zebra in the wild, its mother doesn't fight for it for even a moment? She doesn't miss a hoofbeat, doesn't even stop to look, she just runs to rejoin the herd as though nothing has happened, disappearing into a sea of black and white stripes, and suddenly everything is just the way it was before.

Steve wanted me to get pregnant again, straight away, to disappear into the sea of stripes myself, but I couldn't. I wasn't the same person. It could never be the way it was before.

But I'm OK with that. I mean, if we are all going to have tragedies, if none of us can escape them, then surely we have to learn from them, we have to gain something.

And we have to use what we have gained. Those of us who have fought tooth and nail to overcome tragedy are, after all, if nothing else, proof that such things can be survived.

So we can actually help others survive their tragedies too.

As long as they'll let us.

CHAPTER NINETEEN

I toyed with being a bona fide alcoholic after I got back from Tannington Hall, after Crystal's heartbreaking confession, after I felt I had exhausted all the sensible possibilities for coping with a depressed sister, a wreck of a house and a looming afterlife.

I wanted that bliss of not knowing; that escape from the pain of reality that drugs and alcohol promise. The trouble being that as Harry had always told me, I wasn't a natural. DCI Jane Tennison made it look so easy in *Prime Suspect* — a swig here, a gurgle there, a glass or two of something at lunchtime — but honestly, you have to have the stomach for it.

The night I got back, after talking to Crystal, I tried throwing down a glass of whisky from a bottle I found hiding in the pantry along with three lots of triple sec (don't ask me how they got there, I don't even know what it is) but it was foul. It made my eyes water before I even got it to my mouth.

It tasted like a filthy old puddle that donkeys had peed in and rusty nails had soaked in for centuries.

I spat it out on the floor, then Sparky licked it up and he spat it out too. That's how foul our whisky was. Then I started on the cooking sherry but that wasn't much better. I hadn't noticed when I'd downed it during the early stages of the Harry debacle how much it tasted like vinegar. And not the fancy deli sort of vinegar made by comely virgins on some otherwise uninhabited island off the coast of Sicily or wherever, but the bulk-bin cheap-as-you-like strained-through-the-sweaty-sock-of-a-hormonal-teenage-boy sort. Mind you, I'd had it since 1993 so maybe that's what cooking sherry is supposed to taste like when it's that old. Either way, I threw it out and the next day went to Tesco to stock up on expensive New World wine instead: Chilean reds and New Zealand sauvignon blancs and Australian chardonnays.

It was a Saturday. Tesco was a zoo, and catapulted me into such a black mood with all the healthy people being so unriddled with disease and alive and well yet insisting on moving with glacial speed and bringing their caterwauling brats to run up and down raising merry hell in the booze aisle that when I got home I took to my bed with Sparky and the latest *Hello!* magazine.

To my surprise, mid-afternoon there was a gentle knock at my bedroom door. It was Monty.

'Crystal told me about Poppy,' he said, his beautiful eyes filling with tears. 'Mum, I'm so sorry.'

And when I held out my arms, he walked into them. For a while he was my gorgeous boy again, my perfect son. It was like old times. We hugged each other the way we used to before he got a wife. Despite the circumstances, it was lovely to have him back to myself for those few moments.

Of course, it didn't last.

'I've just spoken to Archie,' he said, pulling away and, embarrassed, wiping a tear from his cheek. 'We're going to head up to Tannington for a few days. Crystal's going to try some reflexology with Poppy. She thinks it could really help.'

I wanted to talk to him about Crystal and her baby, tell him that we'd spoken and she'd given me the telling off I so richly deserved, and that I was sorry for being such a sourpuss.

'You used to call him Grandad,' I said wistfully instead. 'I loved it when you called him that.'

'Yes, but *he* didn't,' Monty said, with a flash of his father's exasperation. 'Please Mum. Let's not get into all that now. Why can't you just let me be my own man?'

'Because you're not a man, you're just a boy!' I exclaimed before I could stop myself. I knew as I was saying it that this would blow away our tender moment yet out it popped. What was the matter with me? Like every other child in the universe, Monty had been telling me since he was two years old that he was a big boy now. Boys never wanted to be boys. They always wanted to be men. And anyone who disabused them of this notion was asking for trouble.

'No, no, I didn't mean that,' I said quickly, trying to recover. 'I know you're a man.' But that came out not the way I meant it either. I said 'man' as in 'Charles' like it was a swear word or a joke. I wished it had been my wrists Poppy slit. I couldn't get anything right.

'Yeah, right, whatever,' my son said, his face teetering on the brink of disgust. 'I'll see you when I see you then.'

'Please, Monty,' I said. 'I'm sorry. I'm just tired.'

He looked vaguely sympathetic for a moment then, my beautiful boy/man. The anger slid off his shoulders, relaxed his eyes, his mouth.

245

'You used to say that all you wanted was for me to be happy,' he said. 'Do you remember that?'

'Of course, I do,' I said. It had been much on my mind of late.

'So now I'm happy but it's not what you want. What happened, Mum?'

It was a good question. What had happened? Well, for a start, it turned out I didn't have a clue what happiness was. I thought I'd had it and I'd been wrong. For years, I had been wrong. And I did desperately want Monty to be happy but I wanted him to be the right sort of happy, the real sort, not the pretend sort or the wrong sort.

'I don't know,' I told him because I didn't want to admit I had no faith in his ability to find what I had not. 'I'm just worried that . . .' But my worries were so many and varied I didn't know where to start. 'I'm just worried,' I said.

'Well don't be, please,' Monty begged. 'Despite not having a job, despite you and Dad, despite even poor Poppy, I'm having the time of my life, Mum.'

And isn't that what I had always wanted him to have? Or had I wanted him to have the time of my life?

I hit my wine supply after I heard him and Crystal leave but I struggled to make the most of it. I probably could have managed a whole bottle on my own if I had started in the morning and kept sipping till bedtime but getting into it later in the day meant I ran out of steam before I got very far. I just didn't fancy it really.

I tried starting earlier the following day but I was retching by the second glass. The trouble was that I felt sick to my stomach in the first place and because I didn't know if this was just the worry or if it was the measles, that made me feel even more worried and therefore more like drinking yet at the same time sicker and less able to do so.

If I could have scored some crack, I probably would have, although I was never much chop at drugs, either. I'd smoked pot twice at student parties and both times fallen asleep and Harry had had to carry me home. And when someone suggested a line of coke at a party a few years later all I could think of was spending Monty's childhood locked up in Holloway jail with all the drug mules and prostitutes. I'd burst into tears, embarrassing everyone there, including Harry, who'd again had to carry me home.

I'd had no wild youth, that was the trouble. And now that I felt like having one, it was too late, my youth had up and left me, and worse, so had everyone else.

Well, there was Will, who would have been perfect, but I was trying to fire him so that I didn't have to see him or smell him ever again as long as I lived (however long etcetera etcetera etcetera).

This was going to make having a wild youth with him quite tricky.

Although, as the hole in the floor downstairs suggested, Will had not taken to being fired quite as much as I'd imagined. I heard him arrive the next morning and stayed in my room attempting to seethe, not easy given my conflicted feelings.

'What are you doing here?' I asked when I finally got dressed and went downstairs to talk to him. It was past lunchtime by then but I'd been rehearsing what I would say for hours. And I'd been changing my clothes. And I'd been putting make-up on and taking it off, then putting it on and taking it off again. Finally, I decided on clean jeans and an old but good button-up shirt, plus a light foundation and some lip gloss. I combed my hair but didn't wear perfume. I wanted it to look like I was making no effort although he had already seen me in baggy-bottomed tracksuit pants and an old T-shirt of Monty's so I didn't know why I was bothering. He would know I had bothered.

'What do you mean what am I doing here? I work here,' Will said, his head and shoulders poking out of the hole, a cobweb smeared on his collar. 'Nice week away?'

'Not particularly, no,' I said as he jumped out of the orifice with athletic ease and stood beside me, wiping his hands on his jeans, then pointing back down into the smelly pit.

'Sid has a mate in the scaffolding business and so we got all this for two and six. Looks like Stan has found some matching recycled floorboards up near Cambridge too. He's gone to have a look at them.'

This did not seem to tally up particularly well with what I had discussed with the two of them before I went to Tannington Hall.

'But what about . . .' I started to say.

'The smell?' he suggested, although that wasn't what I was going to say. 'I know, there was a fox down there, I'm afraid. Or an ex-fox, to be more precise. I gave him an agnostic burial while you were away but the smell might linger for a while. Do you have any scented candles?'

What kind of builder knew about scented candles?

'But I thought I told you,' I said, 'I've gone off the whole idea of a tearoom. I don't want to do it any more and now there's this hole in the floor and all this scaffolding and the pong, not to mention the £30,000. The not having it, I mean.'

Dad's cheque was burning a hole in my bedside table drawer upstairs. I could almost smell the smoke from where I was standing, guiltily unable to stop scratching my neck, which is exactly what body language experts looked for in liars.

'Florence, we are going to do this,' Will said, quite bossily, sort of, but in a gentle reassuring way. 'We have to.'

'But what about . . .' I started again.

'Trust me, Florence,' Will said. 'Can you not just do that? Can you not just trust me?'

The thing is, it's very difficult to fire someone you absolutely want to have sex with on the grounds of never wanting to see them again because of course, deep down, you really do want to see them again no matter how much you try to tell yourself you don't.

'I just can't afford it,' I said, looking at the steel cap of Will's left boot. 'On top of everything it's just . . . I'm so sorry, but you really have to . . .'

'Give me the week, Florence,' Will insisted. Truly, he was making getting rid of him impossible. 'How about that? Just give me the week?'

I'd run out of ways to fire him by then. I'd run out of ways to do anything. 'Is that the time?' I asked instead, pretending to be aghast, looking at the space on my wrist where my watch usually was. I couldn't take another second of him. 'I really have to go up to the kitchen,' I announced agitatedly, and off I took.

The moment I was up there I whipped the cork off another bottle of something fruity from New Zealand. I was shaking my head at my idiocy and contemplating the first sip when Will appeared.

'Tell me what's going on, Florence,' he said.

'I haven't any more money,' I answered, wondering if my nose was growing like Pinocchio's as I spoke. 'I can't pay you,' I added, my snout positively tingling. 'It's all spent, gone, kaput.' My nostrils were going to poke out the window on the other side of the room if I kept this up.

'Yes, I know that,' Will said. 'I'm doing it as a favour. Stan is doing it as a favour. Sid doesn't work for cash anyway.'

I took a slurp of the sauvignon blanc. I'm blowed if I could work out what the fuss was all about. It tasted horribly acidic to me. Like gooseberry juice spiked with flea powder.

'No good?' Will asked, nodding in the wine's direction.

'Not exactly my cup of tea,' I answered, wishing like hell that's what it was but cups of tea don't help you forget your troubles, that's alcohol's job. 'Would you like a glass?'

Will shook his head. 'Don't drink,' he said. 'Sorry.'

I wondered if he was an alcoholic and if it would be rude or insensitive to ask for some pointers.

'Health reasons,' he answered, as though reading my thoughts. 'Mental health reasons mainly. Florence, may I sit down?'

I pulled the bottle of wine closer to myself and nodded.

'What's going on? What's made you change your mind?' he asked as he sat. 'About the tearoom? It can't be the money because we don't need any more just yet. That's not the hold up. We'll work that out, I've told you that. So I'm just wondering, Florence . . .'

I choked down another mouthful of vile gooseberry-flavoured flea juice and said nothing.

'I'm just wondering if it's me,' Will said. 'If it's what happened the other day. Because we may just have gotten our wires crossed and if that's the case then all I can do is say again how sorry I am. In fact, I can't apologise enough. I just couldn't forgive myself if you gave up your tearoom because of me. Because of a misunderstanding about what did or didn't go on upstairs.'

I took another slurp and some sauvignon blanc trickled down my chin. I couldn't even keep the wretched stuff in my mouth.

'Florence?' I nodded so he knew I was listening even though I didn't really want to. 'Because if our wires weren't crossed,' he continued, 'if it wasn't a misunderstanding, if there's something else going on that isn't about upstairs, I would really like to think we could talk about it.'

I nodded again. Swallowed. Licked the sticky wine off my chin. Found myself thinking about the feel of his ribs beneath his shirt, imagined my fingers running over them.

'This is the part where you say something,' Will pointed out, quite politely in the circumstances.

But sadly all the somethings I wanted to say were seriously off limits. I filled my wine glass to the brim again, took another gulp and was about to once more feign being aghast at the time on my non-existent watch when I was saved by the phone.

It was Harry, mortified at the news of Poppy, which he'd just heard from Monty.

'How could you not tell me about this?' he demanded furiously. I shrugged my shoulders at Will in an apologetic fashion and he stood, held up his fingers in an 'I'll give you five' sign and pulling his cellphone out of his jeans pocket, took to the stairs.

'I adore Poppy, Floss,' Harry was saying, although my mind was still stuck on Will's pocket. 'You know that. I'm devastated she'd do something like this and that you wouldn't even think to tell me.'

'I'm devastated too, Harry,' I said, 'about a lot of things.'

'Oh, for God's sake!' There it was, that exasperation that I was noticing so much more now that I felt differently about my husband. Had it always been there? Had I not noticed it before?

'I know you're devastated too,' my exasperated ex-husband continued, 'and I'm sorry, you know I am, but really Floss, just because I'm not there doesn't mean we're not a family. That you and Monty and I aren't still a family.'

'That's exactly what it means,' I cried, fairly exasperated myself by then. 'You not being here puts the complete kibosh on the whole entire family thing, Harry. You have your own family now with the wonderful "Charles" and that stupid little chihuahua.'

'That stupid little what? What are you on about?'

I'd forgotten Charles's pocket-sized dog was only a figment of my funereal imagination. 'I don't have to tell you anything, any more, Harry bloody bollocky Dowling,' I said. 'That's what you get for ruining my bloody bollocky life.'

'Are you drunk?'

I think drunk was taking it a bit far. I was certainly feeling a foreign buzz of confidence that seemed to come with drinking in the early afternoon but I already had a headache and I hadn't even made a dent on my third glass.

'So what if I am?' I challenged Harry.

'Oh, Floss, please, for God's sake. Can't you just . . .'

'Thank you, yes, I can,' I said brightly. 'I'll pass that on. Good day.' And I slammed down the phone.

He might still be a family, but I wasn't. I was just me. I picked up my wine glass and was just about to knock the whole hideous lot back when Will reappeared. He stopped and looked at me and if I was another person, in another life, without all my horrible hidden baggage, I would just have thrown myself at him and begged him to take care of me and look after me and do sweaty, sticky, sensationally filthy things to me.

Pale blue really was his colour. And his face! Handsome, tick; tanned, tick; masculine, tick (underlined, capital letters); and somehow sort of completely understanding despite my obvious lunacy, tick. I could see it in the furrow of his thirty-one-year-old brow, the slight cloudiness in his thirty-one-year-old eyes.

He strode across the kitchen towards me and for a nano second I thought it really was going to be a proper Mills & Boon moment. I even considered a swoon of the not losing consciousness variety. Instead he snatched my glass away, threw the contents down the sink and took me by the hand.

'Come on, you,' he said. 'Go and get some shoes and a coat and meet me downstairs. I've got a surprise.'

Perhaps I was still in swoon mode, because I didn't argue. I did what he told me and put more make-up on while I was at it, plus perfume, and met him down by the hole, which I did my best to ignore while trying very hard not to fall down it. Then we went outside where he opened the passenger door of his pick-up truck and indicated I should jump in.

The truck was yellow, or had been, before rust settled in the places where it had crashed into things or scraped along beside them. But his builder's bits and bobs were neatly tucked away in two locked chests in the open tray at the back, and in the cab it was tidier than the Golf by a country mile.

He had a clipboard, even. And there wasn't one single empty takeaway coffee cup rolling around on the floor. Or a thousand receipts stuck behind the visor. Or lipsticks melted into the dash.

And it smelt nice. Like oranges.

'Where are we going?' I asked as he pulled out of Blomfield Road into Warwick Avenue.

'You'll see,' he said, smiling.

I watched his hands move around the steering wheel, shifting the manual gear lever, flicking on the indicators, as we moved towards Edgware Road. I started to relax. It was a glorious day despite the nip in the air and the city seemed to be exploding with greenery. You could say what you liked about the grime of London but for those few wonderful months in the middle of the year, it shone like an emerald. All of a sudden, I didn't actually mind where I was going, it was just lovely to be going somewhere with someone, especially Will.

As we rounded Marble Arch I started to get a light fluttery feeling in my stomach and when we turned from Park Lane towards Grosvenor Square it became a fully-fledged butterfly. He was taking me to Claridge's.

He drove his truck up to the Brook Street entrance and handed the keys to the doorman who simply nodded a polite greeting, as though he parked such pre-loved vehicles all the time.

'How ever did you get a booking?' I asked, as we crossed the black and white tiled lobby. Usually, you had to book weeks in advance.

'It's always worth a shot,' Will shrugged. 'I called just after they'd had a cancellation, so here we are. Must be my lucky day.'

We were shown to a table in the Reading Room, tucked in the corner of the massive lobby, on the opposite side from the pianist and the double bass player who plonked and plucked soothingly as we passed tables of lunching ladies and businessmen.

The place was full and humming but one of the wonderful things about Claridge's was that no matter how busy it was, there always remained an elegant ambience that spoke of nothing but good taste and extreme comfort.

'You'll be going for the champagne afternoon tea, I expect,' Will said, opening the menu. 'A thirsty person like yourself.'

I stroked the pale green stripes on my Bernardaud china cup. It was French, from Limoges as it happened, but it fit the

Claridge's Art Deco sensibility to a T so I couldn't do anything but love it.

'To be honest, I'm actually not much of a drinker,' I confessed. 'I thought I would try it for a while but it hasn't really taken. I seem to go straight from choking it down to getting the most awful hangover and all I can think of is going to lie in a dark room with a cup of tea and a wet flannel.'

'You should probably chuck it in, then,' Will said. 'Drinking doesn't always pay even when you're really good at it.'

A very pretty blonde waitress came to take our order and I found myself wishing the older, slightly pock-marked waiter on the other side of the room would come to replace her. The staff at Claridge's were known for their inscrutable charm and efficiency but I couldn't believe she wasn't somehow invisibly flirting with Will.

'I'll have afternoon tea with Claridge's Royal Blend,' Will told her politely.

'And I'll have the same with the Rose Congou,' I added crisply. The tea wouldn't go so well with the sandwiches but it seemed wrong to order anything else, given that this was where Rose and I had had so many happy afternoons.

'Is that what happened to you?' I asked Will when the pretty blonde had left. 'Drinking didn't pay?'

'Among other things,' Will answered, looking across the room at a spectacularly sculpted matron in her mid-sixties. I'd spotted her as we'd walked in. Chanel from head to toe, I suspected. 'I can see why you like it here,' he said. 'There's a lot to look at.'

'And the lighting is kind,' I said. There are very few places in the world where everything is just right and Claridge's is one of them. 'Spencer Tracy apparently said that when he died, not that he intended to, he didn't want to go to heaven, he wanted to go to Claridge's.'

I wondered if he was there now. It was definitely the sort of place that an elegant man might haunt, although I thought it was perhaps more of a Cary Grant sort of a place. Our sandwiches arrived and I was entranced to see how they'd been updated since I'd last been. It was now organic chicken and Scottish salmon and the cucumber came with rocket, which I couldn't remember existing in Rose's day.

The pretty waitress poured our tea, leaving it black. Then to my astonishment Will leaned over and delicately put about four drops of milk in my cup, just the way I liked it.

Do you know, in twenty years of marriage Harry had never remembered how I liked my tea? It hadn't bothered me particularly at the time because he so rarely made the tea in the first place but still, he should have known.

I felt the wind quite blow out of my sails. Will couldn't be this perfect, could he? I couldn't deliberately not be having a love affair with the perfect man, could I?

'How did your wife take her tea?' I asked feeling a sudden urge to find his flaws.

'She took it any way it came but she preferred it over-brewed with lots of milk.'

'Right,' I said. 'And why aren't you married to her any more?'

'I treated her appallingly and she can't forgive me,' he said with such forthrightness I nearly choked on my rose-flavoured China leaf. 'I've tried to make amends but it hasn't been easy and it's all my fault, I'm afraid. What's more, it's been terribly difficult for our daughters.'

'You have daughters?'

I tried to hide my surprise, if that's what it was. It had never occurred to me he'd have children. Little girl children. I took a soothing mouthful of tea and tried to ignore whatever was aching inside me.

'Yes. Lucy has just turned eight and Ella is six next month. I don't see them very often but I keep in touch as best I can so that they know how much I think of them.'

'She must be very angry with you, your wife. What did you do?' I asked. 'Did you cheat on her?'

'Yes,' he answered. 'More than once. More than a few times. I was a complete and utter shit, to tell you the truth. I worked in an ad agency in those days and spent most of my time there. I drank too much, I took too many drugs, I stayed out all hours, sometimes for days in a row, and finally I drove my car into a tree when our daughters were in the back seat.'

I put my Dorrington ham with English mustard sandwich back on my pale-green-striped plate. Perhaps I didn't want to know his flaws. Perhaps it was better to imagine that he was perfect.

'Why are you telling me this?' I asked.

Will looked me straight in the eyes and said: 'You know why I am telling you this.'

The thing is that usually I kept what I was actually thinking to myself and talked about something completely different. I was under the impression that's what most people did once they'd reached the age of about four. But when Will spoke it was as though his secret thought bubbles were being popped and escaping into the realm of audible conversation because what he said was so searingly frank. I didn't quite know how to handle this. It felt frightening. I was a person with a lot of secrets to keep contained within my own personal silence, after all. If I contemplated them leaking out willy nilly I wouldn't know where to start with the damage control.

'Were the little girls all right?' I asked retreating to a less confronting subject, although confronting enough, what with the drink and the drugs and the crashing into trees.

'Thankfully, yes,' he said. 'But I could have killed them. And I don't mean if I did it again or the weather was worse or I'd had more tequila, I mean that day, as it was, I could have killed them.'

'I'm so sorry,' I said.

'So am I,' he agreed. 'I'm not trying to ruin your afternoon tea,' he looked around at the room full of people chatting happily as they sipped tea and feasted on bite-sized delicacies, 'but I want you to know everything about me, Florence, warts and all.'

'Well, those are quite some warts,' I had to admit. Although it wasn't the biggest flaw someone had revealed to me in recent weeks and it was nice to hear about it up front instead of, for example, after twenty years of marriage.

'Did your wife boot you out after the tree?' I asked.

'Yes, she should have done it sooner but I made that too hard for her. She's married again now to a very nice sensible chap who my girls love and they've had another little girl of their own.'

How much that hurt I had only started to imagine when our cakes and pastries arrived. I downed a raisin scone and Marco Polo jam with almost obscene haste, then went to work on a chocolate macaroon with tea-flavoured cream filling.

It was divine.

'I can't imagine you being so wild and irresponsible,' I said, when I finally stopped concentrating so hard on my cakes. 'It just doesn't sound like you.'

'It doesn't sound like me now,' Will corrected me. 'But it turns out I was one of those idiots who had to lose it all before they could appreciate what they had in the first place. You know the type, Nick Hornby writes books about us all the time. We're a pretty sad bunch.'

'But what made you like that to begin with?' I asked. 'Was it growing up somewhere wild like Africa or was it spending so much time at boarding school in England?'

'I wish I knew the answer, or I wish there was an answer, but the truth is that I was just a spoiled little shit who got away with murder for far too long. There's no excuse for it. I had great parents, a terrific wife, fantastic job, good friends — although not so much towards the end, they very wisely gave up on me, most of them — and I had many brilliant opportunities in my life but I blew them all because I was a selfish bloody idiot.'

'Oh, I see.'

'Don't look like that, Florence, please. I'm just trying to explain why I am the way I am now. I wasted so much time when I was younger. I messed up a decent woman and two beautiful kids and if I could go back and fix it all I would, but I can't. What I can do is make sure I am never so bloody stupid again.'

I looked at the perfect little fruit tart sitting on the plate in front of me and felt suddenly overwhelmed by the most awful hopelessness.

'I try not to waste time these days, Florence,' Will continued, 'that's all I'm trying to tell you. It's too precious. Life is too precious, every minute of it, that's what I've learned, that's what I'm getting at so — oh God, I've upset you again, I'm so sorry. More tea, I think. I'll get the waitress.'

He motioned for the pretty blonde but I didn't want more tea. I didn't want my fruit tart. All I wanted to do was go home.

Life was too precious for Will to waste his time on me. And that was all he ever would be doing.

WILL

♥ ♥ ♥

God, I dug myself such a hole at Claridge's I couldn't see how I would ever climb out of it.

It's just that I wanted her to know everything there was to know about me. In fact, I couldn't get it out quickly enough. I wanted to lump it all right in front of her in an enormous pile so she could see it all straight away and then we could just get on with the business of, well, whatever was going to happen next.

I suppose I was going gangbusters because I meant what I said when I told her I didn't want to waste time, not a minute of it, and I was losing patience not with her but with the situation. It would never be right between us if I pushed her too far but then there would never be anything between us if she stayed too frightened or too closed off to trust me.

I thought about that a lot while I drove her back to the house. She looked so lost, gazing out at the traffic. Whatever was going on with her was shaking her, right down to the very marrow, as Stan would say.

Yet despite the many setbacks, I still felt what I had always felt; that there was something intangible but enormous hovering in the air between us, linking us, drawing us in as close as we would let it without exploding in our faces. It was still there. Not exactly dangerous, but almost.

And if I was wrong about us, then that almost-dangerous thing would surely be gone but if anything it was stronger.

I've seen it before, the moment when the potential is sucked out of the air; when the gorgeous girl you meet late one night in a bar and think you might just have to marry turns out the next day to love Celine Dion and smoke filterless Marlboros for breakfast and any hope of having a future disappears in an instant.

I'm sure most of us have experienced that moment: the evaporation of something you can't even see in the first place. It's promise, I suppose, mixed with desire but in the case of myself and Florence, or just myself at that point, there was real certainty. It had not evaporated. And if she didn't yet see it, or was stopping herself from feeling it, it didn't mean it wasn't there.

But I knew, as I was driving home to my flat without her that afternoon, the smell of her perfume still wafting in the cab of my truck, that I would have to have enough certainty for the both of us until — well, until what?

It occurred to me then that whatever was stopping her from recognising what we had might not be anything to do with me.

CHAPTER TWENTY

Two days later I was sitting in the Rembrandt Gardens off Warwick Avenue, enjoying the blissful sunshine, literally smelling the roses, avoiding my builder, my son, my daughter-in-law, and my life, when a double stroller bearing two fat pink babies, one asleep and one awake and looking pretty grumpy, was wheeled past me.

The grumpy baby — who had a dissatisfied countenance and small dark eyes — struck me as bearing more than a passing resemblance to my mothball grandmother. Like my grandmother, it could have a pretty face if it put its mind to it, if it released itself, opened itself up, but it didn't. It chose grumpiness.

'Florence?' the woman pushing the stroller asked. When I took my eyes off the contents of the stroller, I saw it was Marguerite, the tea-leaf reader.

'What a lovely surprise,' she said. 'Do you mind if I sit

down?' Before I could answer, she settled the babies in the shade of the London plane tree beside the seat and plonked herself down next to me.

'I was thinking about you yesterday,' she said. 'I walked the girls past your old shop and it reminded me of what a lovely place it used to be to visit. I hardly bother to go in now you're not there. There's no tea, for a start, but there's also too much French furniture — the place is full of it. You can't swing a cat without hitting something from Louis XV. I'm more of a Scandinavian girl myself, when it comes to furniture. Danish especially.' She stopped, as though embarrassed at talking so much, which she had been, and looked over at the babies. That was when I noticed how tired she looked, how her beautiful skin was almost grey, her white Capri pants and cashmere top were uncustomarily wrinkled, her pink coat was marked with something orange and slightly lumpy on the lapel.

'How old are they now?' I asked her as the wakeful, grumpy one started a half-hearted mewling.

'Eleven months on Thursday,' she replied, without the enthusiasm new mothers usually employed. 'I'm sorry,' she said, registering how she sounded. 'I'm just having one of those days.'

'Is it the babies?' I asked, knowing full well it would be. I loved babies but even the jolly good ones were hard work. 'They're such a handful, aren't they? And no one ever tells you that. Or if they do, you never believe them because you think yours will be different. And you've got two. It must be exhausting.'

'It is,' Marguerite said, not without some relief at being able to admit it. 'We had a nanny for a while but she left and I thought I could do it but on days like today I really miss my real job. I don't have enough adult company. I think that's the trouble. I talk nonsense to these two all day long and then when Tim comes home from work I'm too tired to talk sense. I used to have opinions on all sorts of things: elections in foreign countries, complicated tax laws, human rights in China. Now . . . I'm lucky if I can rustle up a preference between mashed bananas and apple purée.'

I wasn't sure I'd ever had an opinion on complicated tax laws but I did remember that frustration at not being able to choose between mashed bananas and apple purée. It was a symbol of having your own brain turn to mush, I suspected, after bringing a child into the world. I didn't know why that happened. I didn't know why anything happened. I was the wrong person for someone having a bad day to be talking to, I imagined. I was having a bad day myself. A bad month. A bad life.

'I started turning my house into a tearoom,' I told Marguerite, apropos of nothing, as her baby's mewling increased in volume.

'You did? How wonderful!' Her face lit up and for a moment her weariness disappeared, restoring the delicate beauty I remembered. 'I've thought about dropping by to see you but I'm not entirely a dropping-by sort of a person. It's a hard habit to pick up if you've never developed it in the past. Like smoking, I imagine. When will it be opening? The tearoom? Then I'll have the perfect excuse to come and visit.'

'Oh, I *started* turning it into a tearoom,' I explained, wishing I had never opened my mouth, realising that apropros of nothing was a stupid reason to say something, 'but I didn't finish. I ran out of . . . well, there are too many other things going on and there was all this rot in the basement and I couldn't quite . . . Anyway, I laid the builder off, and the plumber, although that didn't really have quite as much of an impact as you'd imagine.'

The baby's mewling turned into a full blown roar, which made Marguerite look a hundred years old again, so while she slumped there looking beaten half to death, I plucked the grumpy creature out of the stroller and put her over my shoulder, patting her cute little Tommy Hilfiger-clad back. The roar got louder for a brief moment, but soon turned back into a mewl, which then retreated into a snuffle.

Marguerite smiled gratefully. 'Thank you,' she said. 'I needed that. This.'

I jiggled her daughter against my neck. 'Me too,' I said as a memory flew into my mind from the depths of Monty's babyhood. Me sitting in Holland Park, jiggling his pram and weeping for so long a plain-clothes policeman emerged from the undergrowth and asked me if I was all right at which point I was shamed into going home.

Maybe loneliness wasn't as new to me as I thought it was.

'I just remembered a bad day I had when Monty was about this age,' I told her. 'Which is funny, because if anyone ever asked me if I'd had one I would have said no.'

'Frankly, I would feel a lot better if everyone remembered a lot more of them,' Marguerite sighed. 'I feel like they're only happening to me.'

'Yes, but isn't it comforting to know that years from now you will have forgotten the bad days?' I asked her. 'That they will have faded away and you'll only recall the good ones?'

She considered this. 'I suppose that's why people have more than one child. I had been wondering about that although I won't be in any hurry myself. And anyway, I have two already.'

'I could only ever have one,' I said, 'and I was apparently lucky to even get him.'

'Oh, I am sorry, Florence,' Marguerite was mortified, 'I

must sound terrible. I don't mean to whine or be insensitive, it's just that, well, I don't know what it is.'

I shifted her sleeping baby on to my other shoulder. 'Don't apologise,' I insisted. 'I'm not sure I could have coped with more than one, if the truth be told.' I had never admitted that to anyone. But Harry had been busy lawyering when Monty was a baby and even though it was what I wanted, I had been on my own a lot of the time and it had been hard. 'And I loved Monty so much I couldn't imagine having any love left to give to a brother or sister.'

'I worried about that too,' Marguerite said, 'with having twins. I wondered if they would only each get loved half as much as single children but I think actually love expands to cater for the crowd, if you know what I mean.'

'Or shrinks,' I suggested, which seemed a sad prospect.

'I'm not sure about that,' Marguerite argued gently (it seemed she still did have opinions), 'because you don't stop loving someone if they go away, do you? The amount of love you have for them is still the same, it's just that they're not there to get it. And if someone new comes along, the love for the one who's gone away doesn't get transferred to the new one, it's a whole lot of new love. Oh shit, what am I talking about? You can tell I don't get out much!'

Actually, I thought it was rather lovely, just sitting there in the watery sunshine chatting like two ordinary friends and I told her so.

'It would be jolly nice if we could have a cup of tea and some of your homemade brandy snaps while we were at it though,' Marguerite said. 'Such a shame about your tearoom, Florence. I really thought you were on to something with that but . . . Actually, run that past me again. You started it, then you stopped it, but that didn't have much impact, is that what you said?'

I nodded and kissed the warm sweet hollow at the back of her baby's neck. 'No impact at all as it turns out. I laid off Will, the builder, when I ran out of money and well, inclination, really, but he sort of didn't listen to me so he's still more or less working on it.'

'How peculiar,' Marguerite said. I couldn't have agreed with her more. 'So, apart from you saying that you're no longer doing it, it is still actually happening?'

'Well, yes, I suppose it is.' I hadn't thought of it like that but she was right.

'So, given that, when do you think it might be open for business?'

'Well, it won't be,' I insisted. 'Because I'm not doing it.'

'But if you were?' she insisted right back. 'If it was?'

'If it was I suppose it would be about a month away.' Actually, I didn't have a clue. I would have to buy a kitchen and tables and chairs and I wasn't sure how long that took or where you got those things and anyway I wasn't going to do it. Will would know, but I could hardly ask him, what with him being fired and me not going ahead with it and his not wanting to waste a moment of precious life and everything.

'I hope you'll let us sad new mothers bring our babies to your tearoom,' Marguerite said. 'Not that I know any other sad new mothers but if you let them come there, then at least I could meet some.'

'Well, I won't because it's not happening,' I told her again. 'There will be no tearoom for the sad new mothers to come to.'

'But if there was?'

'There won't be.'

'Oh, I know, but if there was?'

She was persistent, I had to give her that.

'If there was a tearoom at my house which is no longer going to be the case because I'm not doing it, then yes, I would love sad new mothers to bring their babies and meet each other,' I finally agreed. It was quite a strange conversation when I thought about it afterwards.

We chatted for a while about other things then, about her daughters, my son, Harry — whose departure she seemed to know about already — the possibility of the Formosa Street post office closing down, the weather: normal everyday woman-to-woman canal-side chit-chat.

'Florence, I can't tell you how much you have made my day,' she said, when eventually she stood to leave. She took her baby girl from my shoulder, which was just as well as I had cramp in my arm, and put her back, fast asleep, in the stroller. 'I was having such ridiculously dark thoughts this morning and you just swept them all away. I can't thank you enough, really I can't.'

'Don't be silly,' I said. 'I didn't do anything. And by the way,' I added as an afterthought, 'I would love it if you'd drop by to see me at home next time you thought of it.' I was pretty sure I wasn't a dropping-by person either but I was a Marguerite person.

'Who knows?' Marguerite smiled. 'Maybe so many people will start dropping by your house for a slice of cake and some company that you'll find yourself running a tearoom without even meaning to.'

The truth was, she had made my day too. Despite everything we hadn't talked about, that she didn't know and that I hugged close to me like an old vest, the weight of my problems felt lighter than it had in a long, long time.

I was in such a good frame of mind after talking to her that I walked to Tesco and bought vast amounts of expensive chocolate and Dutch cocoa powder for my favourite brownie recipe but ended up giving half of it to Whiffy O'Farrell when I passed him trolling through the Formosa Street skip on my way home.

'I miss our cups of tea,' I told him, 'at the antique shop, remember?'

He gave me the loveliest smile, which I took to mean yes he did remember and that he too missed our cups of tea, but then he bit into one of the chocolate bars and ate it, wrapper and all, which somewhat shook my confidence in his judgement.

He nodded a very polite goodbye, however, and I continued on my way.

At home, Will and Stan had obviously made progress with the dry rot because they were hauling the scaffolding out of the hole and stacking it out the front. I had developed quite a clever policy of not discussing the building project with them by then. It was as though they were working on a neighbour's house, not my own. I tended to lift my eyebrows in mild interest as I passed but did not engage any further.

'We can patch the floorboards and have the kitchen plumbed by this time next week,' Will told me as I slipped through what used to be my hallway. The late sun was streaming in through the tall windows and I had to admit, it would be a jolly nice place to sit and flick through magazines with a good cup of tea and a brandy snap.

I smiled at him and kept going. I'd thought he might have been wary of me since my strange behaviour at Claridge's, but he had just been his usual concerned self as if nothing odd was happening between us at all. I kept catching him looking at me in that peculiar way of his, that knowing sort of way, and he didn't even have the decency to look away and pretend he was doing something else. He just smiled in a slightly guilty fashion and went about whatever he was doing. It bugged me though, that knowing look, because there were very few things of which I could be sure in my life at that point, but one was that Will didn't know me. Not at all. He might think he did, but he didn't. No one did.

When I got up to the kitchen, my mouth watering at the mere thought of my brownie, Crystal was there, mumbling quietly into the phone, but as I passed she raised the volume.

'She's just walked in, I'll pass you right over,' she said, and before I could fully register what was happening she had thrust the receiver into my hands.

It was Young Nick, of course.

'Florence, are you there?' he asked. 'Why haven't you answered any of my calls? Or letters? I've been desperately trying to get in touch with you. We need to talk about your options, to work out what to do next. This isn't something you can sweep under the carpet, I'm afraid. I'm terribly worried about you.'

'I'm so sorry,' I said, trying to keep my voice light and friendly even though what I really wanted to do was shout at him to fuck off and leave me alone and then strangle Crystal with the phone cord until her eyeballs popped out and her nose exploded. She stood just out of arm's reach, her nose looking small and neat, her eyeballs tidily in their sockets, not even pretending she wasn't listening. 'I've been run off my feet with work,' I said gaily, 'and my sister's been very ill.'

'With work?' Nick asked. 'So you went back to the antiques business? You sorted things out with your partner?'

Bugger! I'd completely forgotten I'd told him all about that. 'No, no, another sort of work. Another business,' I said rather lamely, blushing under Crystal's scrutiny.

'Well, just tell them they'll have to wait,' I heard Nick telling someone in the background at his end. 'I don't care. Get a bucket!' I felt a droplet of remorse, then, at causing trouble. But it dried up almost instantly when he turned his attention back to me. 'You just can't ignore this,' he said. 'This is very serious, Florence. We could be talking about your whole life.'

'Yes, I'm well aware of that,' I said, opening the pantry door and stepping into it, to avoid Crystal's unwavering gaze.

'But are you aware that we could also be talking about nothing more than the equivalent of having a wart removed? The danger lies in not finding out, Florence. With the not knowing. You need a CT scan and a consultation with a surgeon. It's the crucial next step. There's just no way around it. You really must deal with this.'

'Why thank you,' I said as evenly as I could manage considering I'd just noticed a whole lot of pongy Asian herbs in the pantry that I certainly hadn't put there. 'I'll take that on board and get back to you, shall I?'

This might assuage my nosy daughter-in-law, I thought. Although when I looked over my shoulder, she had not budged from her watchful position. Nor did she appear particularly assuaged.

'Have you told anybody?' Nick persisted. 'Are you getting any support? You can't do this on your own, Florence. No one can.'

'Oh, that won't be necessary,' I said, a little too quickly perhaps, and then threw in a forced laugh for good measure. 'It's fine just the way it is, thank you so much.'

'There's only one thing you can be sure of,' Nick said, and his voice dropped even lower, became yet more grim, 'and that is that it's not fine just the way it is. Whether what you have is rust or forest fire, Florence, you deny its existence at your peril. At Monty's peril. Do you understand that? I wouldn't be doing my job if I didn't spell it out for you this clearly.

And when I say Monty's peril, I don't just mean that if it's not like removing a wart, if it is more serious, that he might lose his mother. I mean you may have a genetic predisposition to colon cancer. You're young and healthy but something is not right, so it could be a flaw in your genes. And if that's the case, it could be a flaw in Monty's genes too. He might be predisposed as well, Florence. Does that make a difference to you? Monty needs to be tested too. Do you understand?'

My heart was thumping abnormally low in my body. It felt like it was in my stomach.

'Thank you so much for calling,' I said as brightly as I could manage, although my bravado felt like it was being mulched in the kitchen disposal unit. 'I have to go now. I'll speak to you soon. Goodbye.'

I stepped out of the pantry and carefully placed the phone down in the cradle and stood there, staring at the calendar that I noticed for the first time in three months was three months out of date, trying not to shake. Monty? Cancer? I hadn't thought of that at all. If Monty had cancer it would be the end of me, if I wasn't ended already. He could die. Is that what Young Nick meant? Or that he could pass it on to his children and they could die and Crystal had already had one baby die and how terrible would that be if it happened to her again? That would be the most terrible thing of all. And for it to happen to Monty a first time, for his baby to die, it was almost more than I could bear. I was bearing so much already.

I felt the warmth of my daughter-in-law's small tanned hand on my arm then. I wanted to swat it away, to cast her aside, but I couldn't. I was frozen to the spot. 'Florence?' she said. 'What is it? What's the matter?'

'There's asafoetida in my cupboard,' I said. 'And tamarind paste.'

'Florence, you're pale as a ghost! And you're trembling. Please come and sit down.'

'And pomegranate syrup. What do I want with pomegranate syrup?'

'Florence, I think you should . . .'

'How dare you!' I was suddenly so full of uncontrollable rage I could not help but unleash it on her. Poor Crystal. Always there when my fury was getting away on me. I reeled around to face her, flinging her hand off my arm, backing away from her as though she were toxic waste. 'How dare you put these peculiar foul-smelling things in my pantry without telling me first,' I shouted. 'How dare you just march in here with all this foreign bloody muck and throw it about the place, just leave it everywhere, on the shelves, in the pantry, in the kitchen, in my house, *in my house*! Without any permission, without any warning, without checking with me first, without me having asked for any of it, without so much as a by-your-bloody-leave! It's unconscionable! It's bloody criminal! It's so incredibly unfair, I mean how dare you? How, how, how . . .' I don't know when I had started to cry but deep wrenching sobs appeared out of nowhere and, mixed with this awful uncontrollable anger, temporarily removed my ability to breathe.

She should have slapped me, or pushed me out the window, or chopped me into tiny bits and fed me to the dog as I stood there quivering and swallowing great gulps of air, but she didn't.

She steered me to a chair, pushed me gently down into it, got me a glass of water, and then said: 'I don't think this is about pomegranate syrup.'

She sat down next to me, so close I could all but feel her even breath on my hot cheek. 'What's happening, Florence?'

I willed myself not to say a word, to keep quiet, to hold my horrible secret to myself but it was too strong for me. Suddenly, my own thought bubble popped and the terror I felt at what lurked within me burst out into the realm of great gasped half-suffocated spoken-out-loud words.

'I have colon cancer,' I sobbed. 'Bloody bollocky colon cancer. And if I die, no one will care. No one will even notice. It could kill me, it could be killing me right now, as I speak, and it could kill Monty too if I have faulty genes, and I should have done something about it weeks ago when I first found out but I was so scared and then there was Poppy and Will and the rot and I don't want to turn into one of those tragic people you see on the TV, all great big bald head and sad eyes and skinny arms and trying to raise money to go to some far-flung corner of the earth for wheatgerm therapy or . . .'

I was weeping so hard by then my stomach muscles had started to spasm, and I collapsed on the table, my head on my arms, and surrendered to my tears.

Which was when I felt Crystal stroking my hair. This woman I hardly knew and to whom I had been nothing but evil ever since meeting her, sat next to me while I wept, and stroked my hair.

Why this made me even more sad, I don't know. Well, actually, I worked it out. I felt vulnerable. Accepting sympathy means you've dropped any pretence of not needing it and that leaves you raw. Plus I knew that there was no going back from this. It was out. My situation was out. And even if I could contain it as a tiny leak for a while, it would eventually become a raging torrent, claiming the few people I knew and loved just as it was claiming me.

The hair stroking helped, mind you. I know from experience with Monty that it's quite hard to keep that sort of thing up after the first few minutes — it's hard on the wrist — but Crystal never wavered at all.

Finally, I got the sobs under control and eventually the tears. Then she got up to make me a cup of lemon verbena tea. She was very good at being quiet. At waiting. I really liked that about her, actually.

'So, tell me everything,' she said. 'And maybe I can help you figure out what to do next.'

She was the last person in the world I would have imagined baring my soul to but as the secrets leached out of me I began to realise that in a way she was perfect. I didn't have to worry about my relationship with her, for a start, because up until then we hadn't really had one. Or not a meaningful one at any rate. I wasn't in love with her, I wasn't her mother, she hadn't married me then cheated on me with a man, she hadn't given birth to me, she wasn't suicidal. She was probably the person with the least investment in my existence in the whole wide world, other than to not want Monty to bear unnecessary pain on my account, which was something we had in common.

Plus despite her alternative leanings, it turned out Crystal was not particularly psycho-babbly or airy-fairy or tree-huggy, as one might have expected.

In fact, the first thing she did was write a list. She said writing lists helped calm her down when she was stressed about anything because it put problems in order. You could look at a list of things and see how you could tackle each one separately without feeling sick about it, she said. Whereas if they all just stayed jumbled in your mind in one great big sticky ball you never got to consider them individually.

She actually spoke a lot of sense for someone with toe rings and a Chinese tattoo.

And she was enormously efficient, in a secretarial sort

of way, which she said was the result of having been a bank manager in her previous life! A bank manager? Within an hour she had secured an appointment with one of London's top surgeons at his Harley Street clinic the following day. How did these people get bookings so easily? I'm sure I couldn't if I tried — which I supposed I generally didn't.

She offered to come with me and I accepted partly because I was in shock at learning she had once been a bank manager, partly because I had expected her to recommend alternative treatments involving odd herbs and strangely spelt clinics in Switzerland not a Harley Street consultant, and partly because I wanted to keep her on my side so that she wouldn't tell Monty.

'You're going to have to tell him eventually,' she said. 'And Archie and Beth and Poppy and Harry, too, for that matter. They can help you, Florence. We can all help you.'

'But they all have their own problems right now,' I argued. 'And I can't bear to make matters worse.'

'You might make matters better, had you thought about that? You're putting a lot of pressure on yourself trying to keep everyone else happy and it's not necessarily the best thing. Try having a little faith in your family.'

'Can we just try to get through the next couple of days?' I begged her. 'Nick says it might be no big deal, just a little deal, a wart-sized deal. And then I would have worried them all for nothing.'

She agreed, as I knew she would. I wasn't quite ready to let go of my one great big sticky ball.

CRYSTAL

♥ ♥ ♥

Nobody expects me to be practical — maybe because I'm small and blonde — but I am and I always have been.

When Florence told me about her diagnosis the best thing I could think of was to write a list of all the things we needed to do and organise them in order of priority.

It took me one minute on Google and two phone calls to get an appointment with London's most highly recommended colorectal surgeon. You have to love the internet, don't you? His secretary told me there wasn't a chance at first but then she spoke to the consultant himself and came back saying that it appeared they would be able to slot us in after all. I supposed they thought Florence's case was that urgent.

Next, I rang Nick March back to get him to fax a referral over to the surgeon's office. Then I made an appointment for a CT scan the following day, and I changed the time for a job interview I had so I could go with Florence to her appointment. After that I went to buy flowers.

It was all on the list.

You can laugh at lists — and the people who make them — but let me tell you this: some days, when everything else feels totally beyond your control, a few ticks on a piece of paper is about as good as it gets.

CHAPTER TWENTY-ONE

When I woke the next morning I knew my life was about to change. Again. After all, my before and after worlds had collided when I spilled the beans to Crystal and it was inevitable that chain reactions would follow. The first of which was starting with my visit to the rooms of Mr Worthington, Harley Street, at eleven o'clock.

I pushed the unpleasant prospect of another 'internal examination' from my mind with a shiver and cuddled down beneath my quilt, my thoughts turning instead, without me directing them there, to Will. With all I have on my mind, I asked myself, why think of him? Then it occurred to me that I had just watched the bedside clock tick past seven-thirty and I had not heard him let himself in the front door.

Good, I thought, maybe he had finally got the message, given up, gone away. I turned over and curled into a ball. It's just that I had become used to the sound of him letting himself in. It seemed odd for it to be seven-thirty-five and not to have heard it.

I still hadn't heard it by seven-forty-five, nor seven-forty-seven, nor seven-forty-eight. By the time I went downstairs to make my breakfast, it was past eight and I was feeling irritable in the way you do if your socks don't match or your knickers are scratchy. These are not big problems but they can still ruin your day.

Since when had Will become someone I expected to be anywhere at any particular time anyway, I asked myself as I spread honey and apricot jam on a muffin? Mostly I expected him not to be there and he was. Strangely, I had not been as irritated by that as I was currently by finding him absent, as per my wishes. I wasn't entirely sure what that was about.

After breakfast I started to reorganise the pantry alphabetically but ran out of steam by B for baking soda because the shapes weren't working together. I was considering whether colour coding would cause the same problem when there was a timid knock at the front door.

It wasn't going to be Will, because he had a key. Crystal had gone out and was meeting me at Harley Street so it wasn't going to be her either. She had a key anyway, as did Monty, who was off somewhere doing his own thing and not telling me anything about it.

The timid knock repeated itself so I returned the almonds, anchovies and asparagus to their previous positions and went downstairs to see who it was.

Poppy stood on my doorstep, a red beret on top of her orange curls and a suitcase in one hand.

I was so surprised to see her I almost didn't spend a split second scanning the street to see if Will's truck was approaching, which it wasn't.

'Oh, Effie!' Poppy cried, throwing herself at me. 'Can you believe it? It's me! I'm here! It's so good to see you, how utterly divine! I hope you don't mind me coming.'

Of course I didn't mind, but I was astounded. She hated the city usually and I couldn't remember the last time she'd come on her own. Plus, the timing wasn't brilliant. I had Mr Worthington, after all, which I wasn't ready to explain just yet so would have to leave her on her own and lie about where I was going or she would want to come too.

She must have seen the worry on my face. 'Oh, I should have rung,' she wailed. 'I got the first train. Beth said I should have rung but I wanted it to be a surprise.'

I pulled her inside and shut the door.

'Don't be silly, it's fine. It's wonderful. I love surprises. It's just I didn't expect to see you. And — you look so good, Poppy.' She did. Like a different person from the one I had left behind swaddled in a cashmere blanket near the vegie patch at Tannington Hall.

'I've had the most wonderful idea and I wanted to come and tell you about it in person,' she said, pulling off her beret, shaking her curls. She wore long sleeves to cover the scars on her wrists but otherwise she looked the picture of health.

'Oh, look at all this lovely space,' she cried, looking around the abandoned building site that was my home's ground floor, not even noticing the gaping hole in the floor or the scaffolding stacked up or the dust or the lack of builder and plumber. 'And the beautiful light! Oh, it's gorgeous! It's perfect!'

She twirled around from the office side to the TV room side and it was such a pleasure to see her back to being her over-the-top happy little self that the sick feeling I had about my own personal lack of Will in my life drained momentarily away.

'You're pretty gorgeous yourself, Poppy,' I told her, kicking myself for not having the slightest vestige of gluten-free confection in the house. 'You've got some life back in your face.'

She twirled back over to me, took my hand and beamed. 'I feel good. I feel, well, maybe not gorgeous,' she said, 'but so much better and it's because of you.'

'Because of me?' I had spoken to her on the phone every few days and sent a couple of funny cards but other than that I thought I'd been too preoccupied to be much help.

'Yes!' She was practically quivering with excitement. 'Because of what you said to me in the garden at home, about needing to be out in the world not hidden away at home and then I thought of your rot and Daddy's cheque and you having something to look forward to and I knew then that was what I was missing in my life. Something to look forward to. Because the thing I had been most looking forward to never happened to me and that's what was getting on top of me. So I decided I needed another something to look forward to, one that could happen, and then it hit me and it was so obvious, I couldn't imagine why none of us had thought of it before.'

I had no idea what she was talking about but still, just looking at her dancing eyes and twittering hands and radiant face made me want her to have it.

'So are you going to tell me what it is?'

'Well, it's the same thing as you,' she said, with a sweet happy smile, as one arm swept around the vastness of my new over-sized open-plan venture-that-never-was-to-be.

'The tearoom! I want to come and help you run the tearoom.'

An engine roared outside and I used this as an excuse to look out the window to see if it was Will and to plot how I would handle the next few moments. I was in shock. This was a disaster.

'It was Archie's idea really,' Poppy continued, oblivious to my stalling tactic, 'because we were having one of his brainstorming afternoons where he was helping me workshop my skills and to be honest it was getting a bit depressing until we remembered last year at the village fair.'

'The village fair?' I echoed, my mind whirring, as I picked up Poppy's suitcase and headed upstairs.

'Yes, last year I helped on the bric-à-brac stall,' Poppy chirruped behind me, 'doing the change and suggesting things to people. Even Mrs Parsons, you know, the big bosomy lady who plays the Church of England organ, said I had done a wonderful job and she's the one who adds everything up at the end so she should know. So Archie said, "What about Effie's tearoom? Maybe you could do the change and the suggestions at Effie's tearoom?" And at first I thought that was the most ridiculous idea because I wouldn't know what to do. I'd be useless. I'd just get in everybody's way and drive them mad and I don't know the first thing about flour or icing sugar or any of that sort of thing.'

'Lemon verbena tea?' I asked, nodding encouragingly, hoping I didn't look as wretched as I felt. 'Crystal loves it.'

Poppy's eyes, which had been glistening already, moistened even more at this.

'You're getting on? Oh, how wonderful! I'm so proud of you, Eff. And anyway, then I thought, well you could be in the kitchen, doing the baking and making things with the flour and icing sugar, and I could be showing people to their tables and giving them menus and taking their money. I wouldn't ruin everything, I promise I wouldn't.'

'Of course you wouldn't ruin everything!' Why would she think that? Oh, shit! Could I just have one single day when life wasn't full of the most ridiculous complications? How could I tell her there was going to be no tearoom? How could I tell her the thing she had chosen to look forward to was as unlikely at this point as her little redheaded baby?

Another car backfired outside and I crossed to the kitchen window to have a look.

'Are you waiting for someone? Am I in the way?'

'Of course you're not! I'm delighted that you're here. But I do just have to dash out for a bit to a . . .' I tried to think of something Poppy really wouldn't want to do with me. 'To a cheese tasting, I'm afraid,' I told her. 'Twelve different sorts, cow, goat and sheep. But mainly cow,' I emphasised, in case goat and sheep weren't dairy. 'Sorry, didn't know you were coming when I arranged it.'

She grimaced. 'Oh well, I can't be much help in the cheese department, I'm afraid. But I could do a bit of gardening out the front while you're gone,' she suggested. 'It needs a bit of work before we open if we're going to put tables and chairs out there. I thought we could make a couple of sort of garden "rooms" so people could hide away a little bit. What do you think? Rose bushes, obviously, but maybe some tall cosmos and a bit of box hedging and something fragrant like jasmine or daphne?'

'Lovely,' I said. 'Garden away.'

I wasn't going to close her down now. I had Crystal to meet at Mr Worthington's offices. I'd get through that and then I would break Poppy's heart.

I walked to Harley Street: along Regent's Canal, cutting through the park, past the rose gardens, which were blooming in all their glory. The smell was almost hypnotic. For a fleeting moment, I toyed with sitting among the blooms and missing my appointment but as Crystal now knew my situation, I knew any avoidance tactics could only be temporary.

Nonetheless, 'I've got such a headache,' I told her when we met outside Mr Worthington's rooms. 'I wonder if we should come back another time?'

'There is no other time, we were lucky to get this appointment,' Crystal said, opening up her shoulder bag and rustling around inside it. 'I have some tiger balm in here,' she offered. 'Would that help? You can rub it on your temples and it will help calm you.'

I can't imagine what would have calmed me at that point. What with Will not turning up to do the renovations I didn't want and Poppy arriving to help me with the tearooms I wasn't going to have, I was a bundle of nerves. A bundle of nerves who mostly wanted to run away and hide under a rock and never come out again. But that would be at Monty's peril, I had to keep reminding myself.

Mr Worthington's waiting room was a pleasant, peaceful sort of a place but I couldn't keep my legs from jiggling or my hands from fidgeting. After three layers of tiger balm, my eyes were watering but nothing about me was calm.

When the receptionist finally called my name I nearly jumped out of my skin. Crystal stood to come with me, taking me by the elbow and heading me towards Mr Worthington's door.

'No, no!' I cried, panicked. I didn't want anyone talking about my innards in front of her. 'I'll be fine! You wait here. I'll tell you about it afterwards.'

'Actually,' the receptionist intervened, 'we recommend you take a friend in with you, dear. Sometimes it's good to have someone else listening to what Mr Worthington says in case you get confused.'

'He doesn't speak English?' I asked, dimly. It sounded like such an English name.

'No dear, it's more the shock. Sometimes it's hard to remember everything you've been told when you've had a bit of a shock.'

I found it hard to believe that I could be more shocked than I already had been in the past couple of months but while I was trying to work out how to protest further, Crystal steered me towards Mr Worthington's door and into his office — a room that looked so much like the library of a stately home that I almost expected an octogenarian butler to creak through the side door and offer me a sherry.

'It's all a bit *Brideshead Revisited*, isn't it?' I whispered to Crystal as the side door did indeed open. But instead of an elderly manservant, Mr Worthington emerged. He wasn't old and bent over and bearing a silver tray clinking with crystal. He was tall, particularly upright, in his forties I guessed, and dressed dapperly in dark grey, with similarly grey hair and a square jaw.

Crystal made a strange squeak upon seeing him and I guessed she too was expecting someone different but I didn't give it much more thought. I was too busy concentrating on him. He really was very good looking and had lovely warm, twinkly eyes.

'Florence,' he said holding out one of his large, clean hands in my direction. I shook it. It too was warm, which I wasn't sure was such a good thing for a surgeon, sweating on the instruments and all that, but it felt nice anyway. Stanley Morris's dear old mum would certainly approve.

'Google says you're the best person for colons,' I said, my fascination with his good looks waning as I remembered why I was there, My teeth, I realised, were on the brink of chattering.

This was it, the moment of truth. I was in a Harley Street

consulting room talking to a surgeon about my disease. On my own. Well, Crystal was there too, of course, but who was she anyway? And why was she sitting slightly behind me and not saying anything?

'I think Nick March sent you my test results,' I said, somewhat shakily. 'He says it's important to know if it's rust or forest fire — not so much for me, but I have a son . . .' I lost my composure at the thought of Monty.

'Of course,' Mr Worthington said. I thought he shot Crystal a funny look, but I was too busy trying to calm my pending hysterics to properly analyse it.

'Florence, I'm going to give you some advice now that Nick may have already given you but it will help you enormously in the times ahead,' he said in a very calm, authoritative voice, 'no matter what the outcome.'

Outcome? Of what? The advice?

He handed me a tissue, which I took, giving my nose a healthy blow. I turned to look at Crystal and to my surprise she seemed totally shaken. As though some terrible news had just been delivered to her.

'Only worry about what you absolutely know about,' Mr Worthington said to me, putting my mind back where it belonged. 'That's the key. Worrying about anything else is just a waste of time and emotion. I know that seems obvious but honestly, the more information you have, the less your imagination can run away with you so the secret is to find out as much as you can about what your particular problem is — where the cancer is, how it can be treated — and you'll be amazed at how this simplifies things. You no longer have to worry about the "what ifs".'

'But what if —' I started.

'Exactly,' he said. 'You know that feeling you have now?

That sort of overwhelming panic and dread and terror that life as you know it is never going to be the same ever again because it could be that or it could be this or it could be the next thing?'

I nodded. He'd hit the nail right on the head. That overwhelming panic and dread and terror was just part of my waking day now, like breathing.

'We're going to try to eliminate that feeling,' Mr Worthington continued, 'by finding out exactly what it is that we are dealing with and treating it.'

I liked it that he said 'we'. I felt less like just me.

'How will we do that?' I asked and I knew I sounded scared but I felt less so than I had even a moment before.

'I have to be honest with you,' he said, 'your histology shows that you have a very aggressive form of cancer.'

It felt like a punch. The air was sucked out of my lungs. I'd suspected it was bad. I'd known it was bad. And I was right.

'Your tumour was large and flat,' Mr Worthington continued, 'quite unusual for a colon cancer, which makes it a little less predictable. But on the plus side, and it's a big plus, it's been detected fairly early. In terms of finding out more, to eliminate the unknowns, we need to operate, Florence, there is no doubt about that. We need to do a resection, which is when we cut out the bit of colon that has the tumour in it and then we join the bits of colon on either side together again. The operation is relatively straightforward, the recovery period quite manageable, the outcome extremely positive.'

This seemed like so much information I couldn't process it all. The receptionist was right, the shock made it impossible to remember the words even as he said them.

'Surgery?' I asked him, amazed that my voice still worked, that I could control it. 'Couldn't I just have chemotherapy?' I didn't want to lose my hair, of course I didn't, but I didn't want someone making sushi out of my body parts either.

'I'm sorry, Florence, but there's absolutely no doubt that you need surgery. The only truly reliable way to get rid of cancer in the colon is to remove it. Anything else simply doesn't have the same results. It's the first and may in fact be the only step, depending on what we find out when we do further tests. I would do the surgery, which would take around three hours, you would be in hospital for a week, and your recovery at home would take about a month — although someone as young and fit as yourself could well find it a total doddle.'

A week in hospital? A month of recovery? A doddle? I fought to grasp that this was me we were talking about.

'And after this operation,' I hated these words, these horrible sick, old people's words, 'after the recovery, everything would be OK? I would be OK?'

'If the cancer has been contained in your colon, your chances of a full recovery are extremely good.'

If the cancer was contained in my colon, my chances of a full recovery were extremely good. Was that a yes?

'And if it's not contained?' It was Crystal who asked this. She didn't sound like herself. She was obviously as flabbergasted as I was.

'If the cancer has gone through the bowel wall and travelled, there will be traces of it in Florence's lymph nodes, some of which we will remove for testing when we are doing the resection,' Mr Worthington explained. 'Typically, if colon cancer moves it goes to the liver, which is closest, or sometimes the lungs. In either situation, I would most likely recommend more surgery, if appropriate, plus chemo and possibly radiotherapy. The outcome in these cases is not always as positive as the early detection scenario where the cancer is contained, but full recovery is still a possibility.'

So, he could make sushi with my innards *and* I could end up bald?

'Why has this happened to me?' I asked him. 'I've hardly ever been ill. I eat healthily, usually, and I'm fit, usually. What did I do wrong?'

'You most likely did nothing wrong,' he said, 'and you've every right to feel aggrieved. You're outside the statistics in almost every way so I can't answer why this has happened to you. There could be a genetic predisposition that makes you more susceptible to certain cancers and we can test that once we've done the surgery, which will also have an impact on Monty, obviously, even if it's just so he can get in the system in terms of surveillance or . . .'

'Monty?' Had he just mentioned Monty?

'If the genetic testing shows up any faults in your DNA this will be good for Monty, Florence, because he can be tested from now on and early detection is the only really reliable way to . . .'

'But you called him Monty,' I said.

'Of course,' Mr Worthington smiled, 'and if he and Crystal are going to have children then . . .'

'If Monty and Crystal have children?'

Mr Worthington looked at Crystal, clearly puzzled. 'Why, yes,' he said. 'I know it has been difficult for you but . . .'

'What's been difficult for me?' I turned to Crystal, puzzled myself. She was chewing her bottom lip, looking sicker than I was. 'What's going on here? Did you talk to him before I got here?'

Mr Worthington laughed. 'Well, of course, she's talked to me,' he said.

Then as I turned back to him, still totally bewildered, I

watched comprehension drop down over his face like a dance-hall curtain.

'Oh, fuck,' he breathed, leaning back in his chair and closing his eyes. 'Oh fuck, oh fuck, oh fuck.'

Now, I wasn't at all *au fait* with the medical protocol of the day but this seemed a mightily inappropriate response towards a patient discussing a life-threatening illness and its treatment.

Crystal then totally floored me by saying to him: 'I had no idea it was you. I didn't know your surname. I didn't know exactly what you did. And I didn't know you did it here.'

'Did what?' I asked again, dimly. 'Did what here?'

'I assumed you came to me on purpose,' Mr Worthington said to Crystal. 'Because you knew this was my field. It never occurred to me for a moment — it just seems so outrageously bloody awful, otherwise. Oh fuck, oh fuck, oh fuck.'

'Will someone please tell me what the hell is going on?' I demanded. 'What's all this "oh fucking" about?'

There was a hideous silence, while the other two stared at each other with ill-disguised horror.

'I'm so sorry, Florence,' Crystal finally said, 'but this is Charles.'

'Charles?' I repeated dimly. Was I supposed to know what that meant? I only knew of one other Charles, or 'Charles' as I called him. And he was a something or other at the Whittington and I hadn't even met him nor did I want to.

Oh, please, no.

'*That* Charles?' Now I was in shock. '*Harry's* Charles?' No! Where was the dog, the green suit, the awful orange hair? It simply couldn't be Charles, Harry's Charles. It just simply could not be. For many reasons. Too many.

'Please tell me,' I implored him. 'Please, please, please tell me that I haven't been sitting here discussing my colo-rectum with my gay ex-husband's new boyfriend.'

There was another dreadful silence into which mushroomed the certitude that this was exactly what we had been doing.

'Oh fuck,' I said myself. Just when you think your life could not possibly get any worse, it does. Enormously.

I wasn't sure what the standard procedure was for dealing with this kind of colossal cock-up but as I reeled with the implications of what had just gone on, Charles leaned forward, pressed a buzzer on his desk and said into whatever contraption it was: 'So sorry to bother you, Evelyn, but do you think we could have tea for three in here? The Lady Grey, if you wouldn't mind, leaf of course. And some of those lemon biscuits from Fortnum's, not the Duchy of Cornwall ones but the other ones. Thank you, Evelyn, much appreciated.'

I knew from made-for-TV movies that alcoholics usually had to hit rock bottom before they could give up the booze and start to turn their lives around. But I'd often wondered how they knew where rock bottom was when everything before rock bottom could also have been rock bottom or at least felt like it at the time.

And although I had made a hash of being an alcoholic, I wouldn't be an alcoholic's elbow as Rose would have said, but sitting there in Charles's office I nonetheless recognised the skull-cracking thump of rock bottom being hit.

When you get there, it's obvious.

I probably could have sunk further. It was humanly possible. I could have abused the man who stole my husband and stormed out of his office. I could have gone home, packed my bags and run away to a dingy bedsit in Brighton. I could have lived out my days all alone eating greasy fish and chips and watching telly and talking to no one.

But here was the thing. In storming out of the office, I would alert Crystal and Charles to my departure. In going home to pack my bags I would alert Poppy who would tell my parents. Plus I also ran the risk of running into Monty who would find out anyway via Crystal, as would Harry via any of the three of them.

And then there was Will.

He would surely notice if I didn't turn up to ignore his hole and remind him that his services weren't needed. And even if he never came back to the house, Stanley probably would and he would hear from Crystal or Monty or Poppy and tell Will I'd run away to Brighton and Will might just come and fetch me, so that was that. My chances of living out a lonely life eating greasy fish and chips and watching telly were already shot.

I had an aggressive form of cancer that required immediate treatment; I had a suicidal sister who believed her only chance at happiness was to work in the tearoom I was no longer opening; I had just spilled my guts — literally — to the chap who was shagging my husband.

I should have felt like jumping out the nearest window but I didn't. Something was nagging at me and stopping me from spiralling further downward, below rock bottom. Something was happening to me. Something had changed. Something was pointing me in a different direction.

Maybe it was the realisation, the sudden urgent utter conviction that Crystal, Monty, Harry, Poppy, Mum, Dad, Stanley, and Will would all fight to keep me from my lonely bedsit in Brighton.

Maybe it was that Charles, previously known as 'Charles', had just coped with excruciating embarrassment by producing a pot of Lady Grey, leaf of course, and lemon biscuits, for heaven's sake.

The truth was that I'd never felt more like a cup of tea and a biscuit in all my life.

And the other truth was that I was no longer alone.

CHARLES

♥ ♥ ♥

At first, I just wanted the floor to open up and swallow me whole then spit me out in Mexico or China or somewhere far, far away where no one would ever find me no matter how hard they looked.

Really, you could not dream up such a dreadful coincidence. But as Florence herself pointed out later, it really wasn't such a coincidence at all when you thought about it. There was she, in London, being in need of a specialised surgeon, and there was I, in London, being one. I had assumed Crystal knew I had rooms in Harley Street as well as being a consultant at the Whittington but why would she? I'd never thought to spell it out.

Had I, no doubt we could have avoided the whole sorry disaster altogether.

Although of course it wasn't a disaster, in the end. There was a moment, after it became clear to her who I was, when if she'd had a gun I think she would have pulled it out and shot me. And who could have blamed her? As it was, she did not appear to be armed. She just sat there looking like she really wished she was, during which all I could think to do was to ask Evelyn to bring in some tea.

There's no problem can't be solved by a cup of tea, my grandmother always used to say, and while I didn't particularly think of this when I first asked for it, I thought it afterwards because no sooner had I taken my finger off the intercom button than Florence started to laugh.

She's a very attractive woman anyway, but when she laughs she's quite beautiful. I could see then what Harry had seen in her, why it must have been so hard for him to leave, despite the circumstances. Without seeing her in the flesh I hadn't truly appreciated his position. I'd just thought, if your heart's not in it, get out, old man. But having her sitting there, laughing, after such a dreadful thing had just happened, I fell in love with her a little myself. She was quite captivating.

And then Crystal, poor Crystal, whom I really should have noticed had got such a fright to begin with, also started to laugh. An Australian laugh is never quite as catchy as an English one, of course, but hers was pretty infectious all the same. Despite the fact that mortification still clung to my own innards in spasms, I too joined in the laughter.

I laughed till Florence cried, and then Crystal cried too, and then Evelyn brought in the tea. She's seen plenty of tears before so wasn't at all fazed.

'It just can't keep getting worse,' Florence said as I poured for her. 'It just can't. Not everything. Something has to start getting better.'

'It will,' I told her and that wasn't an empty promise. I didn't know all there was to know at that stage about her illness but I knew about her life. And just having Crystal there with her in my office to discuss her treatment was the beginning of the something getting better. 'I can help you,' I said.

And she thanked me. Very sweetly, she thanked me. Then told me her own lemon biscuits were better than the Duchy of Cornwall and the other ones put together.

CHAPTER TWENTY-TWO

When my taxi pulled up outside the house Will's truck was in my driveway and for the first time since I had met him I allowed whatever was stirring inside me to rise to the top.

Anticipation was the cherry on my cupcake in this particular instance.

Anticipation. It was a sensation that had been missing in my world in recent times and allowing it to envelop me felt like being rolled in chocolate and sprinkled with Cadbury Flake.

I ran up the outside stairs of the house and flung open the door to find Will mid-conversation with Poppy, who still had her gardening gloves on. I checked her face to see if he'd mentioned I had put a halt to the tearoom, at which point I noticed there were bits of what was obviously a semi-industrial kitchen stacked in the far corner by the back door.

'Don't be cross,' Will said, 'but I got it for a song. A mate of Sid's has just closed down his gastro pub in Mile End and he was virtually giving this away but I had to collect it this morning so —'

'It'll be perfect, don't you think?' Poppy interrupted, clasping her hands excitedly in front of her. 'I was just telling Will about the plan, the me-helping-you plan.'

Will and I looked at each other. He was silently pleading with me, I could tell, to go ahead, to do it, and I was silently pleading the exact same thing.

'Is something wrong?' Poppy asked.

'No,' Will and I answered simultaneously.

Then more silence. Not the dread-laden, are-you-really-my-husband's-boyfriend sort of silence that I had so recently experienced but an electric anticipatory could-you-really-be-my-own-boyfriend sort of silence, which is not really a silence at all. Well, you can't hear anything, but you can feel it.

'Oh my God,' Poppy said, her jaw dropping open as she looked from me to him and back again. 'You two!'

I had so much to say it had all got stuck in my chest then dropped to my hands, which hung heavy and motionless at my sides. I couldn't remember what I usually did with them.

Even Will seemed incapable of speaking, of moving, his eyes still just searching mine.

'I am just going to go outside and finish pruning the . . . erm, I'll find something to prune,' Poppy said and headed for the door. 'Oh, my God,' she mouthed at me behind his back before she disappeared. 'Oh, my God!'

We stood there on opposite sides of the room for I don't know how long. Probably not long at all but it felt like forever. I was almost scared to breathe. I was almost scared to do anything. Almost.

'Whatever you have to tell me, it's OK,' Will finally said.

'Honestly. It's OK.'

And just like that, I wasn't scared any more.

'I believe you,' I told him. Then we walked towards each other and he took me in his arms. That was it. He just took me in his arms. I nestled there, against his chest, breathing him in, feeling his heart beating against my shoulder, smelling him, and if I had died right then and there, I truly believe I would have died happy.

This is what it's about, I thought. This is what life is about. And it could all end in a minute, or tomorrow, or next week, or next year, but it wasn't ended just yet and it felt utterly glorious.

'I have cancer,' I said into the softness of his shirt and he clutched me even tighter then, rocked me gently from side to side. 'It's in my bowel, or my colon, or whatever it's called, and it's very unsexy and it might be in other places too but I'm not sure. Although I think I'm going to die, which is why I didn't want to open the tearoom and I didn't want anything to happen between us because if this kills me you'll be left all on your own and I just couldn't bear that.'

He folded me tighter still into his body.

'I knew there was something going on,' he said. 'I thought there might be someone else.'

'But isn't this worse?' I asked, my eyes scrunched closed against the possibility. 'Isn't this much, much worse? I might die, Will.'

He pulled back then, but only enough to take me by my shoulders and look me in the eyes again.

'But you might not,' he said.

'But I might,' I said again.

'Florence, you might *not*. And anyway, if we only have one hour together it will still be the best hour of my life.'

'Are you telling me you only have an hour?' I asked him. You don't go from being glass-half-empty to glass-half-full in an instant, after all.

'I'm telling you I have forever,' Will answered. 'We both do. I will look after you forever, Florence, no matter how long that is. In sickness and in health, I will look after you. I don't care if you live till the end of next week or till you're a hundred.'

'I'm very close to a hundred now,' I said. 'But I've decided that doesn't matter.'

I remembered my dream then, the one where Will had told me that he loved me, that he would always be there for me, that with him beside me I had nothing to fear and never would ever again.

So I surrendered, that moment: I surrendered to whatever life had in store for me. I'd survived on my own two feet without a job, without a husband, without my son, without a compliant digestive system. I knew I could do it, I knew I could survive, but I also knew now that there was more to life, more to living, than just surviving.

Maybe rotten things did happen in threes. Or maybe they happened in sixes. But do you know what I discovered that day? You don't have to count them.

Will moved in more or less straight away. Time was precious, after all. And in the circumstances, once everyone knew what the circumstances were, everyone who knew and loved me agreed it was the best possible outcome.

I had my surgery — Charles did indeed do the honours — and it went exceedingly well. I recovered in less than four weeks. I took each day after that as it came.

One of the best days was about five months later when we opened Rose's to the public. It took longer to buy tables and chairs and cake forks and napkins than I had ever imagined and it took a while to fully regain my strength but everyone pitched in and helped. Even Marguerite, who became a regular at dropping in well before the doors were opened to the public, proved indispensable when it came to sourcing non-matching china. Plus she bumped into Sinead, the cleaner from my old shop, crying outside the tube station because she'd been dumped by her fiancé of one day, so we got a cleaner too. Then it was just a matter of me making the cakes and Poppy making the suggestions and taking the money.

We opened with a grand gala to which everyone near and dear to me, to us, was invited. The food was a triumph. There were plain scones and cheese ones and date ones made from spelt flour (for Poppy) yet still, amazingly, quite delicious. There were brandy snaps with triple sec filling, there were tiny strawberry tarts, there were chocolate cupcakes, berry cupcakes, lemon cupcakes, chocolate-berry-lemon cupcakes. There were éclairs, there were bite-sized quiches, there were cucumber sandwiches, there was tiramisu served in shot glasses (Monty's idea) and sugar-free carob balls that were at least chock full of macadamia nuts (Crystal's idea). There were cherry and pinot noir dark chocolate truffles, made by my gorgeous man and adorning the top stack of each three-tiered tray on every one of the tables in our beautiful garden.

Mum and Dad were there positively brimming with pride; Stanley Morris was there with his daughter; Marguerite with her husband and twins; Charlotte and Martin and the girls came (and brought a pockmarked French jardinière of course). We'd made friends again, Charlotte and I, partly because life was too short to keep grudges and partly because Abigail was very good at washing dishes.

Crystal invited her Earls Court crowd who turned out to be from her banking past and quite presentable, plus the exact types who might like a spot of afternoon tea by the canal on a regular basis.

Rosalie, the cat woman, who used to come into the antique store to look at picture frames, arrived with Julia from the real estate agency. They'd started a film club together and got chatting with Rupert, the schoolteacher, who said he'd love to join and the three of them retreated to a corner to debate *Five Easy Pieces*.

Even Whiffy turned up.

I'd given him his invite at the Formosa Street skip, and while he wouldn't come inside or sit at one of the tables in the courtyard, he drank a cup of lapsang souchong sitting on the kerb and ate three wild duck sandwiches in quick succession before making a very polite thank you and peeing through the rails on the bridge into the canal.

More exciting than that, though, and infinitely better smelling, Will's ex-wife Natasha came. He'd asked her to but she'd given him every reason to think she would rather stick needles in her eyes so it was an extra thrill to see her climb out of her car with Terry, her husband, and the three children. Will's two girls were beautiful, just like their mother. Terribly polite, especially towards him, but I suspected they had inherited his kindness and compassion just by the way they treated other people, and he was amazing with them. I know he must have wanted everyone to leave so he could just concentrate solely on them, not waste a precious moment, but he stayed low key, subtly getting them to help so they were always near, but not making a fuss that would embarrass them, or Natasha.

'They take after you,' I said to her as I offered her a cupcake. 'What beautiful children.'

'Thank you,' she said and we watched Will pour a cup of tea for Edith, of the bad mornings, whom I'd bumped into at

Tesco and invited along, to her great joy. She had a gentleman friend, Ted, who she'd met at the library.

'He's so different now,' Natasha said, looking at Will, with perhaps a trace of wistfulness. 'I wish he could have been like that . . .'

I knew what she meant. I'd done more than my share of wishing things could have been different. As if to prove this point, Charles and Harry arrived and I pointed them out to her.

'My ex,' I said, 'with his boyfriend.'

Her mouth dropped open, but she had the presence of mind to close it as Charles and Harry came over to kiss me hello.

'You get on so well with him,' she marvelled when they moved in the direction of Poppy who was surrounded by children. 'How do you do it?'

'Well, once I finished hitting him with bananas, hating him, resenting him, and, oh, did I mention hitting him with bananas? I had to admit that he was happier and so, the way things have worked out, am I.'

Natasha looked at her husband, Terry, who was wiping raspberry jam off the hands and face of their littlest girl and smiled.

'You might just be on to something there,' she said, and then she got a look on her face I had well become accustomed to. 'And you,' she said, her head listing to one side, 'are you all right? Will said you'd not been well.'

'I'm well right now,' I said. 'And that's what counts.'

I couldn't tell her that as long as Will was with me, telling me he loved me, that I was beautiful no matter what scars, internal or external, I bore, I was all right. He and the moment we were in were all that mattered. Everything else was a bonus.

Life wasn't perfect, of course it wasn't. I was moody, sometimes scared, sometimes angry. Will did his best to stay on an even keel but I drove him mad sometimes, I knew that. He told me. We argued. We made up. We expressed our feelings!

Natasha and I watched as he picked up his younger daughter Ella and sat her on a table to do up her shoe.

'I am a bit *carpe-diem*-ish these days,' I suddenly said to her, 'so forgive me if I am speaking out of turn but Will would love to see more of the girls and so would I. The odd weekend, perhaps, or a few days in the school holidays, if you thought that was appropriate? Whatever you think. We'd fit in completely.'

I knew what it felt like to let go of anger, resentment, hurt. I knew how hard it was.

'He always had it in him to be a good father,' Natasha said, softly. 'I suppose the timing just wasn't right. Let me talk to Terry.' We smiled at each other and it was a rather lovely, hopeful moment.

I sat down then, a familiar tired-but-happy feeling washing over me and I watched Poppy dance around with one of Marguerite's twins: the one that looked less like mothball Granny.

Will took the opportunity to sweep Ella up in his arms then and danced her over to my sister, where the four of them did an impromptu family waltz around the cosmos she had planted and he had fertilised.

I caught Monty's eye. He was sitting on the steps in the sunshine and when I looked at him he smiled at me and I felt so loved, so understood, I wanted to weep tears of sheer gratitude.

Here was my family, drinking tea and eating cupcakes in

my grandmother's garden and together we could face whatever rotten things came our way.

Because if I'd learned anything in recent months it was that there really is no escaping the fact that life can simply be horribly unfair.

In the past I think I had corralled rotten things into groups of three because at some level it gave me the impression I was controlling them, keeping track of them. In my world I believed the universe would only dish out so much shite before it realised it had overdone it and corrected matters.

That, of course, turned out to be nonsense.

The truth is that sometimes the shite just keeps on coming and that is what is so unfair. But here's the thing: it's never all shite. If you can wake up in the morning for just long enough to breathe in and out and see the sun shining, you're already surviving it. You're already if not getting around it, at least getting over it, getting past it.

And who knows what can happen then?

Just look at me. I was on the biggest roll of rotten things known to mankind when I met the love of my life. The love of my life! Had I not been fired by my partner, abandoned by my husband, heartsick over my son and struck down by measles, would Will and I still have found each other? And if we had found each other, would we still have ended up together?

I don't know, and in many ways it doesn't matter. Will is right, every moment is precious, too precious for questions that can't be answered. Really, you're better off just looking at what you've ended up with (however you've ended up with it), trying to ignore the rottenness of that and celebrating the wonderfulness of something else.

'On top of everything, how can I bear this?' I used to ask myself in bleaker days.

On top of everything. Looking up from the bottom of a half-empty glass, it's a pretty grim place.

But looking down from the rim of a half-full one? That's a different story.

On top of everything is exactly where I was that afternoon in Rose's garden.

Will and Poppy, still holding the children, danced around the new jardinière — a little bit of Provence in Little Venice, oh well! — the dappled light of the tree of heaven picking up the coppery glint of Poppy's hair, sliding over Will's broad shoulders as he waltzed with his daughter. Sparky licked my toes and looked mournful. My mother kissed my father. Crystal went and sat on Monty's knee. A warm feeling so delicious it could have been hot chocolate mousse suddenly surged through me, starting at my toes, my fingers, the top of my head, and rushing towards my heart.

I looked at Will, so ready to be a good father, and Poppy, so desperate to be a mother, dancing past each other in the sunlight and I had the most wonderful idea.

If ever there was a man to bring an angel into the world, it was this one. He wouldn't be doing it with me, for many reasons I was past that, but maybe with my blessing, if he was willing, while her ovaries were still in good operating order, he could do it with Poppy. He was the perfect non-puppy-killing flesh-and-blood man, after all.

They both laughed at something, then looked over at me.

Moments like that, I truly treasured.

MONTY

♥ ♥ ♥

There's a great deal of talk at film school about influences, about inspiration, but every time I think about the guys I consider the directing heroes — the Coens, Scorsese, Quentin Tarantino — I still go, 'Yeah, fantastic, but that's just film-making, isn't it, that's make-believe. It's life that really counts. It's living.'

My mother, Florence Petal Rainbow Dowling, worked out how to live better than anyone else I have ever met, which is why my graduation project is about her. Not the coolest thing in the world, admittedly, to make a film about your mum, but she taught me more about following your heart than anyone else ever could, and what better inspiration could a filmmaker, a son, a person, hope for?

Actually, my mother said she only really started to live when the opportunity to keep doing so was taken away from her, which in her opinion showed that it's never too late.

She was a great wife — both her husbands tell me — and a wonderful mother, a good daughter, a devoted sister and a truly nice person, which doesn't sound like much but it was one of her ambitions, to be a nice person, and she really got there, I think. She was always there. Or close, anyway.

Of course, she did spend her first thirty-nine years worrying too much and waiting for rotten things to happen to her. Then when they did, and some of the things were obviously, really, truly rotten, she realised she could have a lot more fun not waiting for them.

So, you know what she did then? She just stopped seeing the rot.

This is a woman whose career and marriage ended basically in one day, after all, but who then turned her rather falling-down old house into one of London's top tearooms. Not only that, she fell in love with the builder who helped her. She married him. She had the time of her life with him, as she was so fond of saying.

As time went on, despite the circumstances, her appetite for — well, cakes, obviously, and slices and biscuits and anything covered in chocolate — but also for life just grew and grew and grew.

She went on safari to Africa because she wanted to see the zebras, she went to Australia because she wanted to meet my in-laws, she went to Paris because she wanted to have macaroons at Ladurée, she even went to Greece on holiday to do nothing at all although Will, the builder, says it was the most exhausting holiday he's ever been on.

And despite the fact that physically she weakened and waned, often in front of our very eyes, her capacity for sheer joy outweighed anything else about her and I think this helped all of those who loved her, actually, to deal with the inevitable: her leaving us.

'I'm just so lucky,' she would say to me, over and over again even on days when she could barely open her eyes, let alone get out of bed.

Lucky? The woman was dying.

'Yes, but not today,' she'd say as she reached for a cherry truffle or a brandy snap or Will.

She never wanted to be the star of this show, by the way, partly a hair issue, she told me, but partly because she was too busy baking for the tearooms, packing picnics, swimming at the

Heath, helping Poppy make dreamcatchers for her stall, learning reflexology, darning holey caftans.

'Don't ask me!' was her response when I asked what it was like having Stanley Morris turn up just after her life-changing roll of rotten things started spiralling out of control. 'Ask Stanley Morris!'

And so I did. And so this is how we, her family and friends, saw her during this crucial turning point, when she basically chose the joy of living over the fear of dying.

She saw a rough cut, by the way, before she became too ill, which made her laugh so much I nearly had to call an ambulance.

'I'm such a nitwit,' she said. 'But a nice nitwit, don't you think?'

So this is it, a film about my mum. She is missed. God, how she is missed. But she is remembered. Having just become a father myself — twin boys, she would have been mad about them — I feel even more inspired now to be like her, to seize the day, to choose life, as her hero George Michael might put it.

Or, just as apt but maybe not quite so '80s boy band, to choose living.

ACKNOWLEDGEMENTS

♥ ♥ ♥

I feel like I have been researching this book my whole life in which case I really should have kept better notes as I can't quite remember whom to thank.

I will start with my late grandmother, widely known as Lil, because I associate memories of her so strongly with the smell and taste of good old-fashioned baking. Whenever we visited her little house in Alexandra, Central Otago, she would be pulling something delicious out of her oven, be it afghan biscuits, Neenish tarts, caramel slice, spiced apple shortcake, kiwi biscuits, Louise cake and Belgian biscuits (just like the bought ones!) to name but a few.

And as my mother (no slouch on the baking front herself) reminded me recently, my grandmother didn't even have a whole oven to pull the delicacies out of. It was what I think was called a rangette — a free-standing mini oven with two hob elements and a small cooker. This did not stop her from filling the cake tins and, subsequently, her grandchildren.

There seems to be some sort of common connection with grandmothers and afternoon tea. Maybe it's because seeing Grandma is usually a treat? Or maybe it 's because Grandma doesn't want to be anywhere near the vicinity at proper mealtimes when the hysterics and mashed parsnips are flying.

Anyway, afternoon tea seems to be enjoying something of a

comeback as does home baking. I baked quite a bit when I was younger but then went on a diet for the next 30 years so didn't bother. After researching my novel, *By Bread Alone*, however, I got the bug for making bread; cakes, slices and biscuits soon followed and continue to do so.

My chocolate and banana cake with fresh raspberries (see page 183) even managed to take out the top prize in the ladies' cake section at the 2008 Lake Hayes A & P show, I'll have you know. Never has my chest been quite so puffed up with pride. Nor my waistband, from repeatedly testing the recipe.

Taking afternoon tea is, in my opinion, one of life's great pleasures and therefore the perfect topic to research. I am eternally grateful to the people who have helped me explore the intricacies of this most delightful of snacking opportunities.

George Peacock at Peacock's in Ely, near Cambridge, did indeed turn his daughters' bedrooms into tearooms and his bustling riverside premises provided much inspiration for the fictional Rose's. Claridge's remains my favourite London tea spot, although the Wolseley isn't too bad and it's hard to beat Patisserie Valerie in Old Compton Street for its amazing window display of cakes and pastries.

Ladurée in Paris just has to be visited for the macaroons, but don't miss the hot chocolate at Angelina's and, whatever you do, make sure you go and get talked into buying $75 of Darjeeling first flush from the delightful boy in the linen jacket at Mariage Frères. It makes about two cups of tea but you will so enjoy the experience of meeting him.

Stephen Twining from Twining's Tea was crucial in providing a tea and food matching session at the company's English headquarters — plus two lunches. This puts him at the top of my list for people to research things with.

Jane Pettigrew and Tim Clifton from the UK Tea Council

provided a most enlightening few hours of hard-core tea tasting in London and Bonnie Kwok proved to be a delightful companion for one of my most heavenly afternoon teas ever, at the Peninsula in Hong Kong.

Harriet Allan at Random House New Zealand has done a wonderful job of not hitting me on the head with a cricket bat for repeatedly missing my deadlines, while Jennifer Balle has worked her usual magic on the publicity (not to mention tea and sympathy) front.

Then there's Ann Clifford, who has edited five of my novels now, and is still an outstanding editor and irreplaceable support but also, more importantly, a trusted and much-loved friend. Plus, this time, we went all modern and edited on the computer. I miss the red wine stains but not having bits of paper fly away in the wind (or the dog).

Last, but by no means least, this book is dedicated to anyone having a bad day, and we all know they exist, but it's also dedicated to all the real-life Wills out there, about whom some of you may be a little more doubtful.

My sister-in-law Nicki Robins died of colon cancer in June 2007 but not before she fell in love with one such Will. He never made truffles, as far as I know, but according to Nicki, when she finally told him she had a terminal illness, he simply said: 'Girlfriends: there's always something wrong with them,' and got on with the business of being her boyfriend.

That, in my mind, means he whips Indiana Jones's butt in the hero stakes.

Yes, if ever there was a girl to laugh in the face of life's unfairness, it was Nicki. And while unfairness, curse it, ultimately got the better of her she proved above all — to me anyway — that it's not how much time you have that counts; it's what you do with the time you have.

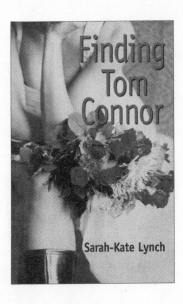

'the most hilarious and irreverent New Zealand novel in years.
A wickedly funny debut' *Sunday Star-Times*

'This book is laugh-a-minute . . . fast-paced and funny'
Waikato Times

'a romantic and rollicking good read . . . hits the spot with its
light-hearted look at life and love' *Next*

'a frothy, hilarious read' *Dunedin Star*

'a truly lovely read — as moreish as a sweet, creamy cheese which
tickles you with pepper on its way down. *Blessed Are* is seductive,
feel-good but not pulpy. It fills you up, like cheese itself. But it
bubbles, too, like champagne.' *Weekend Herald*

'funnier than anything I've read in recent years' *The Press*

'Sheer entertainment' *Next*

'Self-assured, witty, well-structured and a jolly good read' *She*

'A tasty, surprising, frequently hilarious and occasionally tearful
experience' *Otago Daily Times*

'page-turning moments of drama and laugh-out-loud humour'
The Dominion

'fluent, zesty prose' *The Evening Post*

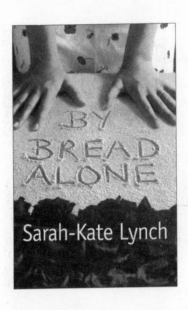

'*By Bread Alone* is the third truly, madly, deeply humorous novel from this gifted writer.' *Next*

'By George, she's got it. Our very own Sarah-Kate Lynch has cracked the chick-lit nut. *By Bread Alone* makes for perfect holiday reading.' *The Dominion Post*

'without a doubt *By Bread Alone* is going to be the season's mega-hit . . . it's the perfect chill-out holiday read. Sarah-Kate has woven a tale full of fabulous characters, delightful dialogue and her trademark humour, underscored by a poignancy that is both surprising and deeply moving. Described so magically that you can see the colours, smell the "apple starter" and taste the sourdough.' *Femme*

'*By Bread Alone* is evocative without being mawkish, entertaining enough to elicit laughter and at times so sad it brought forth a tear or two . . . witty, charming, faithfully passionate to its subject and emotionally adept. If only this book was a man' *Sunday Star-Times*

'as delectable and easy to read as the sumptuous cuisine
described in it' *Next*

'a deftly turned tale' *Canvas, New Zealand Herald*

'The pleasure for the reader is in Lynch's exuberant wit, her wicked
observations, her wacky plot detours . . . and her delight in food'
The Dominion Post

'great escapist summer reading' *Otago Daily Times*

'Lynch writes with great pace, an easy style and plenty of humour'
The Press

'Funny, touching and delicious! A perfect summer read'
View, Herald on Sunday

'Impeccably researched, it reads like a dream'
The Dominion Post

'As light and airy as champagne . . . it fizzes along and is very funny'
North & South

'this enjoyable novel would be a perfect summer holiday
accompaniment for those seeking a soupçon of escapism' *The Press*

'one of the books I've most enjoyed in years'
Her Business